ESSENTIAL FRENCH

PHRASEBOOK & DICTIONARY

Nicole Irving, Leslie Colvin and Kate Needham

Illustrated by Ann Johns

Designed by Lucy Parris
Edited by Susan Meredith

Language consultants: Renée Chaspoul, Annick Dunbar,
Zina Rahouadj and Lorraine Beurton-Sharp.

Cover designed by Stephen Wright
and Andrea Slane.
With thanks to Lucy Owen.
Cover photographs: Eiffel Tower © AP;
poster © Historical Picture Archive/CORBIS;
road signs © Adam Woolfitt/CORBIS.

The material in this book was originally published in
two separate volumes: *Essential French* and
Essential French Dictionary.

Original designs by Adrienne Kern and Kathy Ward.

First published in 2000 by Usborne Publishing Ltd, Usborne
House, 83-85 Saffron Hill, London EC1N 8RT, England.
www.usborne.com
Copyright © 2000, 1994, 1990 Usborne Publishing Ltd.

Printed in Italy.

Contents

About the phrasebook

This book gives simple, up-to-date French to help you survive, travel and socialize in France. It also gives basic information about France and tips for low budget travellers.

Finding the right words

Use the Contents list on page 3 to find the section of the phrasebook you need. If you don't find a phrase where you expect it to be, try a related section. There are food words, for example, on several pages. If you still can't find the word, try looking it up in the dictionary.

Go for it

Remember that you can make yourself clear with very few words, or words that are not quite right. Saying "Paris?" while pointing at a train will provoke *oui* or *non* (yes or no). The French listed on the opposite page is absolutely essential.

You will feel more confident if you have some idea of how to pronounce French correctly and of how the language works. If French is new to you, try looking through the sections on pages 55-60. A good pronunciation tip is to make your voice go up at the end of a question. This will help it to sound different from a statement.

Being polite

Words like *excusez-moi* and *pardon* (excuse me), *s'il vous plaît* (please) or *merci* (thank you) make anything sound more polite and will generally guarantee a friendly response.

There are other ways of being polite in French. The words *Monsieur* (Sir) and *Madame* (Madam) are often used to address older people whose names you don't know, e.g. *Bonjour, Monsieur* (Hello, Sir) or *Merci, Madame* (Thank you, Madam).

French has two different words for "you": *tu* and *vous*. You can use the casual *tu* for a friend, or someone your own age or younger. It is important, though, always to use the polite *vous* when you talk to an older person, whether you know them or not. Saying *tu* to someone who doesn't expect it can be very rude. For more than one person, always use *vous*. In this book *tu* or *vous* is given depending on the situation. Sometimes you will have to judge which is best, so both are given. If you are ever in doubt, say *vous*.

The language in this book is everyday, spoken French, ranging from the formal to the colloquial. An asterisk after a French word shows that it is slang or fairly familiar, e.g. boring: *rasoir**. Two asterisks indicate that a word is strong slang and could be considered very impolite.

Masculine or feminine?

Adjectives with two forms in French are given twice, e.g. green: *vert/verte*. The first is masculine (m) and the second is feminine (f). You can find out more about masculine and feminine in French on pages 56 and 57.

Excusez-moi, nous sommes perdues.
Excuse me, we're lost.

Vous allez où?
Where are you going?

4

yes	oui
no	non
maybe	peut-être
I don't know.	Je ne sais pas.
I don't mind.	Ça m'est égal.
please	s'il vous plaît/s'il te plaît
thank you	merci
excuse me	pardon, excusez-moi
sorry	pardon, désolé/désolée
I'm very sorry.	Je suis désolé/désolée.
It's nothing/ Don't mention it.	Ce n'est rien.
hello	bonjour
goodbye	au revoir
hi	salut
bye	salut
good morning	bonjour
good evening	bonsoir
good night	bonne nuit
see you soon	à bientôt
Mr, Sir	Monsieur
Mrs, Madam	Madame
and	et
or	ou
when?	quand?
where is?	où est?
why?	pourquoi?
because	parce que
how?	comment?
how much?	combien?
How much is it?	C'est combien?
how many?	combien?
What is it/this?	Qu'est-ce que c'est?/ C'est quoi?
it/this is	c'est
is there?	est-ce qu'il y a?/il y a?
there is	il y a
I'd like	je voudrais
could I have?	je peux avoir?

Jean est là, s'il vous plaît?
Is John there please?

Getting help with French

I don't understand.
Je ne comprends pas.

Can you write it down?
Vous pouvez me l'écrire?
Tu peux me l'écrire?

Can you say that again?
Vous pouvez répéter?
Tu peux répéter?

A bit slower, please.
Un peu plus lentement, s'il vous/te plaît.

What does this word mean?
Que veut dire ce mot?

What's the French for this?
Comment on dit ça en français?

Have you got a dictionary?
Vous avez un dictionnaire?
Tu as un dictionnaire?

Do you speak English?
Vous parlez anglais?
Tu parles anglais?

Plus lentement, s'il te plaît.
Slower, please.

Signs you may see

Sortie de secours	**Emergency exit**
Attention	**Beware**
Chien méchant	**Beware of the dog**
Défense d'entrer	**Keep out, no entry**
Interdit de fumer	**No smoking**
Propriété privée	**Private property**
Danger	**Danger**
Eau potable	**Drinking water**
Eau non potable	**Not drinking water**
Baignade interdite	**No swimming**
Camping sauvage interdit	**No unauthorised camping**

Asking the way

Je suis perdu.
I'm lost.

Vous pouvez m'aider, s'il vous plaît?
Can you help me, please?

Où est l'office du tourisme?
Where is the tourist office?

Vous pouvez me dessiner un plan?
Can you draw me a map?

Est-ce qu'il y a des toilettes publiques par ici?
Is there a public toilet around here?

Fact file

Most large towns have an *office du tourisme* (tourist office), sometimes called *syndicat d'initiative*. It's often near the station or town hall. In tourist areas even small towns have one, but opening times may be restricted. Most tourist offices will provide town plans and leaflets on local sights free of charge, and some sell maps and booklets. They also give advice on places to stay and travel arrangements. They often employ someone who speaks English.

Go straight ahead.
Allez tout droit.

It's on the left/right.
C'est à gauche/à droite.

Follow the signs for Blois.
Suivez les panneaux pour Blois.

Go left/right.
Allez à gauche/à droite.

Take the first on the left.
Prenez la première rue à gauche.

Take the second turning on the right.
Prenez le deuxième tournant à droite.

It's ...	C'est ...
Go ...	Allez ...
Carry on ...	Continuez ...
straight ahead	tout droit
Turn ...	Tournez ...
left, on the left	à gauche
right, on the right	à droite
Take ...	Prenez ...
the first	le premier/la première
the second	le/la deuxième
the third	le/la troisième
the fourth	le/la quatrième
turning	le tournant
crossroads, junction	le carrefour
roundabout	le rond-point
traffic lights	les feux
pedestrian crossing	le passage piétons
subway	le passage souterrain
Cross ...	Traversez ...
Follow ...	Suivez ...
street	la rue, le boulevard
road	la route
path	le chemin, le sentier
main street	la rue principale
square	la place, le square
motorway	l'autoroute
ringroad	le boulevard périphérique

one way	sens unique
no entry	sens interdit
no parking	stationnement interdit
car park	un parking
parking meters	des parcmètres
pedestrian area	une zone piétonne
pedestrians	piétons
pavement	le trottoir
town centre	le centre-ville
in town, to town	en ville
area, part of town	le quartier
outskirts, suburbs	la banlieue
town hall	la mairie, l'hôtel de ville
bridge	le pont
river	la rivière
park	le jardin public
post office	la poste, les PTT
shops	les magasins
church	l'église
school	l'école
museum	le musée
railway line	la ligne de chemin de fer
just before the	juste avant le/la
just after the	juste après le/la
to the end of	jusqu'au bout de
on the corner	au coin
next to	près de
opposite	en face de
in front of	devant
behind	derrière
above	au-dessus, en haut
below	au-dessous, en bas
over	par-dessus
under	en dessous
in	dans
on	sur
here	ici
there	là
over there	là-bas
far	loin
close, near	près (de)
nearby	tout près, juste à côté
near here	près d'ici
around here	dans les alentours, par ici
somewhere	quelque part
in this area	dans ce quartier
l0 minutes walk	à dix minutes de marche
5 minutes drive	à cinq minutes en voiture
on foot	à pied

Quel est le meilleur chemin pour aller au camping?
What's the best way to the campsite?

Vous pouvez me montrer sur la carte?
Can you show me on the map?

Où est la plage la plus proche?
Where's the nearest beach?

C'est loin?
How far is it?

Pour aller à l'auberge de jeunesse, s'il vous plaît?
How do I get to the youth hostel?

7

Getting information

A quelle heure est le prochain train pour Toulouse?
What time is the next train to Toulouse?

Combien de temps dure le voyage?
How long is the journey?

Je dois changer?
Do I have to change?

Fact file

The *SNCF* (French railways) runs an extensive rail network and operates some bus services. Fares are cheapest during the off-peak *période bleue* (blue period). Before you get on a train, look for the sign *Compostez votre billet* (Stamp your ticket), stamp it in the orange machine, then hang on to it. *TGV* are high speed trains – you reserve in advance and may pay a supplement. *Autotrains* are the slowest, stopping trains. The under-26 InterRail and Eurail passes are valid throughout the country.

The Paris *métro* is easy to use; maps are free from stations. Check the number of the line you want and the direction – the last stop on the line gives you this, e.g. *direction Pont de Neuilly*. The same tickets are valid on the *métro*, buses and the central zone of the *RER* (Paris express trains). A book of ten tickets or a *carte orange* (weekly travel pass) works out cheaper than single tickets. These are available from *tabacs* (tobacconists) as well as stations. For a book of tickets, ask for *un carnet*.

Je change où pour la gare St-Lazare?
Where do I change for St-Lazare?

Qu'est-ce qu'on vient d'annoncer?
What did they just say over the loudspeaker?

C'est quel quai pour les Halles?
Which platform for Les Halles?

Tickets

Où est-ce que je peux acheter un billet?
Where can I buy a ticket?

Un aller simple pour Avignon, s'il vous plaît.
Can I have a single to Avignon?

J'ai droit à une réduction?
Can I get a reduction?

Comment marche cette machine?
How does this machine work?

English	French	English	French
I'd like to reserve a seat.	Je voudrais réserver une place.	**youth fare**	tarif jeune
railway station	la gare	**ticket (bus/tube)**	un ticket
underground station	la station de métro	**ticket (train)**	un billet
		a single	un aller simple
bus station	la gare routière	**a return**	un aller et retour
bus stop	l'arrêt d'autobus	**book of tickets**	un carnet de tickets
train	le train	**supplement**	un supplément
underground train	le métro	**left luggage locker**	le casier de consigne
tram	le tramway	**track**	la voie
bus	l'autobus	**connection**	une correspondance
coach	le car	**timetable**	l'horaire
leaves at 2 o'clock	part a deux heures	**arrivals/departures**	arrivées/départs
arrives at 4 o'clock	arrive à quatre heures	**long distance**	grandes lignes
first/last	le premier/le dernier	**local, suburban**	banlieue
next	le prochain	**every day**	tous les jours
cheapest	le moins cher	**weekdays**	semaine
ticket office	le guichet	**Sundays and bank holidays**	dimanches et jours fériés
ticket machine	un distributeur automatique	**in the summer time**	pendant l'été
fare	le tarif	**out of season**	hors saison
student fare	tarif étudiant	**except**	sauf

Buses

C'est bien le bus pour Versailles?
Is this the right bus for Versailles?

Où va cet autobus?
Where does this bus go?

Vous pouvez me dire où je dois descendre?
Can you tell me where to get off?

Travel: air, sea, taxis

Je voudrais confirmer mon vol.
I'd like to confirm my flight.

A quelle heure je dois faire enregistrer les bagages?
What time should I check in?

Où est-ce que je fais enregistrer mes bagages?
Where do I check in?

Fact file

Airports and ports usually have signs and announcements in English. There's often a *navette* (bus shuttle) from the airport into town.

Taxis have a standard pick-up charge plus a metered fare; each large bag is charged extra. Taxis often take only three passengers, but they can be good value.

Mes bagages ne sont pas arrivés.
My luggage hasn't arrived.

Madame Duclos est supposée me rencontrer.
Mrs Duclos is supposed to be meeting me.

Where is the taxi stand?
Où est la station de taxi?

Take me to ...
Emmenez-moi à ...

What's the fare to ... ?
C'est combien pour aller à ... ?

Please drop me here.
Laissez-moi ici, s'il vous plaît.

airport	l'aéroport
port	le port
aeroplane	l'avion
ferry	le ferry
hovercraft	l'aéroglisseur
flight	le vol
the English Channel	la Manche
rough	agité/agitée
calm	calme
I feel sea sick	j'ai le mal de mer
on board	à bord
suitcase	une valise
backpack/rucksack	un sac à dos
bag	un sac
hand luggage	des bagages à main
trolley	un chariot
information	renseignements
customs	la douane
passport	le passeport
departure gate	la porte (de départ)
boarding pass	la carte d'embarquement
foot passenger	passager sans véhicule
No smoking section	Non-fumeurs
travel agent	l'agence de voyages
airline ticket	un billet d'avion
cut price	à prix réduit
standby	sans garantie
charter flight	un vol charter
flight number	le numéro de vol
a booking	une réservation
to change	changer
to cancel	annuler
a delay	un retard

Fact file

You can hire bikes from bike shops and some train stations. To find out about taking a bike on a train, see *SNCF* leaflet *Guide du train et du vélo*.

You can ride mopeds from age 14, but must be insured and wear a helmet. Remember the French drive on the right. When you get to a town, follow signs for *Toutes/ Autres directions* (all/other directions) until you see the signs you want.

Je suis tombé en panne.
I've broken down.

Où est le garage le plus proche?
Where's the nearest garage?

Give way to traffic coming from the right.
Priorité à droite.

Fill it up, please.
Le plein, s'il vous plaît.

I have a puncture.
J'ai crevé.

The engine won't start.
Le moteur ne démarre pas.

The battery's flat.
La batterie est à plat.

How much will it cost?
Ça va coûter combien?

for hire
à louer

Can I hire ... ?
Je voudrais louer ...

Where are you going?
Tu vas où?/Vous allez où?

I'm going to St-Jean-de-Luz.
Je vais à St-Jean-de-Luz.

town centre	centre-ville
give way	cédez le passage, priorité à droite
toll	le péage
insurance	l'assurance
driving licence	le permis de conduire
(car) documents	les papiers
crash helmet	un casque
petrol station	une station-service
petrol	de l'essence
lead-free petrol	de l'essence sans plomb
oil/petrol mixture	du mélange
garage, repair shop	un garage
oil	de l'huile
litre	un litre
car	une voiture/une bagnole*
bicycle	un vélo
moped	un vélomoteur
motorbike	une moto
radiator	le radiateur
lights	les phares
chain	la chaîne
wheel	la roue
gears	les vitesses
cable	le câble
pump	la pompe
tyre	le pneu
inner tube	la chambre à air

Je ne sais pas ce qui ne va pas.
I don't know what's wrong.

Les freins ne marchent pas.
The brakes don't work.

Vous pouvez réparer ça?
Can you fix it?

Accommodation: places to stay

At the tourist office

Vous avez une liste de campings?
Do you have a list of campsites?

Fact file

The *office du tourisme* or *syndicat d'initiative* (tourist office) will supply lists of places to stay. Cheaper options include *auberges de jeunesse* (youth hostels) - a good idea in towns and cities; *gîtes d'étape* - basic hostels in walking or cycling areas; and *relais routiers* - restaurants with basic rooms. *Chambres d'hôte* is bed and breakfast accommodation in someone's home but this may be no cheaper than a basic hotel.

Camping

Fact file

There are lots of *campings* (campsites). The local *camping municipal* is often the cheapest.

Is there a campsite around here?
Est-ce qu'il y a un camping par ici?

Where are the showers?
Où sont les douches?

tent	une tente
caravan	une caravane
hot water	l'eau chaude
cold water	l'eau froide
drinking water	l'eau potable
camping gas	une cartouche de camping gaz
tent peg	un piquet
mallet	un maillet
sleeping bag	un sac de couchage
torch	une lampe de poche
matches	des allumettes
loo paper	du papier hygiénique
can opener	un ouvre-boîte

Il y a un emplacement de libre?
Do you have a space?

On est trois avec une tente.
There are three of us with a tent.

Il y a un magasin?
Do you have a shop?

On peut boire l'eau du robinet?
Is it OK to drink the tap water?

Hotels

Vous avez une chambre?
Do you have a room?

C'est complet.
We're full.

Vous connaissez un autre hôtel par ici.
Is there another hotel nearby?

Combien coûte la chambre?
How much for a room?

Fact file

Ungraded and 1 and 2 star *hôtels* are the cheapest. Most have rooms for three or four people which cuts costs. *Demi-pension* (half-board) and *pension* (full board) can be good value.

Le petit déjeuner est compris?
Does that include breakfast?

Je peux voir la chambre?
Can I see the room?

Rooms to let
Chambres à louer/Chambres d'hôte

There are three of us.
Nous sommes trois.

Combien de nuits?
How many nights?

How much do you want to pay?
Combien vous voulez payer?

Can I leave a message for someone?
Je peux laisser un mot pour quelqu'un?

Can I have my passport back?
Vous pouvez me rendre mon passeport?

one/two night(s)	une/deux nuit(s)
room	une chambre
single	pour une personne
double	pour deux personnes
with three beds	avec trois lits
clean	propre
cheap	pas cher/chère
expensive	cher/chère
lunch	le déjeuner
dinner (evening)	le dîner
key	la clé
room number	le numéro de la chambre
registration form	une fiche

Je cherche une chambre pour deux personnes.
I'm looking for a room for two people.

Vous pouvez me réserver une chambre?
Can you book a room for me?

Accommodation: staying with people

Greetings

Bonjour.
Hello.

Comment ça va?
How are you?

For more polite or formal greetings, say *Bonjour* followed by *Monsieur* or *Madame*. Also use the polite *vous* form: *Comment allez-vous?* (How are you?) (See page 4.)

Où est-ce que je peux mettre mes affaires?
Where can I put my things?

Je dors où?
Where am I sleeping?

A quelle heure est le petit déjeuner?
What time do you have breakfast?

Tu peux me réveiller à sept heures?
Could you wake me up at seven?

Washing

Comment marche la douche?
How does the shower work?

Is it OK if I have a bath?
Je peux prendre un bain?
Do you mind if I wash a few things?
Je peux laver quelques affaires?
Where can I dry these?
Où est-ce que je peux faire sécher ça?

bathroom	la salle de bain
bath	un bain
shower	une douche
toilet	les toilettes, les cabinets
bidet	le bidet
towel	une serviette
soap	du savon
shampoo	du shampooing
toothpaste	du dentifrice
toothbrush	une brosse à dents
deodorant	un déodorant
hairdryer	un sèche-cheveux
hairbrush	une brosse à cheveux
washing powder	de la lessive

Being polite

Je peux payer quelque chose?
Can I pay my share?

Non, ne t'inquiète pas.
No, don't worry.

C'est gentil à vous de me recevoir.
It's nice of you to let me stay.

Tout va bien.
Everything's OK.

alarm clock	un réveil
sleeping bag	un sac de couchage
on the floor	par terre
an extra ...	un/une autre ...
blanket	une couverture
quilt, duvet	une couette
sheet	un drap
pillow	un oreiller
bolster	un traversin
electric socket	une prise
needle	une aiguille
thread	du fil
scissors	des ciseaux
iron	un fer à repasser
upstairs	en haut
downstairs	en bas
cupboard	un placard
bedroom	la chambre
living room	le salon
kitchen	la cuisine
garden	le jardin
balcony	le balcon

I'm tired.
Je suis fatigué/fatiguée.

I'm knackered.
Je suis crevé/crevée.

I'm cold.
J'ai froid/froide.

I'm hot.
J'ai chaud/chaude.

Can I have a key?
Je peux avoir une clé?

What is there to do in the evenings?
Qu'est-ce qu'on peut faire le soir?

Where's the nearest phone box?
Où est la cabine téléphonique la plus proche?

Saying goodbye

Merci pour tout.
Thank you for everything.

Au revoir.
Goodbye.

C'est combien pour appeler l'Angleterre?
How much is it to call Britain?

Je peux utiliser votre téléphone?
Can I use your phone?

Je veux payer la communication.
I'll pay for the call.

For more about making phone calls, see page 17.

Banks

Je voudrais changer de l'argent.
I want to change this.

Vous prenez les eurochèques?
Do you accept eurocheques?

Je peux voir votre passeport?
Can I see your passport?

Post office

Pardon, il y a une boîte aux lettres par ici?
Where's the nearest postbox?

Je voudrais un timbre pour envoyer ça.
Can I have a stamp for this?

Fact file

The unit of currency is the French *franc* (FF) or, from 2002, the euro. 1 FF = 100 *centimes*. Most banks are open Monday to Friday 9am to 12 noon and 2pm to 4pm. Some open on Saturday and close on Monday. *Bureaux de change* (foreign exchange offices) are often open outside banking hours but will probably give a poorer rate of exchange.

Money problems

J'ai perdu mes traveller's chèques.
I've lost my traveller's cheques.

Les numéros de la série sont ...
The serial numbers were ...

Comment je fais pour en avoir d'autres?
How do I get replacements?

J'attends de l'argent; il est arrivé?
I'm expecting some money; has it arrived?

bank	une banque	**directory**	un annuaire
cashier's desk, till	la caisse	**phone number**	le numéro de téléphone
foreign exchange	un bureau de change	**wrong number**	le mauvais numéro
enquiries	des renseignements	**reverse charge call**	un appel en PCV
money	de l'argent	**Hang on.**	Ne quittez pas.
small change	de la monnaie		
notes	des billets		
traveller's cheques	des traveller's chèques,		
	des chèques de voyage		
credit card	une carte de crédit,		
	une carte bancaire		
exchange rate	le cours du change		
commission	la commission		
money transfer	une mise à disposition		
post office	une poste, les PTT		
postcard	une carte postale		
letter	une lettre		
parcel	un colis		
by airmail	par avion		
by registered post	en recommandé		
stamp	un timbre		
telephone	un téléphone		
telephone box	une cabine		
	téléphonique		
mobile phone	un portable		

The cashpoint machine (ATM) has swallowed my credit card.
Le distributeur (DAB) a avalé ma carte de crédit.

Where can I send an e-mail?
Où est-ce que je peux envoyer un e-mail?

Fact file

A few phone boxes take coins but most take *télécartes* (phonecards). You can receive incoming calls if the number is shown in the box. There are also phones in post offices and cafés. These are often metered and you pay after the call. You can buy phonecards and stamps from post offices or *tabacs* (see page 24). For useful phone numbers see page 49.

Phones

Ce téléphone ne marche pas.
This phone doesn't work.

C'est bien l'indicatif pour Lyon?
Is this the code for Lyon?

Allô, Sylvie est là, s'il vous plaît?
Hello, is Sylvie there, please?

Dites-lui que j'ai appelé, s'il vous plaît.
Please tell her/him I called.

Elle rentre quand?
When will she be back?

Elle/il peut me rappeler?
Can she/he call me back?

Mon numéro est le ...
My number is ...

Je peux laisser un message pour ...?
Can I leave a message for ...?

Cafés

café	un café, un bar, un café-brasserie
at the bar	au comptoir
Cheers!	A ta/votre santé!
something to drink	quelque chose à boire
something to eat	quelque chose à manger
snack	un casse-croûte
black coffee	un café, un express
(large) white coffee	un (grand) crème
decaffeinated	décaféiné, déca
white decaff.	un déca-crème
tea (with milk)	un thé (au lait)
hot chocolate	un chocolat chaud
fruit juice	un jus de fruit
orange juice	un jus d'orange
coke	un coca
still mineral water	de l'eau (minérale) plate
fizzy mineral water	de l'eau gazeuse
beer (bottled)	une bière
beer (draught)	une pression, un demi
bottle of ...	une bouteille de ...
half a bottle of white wine	une demi-bouteille de vin blanc
glass of red wine	un verre de vin rouge
milk	du lait
sugar	du sucre
ice	avec des glaçons
slice of lemon	une tranche de citron
cheese/ham sandwich	un sandwich au fromage/jambon
omelette (plain)	une omelette (nature)
ice cream	une glace

Fact file

Cafés are open varying hours for drinks, snacks, meeting up with friends or using the loo and phone. Prices vary. If you sit down, a waiter serves you. Drinks may be cheaper if you stand at the bar. Tea comes with lemon – ask for milk if you want it. Try *citron pressé* or *orange pressée* (freshly squeezed lemon or orange) – you add your own water and sugar. Snacks include *croque-monsieur* (toasted ham and cheese sandwich).

On prend un café?
How about a cup of coffee?

Cette chaise est libre?
Is this chair free?

Je peux voir la carte?
Can I see the menu?

Un café, s'il vous plaît.
A black coffee, please.

Vous avez des milk-shakes?
Do you have milk-shakes?

Eating out

Choosing a place

On va où?
Where shall we go?

Je n'aime pas les pizzas.
I don't like pizzas.

Si on allait manger un hamburger?
What about a hamburger?

French food	la cuisine française	**sausages**	des saucisses
Moroccan food	la cuisine marocaine	**mixed salad**	une salade composée
cheap restaurant	un restaurant pas cher	**green salad**	une salade verte
fast-food	la restauration rapide	**spaghetti**	des spaghettis
take-away kiosk	un endroit vente à emporter	**rare**	saignant
menu	la carte	**medium**	à point
starter	l'entrée	**well done**	bien cuit
main course	le plat principal	**mustard**	la moutarde
dessert	le dessert	**salt**	le sel
price	le prix	**pepper**	le poivre
soup	de la soupe, du potage	**dressing**	la vinaigrette
fish	du poisson	**mayonnaise**	la mayonnaise
meat	de la viande		
vegetables	des légumes		
cheese	du fromage		
fruit	des fruits		
chips	des frites		

Is everything all right?
Tout va bien?
Yes, it's very good.
Oui, c'est très bon.

Deciding what to have

Je peux en avoir un sans fromage?
Can I have one without cheese?

C'est quoi, ça?
What's that?

Un comme ça, s'il vous plaît.
One of those please.

Problems

J'ai demandé un steak frites.
I ordered steak and chips.

Ce n'est pas assez cuit.
This isn't cooked enough.

Vous n'avez pas de ketchup?
Don't you have any ketchup?

S'il vous plaît!
Excuse me!

L'addition s'il vous plaît.
Can we have the bill please?

Je n'ai pas commandé ça.
I didn't order this.

Fact file

Standard French dishes are *steak frites* or *poulet frites* (steak and chips or chicken and chips). Try the *spécialités régionales* (regional specialities) or *couscous* (a North African dish). Red meat is often served rare. Ask for *très, très cuit* if you want it very well done.

Restaurants are sometimes called *brasseries*. Look out for *le menu*, *le menu du jour* or *le menu touristique* (set menu) which is displayed outside with its price. It is usually three courses and is cheaper than eating *à la carte*. *Le plat du jour* (dish of the day) is often good value.

Cafés do snacks and simple meals (see page 18) but they can be pricey. Look out for stalls selling *crêpes* (pancakes with various fillings), *galettes* (wholewheat pancakes) and *gaufres* (waffles), and for fast-food places. These should be cheaper.

Tipping in cafés and restaurants is normal practice but *service compris* means service is included. *Service non compris* means it is not, so it's best to leave a tip of about 10%.

Best times to eat out are lunch at 12 noon or 1pm and dinner at about 8pm.

Fact file

Breakfast is coffee (or tea or hot chocolate) with a *croissant, pain grillé* (toast) or *tartine* (bread with butter and jam). At home *café au lait* (coffee and plenty of hot milk) served in a bowl is standard and it's fine to dunk whatever you are eating.

Meals are often three courses. Salad can be a separate course. Cheese comes before pudding which is often fruit.

Enjoy your meal.
Bon appétit!

I'm hungry/thirsty.
J'ai faim/soif.

I'm not hungry/thirsty.
Je n'ai pas faim/soif.

A table!
It's ready.

Servez-vous!
Help yourselves.

C'est fait avec quoi?
What's in this?

Tu peux me passer le beurre?
Can you pass the butter?

Ça me suffit, merci.
I've had enough thanks.

Tu veux de la salade?
Would you like some salad?

C'était délicieux.
That was delicious.

Un tout petit peu.
Just a little.

Encore un morceau de pain?
Some more bread?

Helping

Je peux vous aider?
Can I help?

Je peux mettre la table?
Can I lay the table?

Je peux faire la vaisselle?
Can I do the washing-up?

meal	le repas	**rice**	du riz
breakfast	le petit déjeuner	**dried beans**	des haricots secs
lunch	le déjeuner	**potatoes**	des pommes de terre
dinner (evening)	le dîner	**onions**	des oignons
bowl	un bol	**garlic**	de l'ail
glass	un verre	**tomatoes**	des tomates
plate	une assiette	**peppers**	des poivrons
knife	un couteau	**green beans**	des haricots verts
fork	une fourchette	**peas**	des petits pois
spoon	une cuillère	**courgettes**	des courgettes
cereal	des céréales	**aubergines**	des aubergines
bread	du pain	**spinach**	des épinards
jam	de la confiture	**cabbage**	du chou
margarine	de la margarine	**cauliflower**	du chou-fleur
chicken	du poulet	**chicory**	des endives
pork	du porc	**raw**	cru/crue
beef	du boeuf	**(too) hot, spicy**	(trop) épicé/épicée
veal	du veau	**salty**	salé/salée
liver	du foie	**sweet**	sucré/sucrée
pasta	des pâtes		

Special cases

Je n'aime pas le poisson.
I don't like fish.

Je suis végétarien. [†]
I'm a vegetarian.

Je ne supporte pas les oeufs.
I'm allergic to eggs.

[†]If you're female, say *Je suis végétarienne.*

Je peux vous aider?
Can I help you?

Je voudrais ça.
I'd like that.

Ça coûte combien?
How much is it?

Fact file

Opening times vary but bear in mind that many shops close for lunch and close on Monday. Most shops are open Tuesday to Saturday 9am to 12 noon and 2pm to 7pm. Small food shops may open on Sunday morning and others on Monday. Department stores and big supermarkets stay open all day Monday to Saturday. In the south, shops open earlier, close longer for lunch and stay open later. Look out for signs on shop doors: *Heures d'ouverture* (opening hours) or *Fermeture hebdomadaire* (closed each week on ...).

A *tabac*, sometimes part of a bar, sells stamps, phonecards, sweets etc., and may sell bus/*métro* tickets. *Drogueries* (hardware shops) sell handy things for camping but try a *magasin de sport* for camping equipment proper.

It is generally cheaper to buy everday things in chain stores such as *Monoprix* or *Prisunic,* or in supermarkets, rather than in smaller, specialist shops.

The cheapest, easiest way to buy food is in a hypermarket or supermarket. Specialist food shops may be more pricey, but offer more choice and are worth a visit. *Charcuteries* or *traiteurs* (delicatessen) sell salads, quiches, pizzas, etc., as well as *charcuterie* (cured and cold meats, pâté, salami etc.). In small places with no baker, the sign *dépôt de pain* means fresh bread is stocked. Markets are held regularly and are good for food, local produce, cheap clothes etc. There are few greengrocers. People buy fruit and vegetables from market stalls, supermarkets or a *supérette* (small supermarket).

Vous pouvez me l'écrire s'il vous plaît?
Please write that down.

Très bien.
That's fine.

C'est quatre-vingt-six francs.
It's 86 francs.

Je le prends.
I'll take it.

shopping centre	un centre commercial
shop	un magasin
department store	un grand magasin
market	un marché
hypermarket	un hypermarché
supermarket	un supermarché, un libre-service
small supermarket	une supérette
grocer	une épicerie
baker	une boulangerie
cake shop	une pâtisserie
sweetshop	une confiserie
butcher	une boucherie
delicatessen	une charcuterie, un traiteur
fruit/veg stall, greengrocer	un marchand de fruits et légumes
fishmonger	une poissonnerie
healthfood shop	un magasin de produits diététiques
hardware shop	une droguerie, une quincaillerie
chemist	une pharmacie
camera shop	un magasin de photos
gift shop	un magasin de cadeaux
tobacconist	un tabac, un bar-tabac
newsagent	un marchand de journaux
bookshop	une librairie
stationer	une papeterie
record shop	un magasin de disques, un disquaire
computer store	un magasin d'informatique
video shop	un magasin de location vidéo
flea market	un marché aux puces
junk shop	une brocante
sports shop	un magasin de sport
shoe shop	un magasin de chaussures
heel bar	un talon minute
hairdresser, barber	un coiffeur
launderette	une laverie automatique
travel agent	une agence de voyages
browsers welcome	entrée libre
open	ouvert/ouverte
closed	fermé/fermée
entrance	l'entrée
exit	la sortie
checkout, till	la caisse
stairs	l'escalier
price	le prix

Où sont les magasins?
Where's the main shopping area?

Vous vendez des piles?
Do you sell batteries?

Où est-ce que je peux en trouver?
Where can I get some?

Où est-ce que je peux faire réparer ça?
Where can I get this repaired?

Où est-ce que je peux trouver des lunettes de soleil?
Where's a good place for sunglasses?

Je peux vous aider?
Can I help you?

Je peux voir ça?
Can I see that?

Il coûte combien?
How much is it?

Je regarde seulement.
I'm just looking.

Je vais réfléchir.
I'll think about it.

sunscreen	un écran total
make-up	du maquillage
(hair) gel	du gel (pour les cheveux)
hair spray	de la laque
tampons	des tampons
tissues	des mouchoirs en papier
razor	un rasoir
shaving cream	de la crème à raser
painkiller	un calmant, un analgésique
contact lens solution	de la solution de nettoyage (pour des lentilles)
plasters	des pansements
film	une pellicule
English newspapers	des journaux anglais
postcard	une carte postale
writing paper	du papier à lettres
envelope	une enveloppe
notebook	un carnet
pen	un stylo
pencil	un crayon
poster	une affiche
stickers	des autocollants
badges	des badges
sunglasses	des lunettes de soleil
jewellery	des bijoux
watch	une montre
earrings	des boucles d'oreilles
ring	une bague
purse	un porte-monnaie
wallet	un portefeuille
bag	un sac
smaller	plus petit/petite
cheaper	moins cher/chère
another colour	d'une autre couleur

Je voudrais une crème solaire.
I need some suntan lotion.

Il n'y a pas plus grand?
Is there a bigger one?

Je voudrais une baguette.
I'd like a baguette.

Je voudrais pour quinze francs de raisin.
Can I have 15 francs worth of grapes?

Je voudrais une petite tranche de ce pâté.
Can I have a small piece of that pâté?

carrier bag	un sac plastique
small	petit/petite
big	gros/grosse
a slice of	une tranche de
a bit more	un peu plus
a bit less	un peu moins
a portion of	une part de
a piece of	un morceau de
a kilogram	un kilo
half a kilo	une livre
250 grammes	deux cent cinquante grammes
organic	biologique, naturel
French salami	du saucisson
quiche	une quiche
bread	du pain
roll	un petit pain
cake	un gâteau
croissant	un croissant
doughnut	un beignet
sweets	des bonbons

chocolate	du chocolat
crisps	des chips
apples	des pommes
pears	des poires
peaches	des pêches
nectarines	des brugnons, des nectarines
plums	des prunes
cherries	des cerises
raspberries	des framboises
strawberries	des fraises
melon	un melon

Fact file

As a change from *croissants*, try *un pain au chocolat/aux raisins* (pastry filled with chocolate/currants), or *une brioche* (a soft, slightly sweet loaf or bun). *Une ficelle* is a thin *baguette*. Wholemeal bread is *du pain complet*.

Un peu plus, s'il vous plaît.
A bit more please.

Comme ça?
Like that?

Oui, ça suffit, merci.
OK, that's enough, thanks.

clothes	les vêtements
shirt	une chemise
T-shirt	un tee-shirt
vest top	un débardeur
sweatshirt	un sweat-shirt
jumper	un pull
fleece	une polaire
dress	une robe
skirt	une jupe
trousers	un pantalon
shorts	un short
jogging bottoms	un pantalon de survêtement
top	le haut
bottom	le bas
trainers	des baskets
shoes	des chaussures
sandals	des sandales
boots	des bottes
belt	une ceinture
jacket	une veste
waterproof	un imper(méable)
underpants	un slip, un caleçon
knickers	un slip, une culotte
bra	un soutien-gorge
tights	un collant
socks	des chaussettes
swimsuit, trunks	un maillot (de bain)
a small size	une petite taille
a medium size	une taille moyenne

Fact file

You can usually exchange purchases within 28 days. For cheap clothes, try stores such as *Eurodif* or *Districenter*, or hypermarkets. *Un dépot - vente de vêtements* is a second-hand clothes store and *un magasin de dégriffés* is a designer seconds store. You will also come across charity shops.

a large size	une grande taille
too big	trop grand/grande
smaller	plus petit/petite
long	long/longue
short	court/courte
tight	serré/serrée
baggy	large
style	un style
look	un look
fashionable	à la mode
trendy, cool	branché/branchée*
untrendy	ringard/ringarde*
out-of-date	démodé/démodée
smart	chic
dressy	habillé/habillée
scruffy	crado*, minable
second-hand	d'occasion
fun	chouette*
sale	les soldes
changing room	la cabine d'essayage

On peut venir en jean?
Are jeans all right?

Je peux emprunter ta veste?
Can I borrow your jacket?

J'apporte mon maillot?
Shall I bring my swimming stuff?

Music

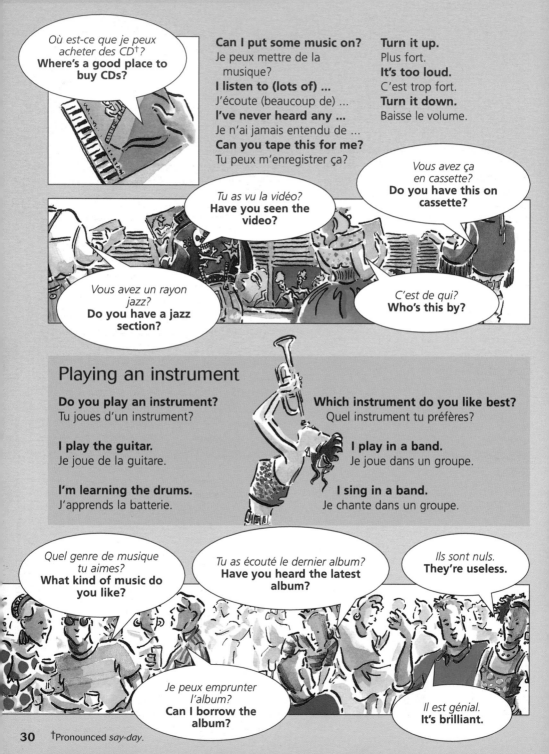

Où est-ce que je peux acheter des CD†?
Where's a good place to buy CDs?

Can I put some music on?
Je peux mettre de la musique?
I listen to (lots of) ...
J'écoute (beaucoup de) ...
I've never heard any ...
Je n'ai jamais entendu de ...
Can you tape this for me?
Tu peux m'enregistrer ça?

Turn it up.
Plus fort.
It's too loud.
C'est trop fort.
Turn it down.
Baisse le volume.

Vous avez ça en cassette?
Do you have this on cassette?

Tu as vu la vidéo?
Have you seen the video?

Vous avez un rayon jazz?
Do you have a jazz section?

C'est de qui?
Who's this by?

Playing an instrument

Do you play an instrument?
Tu joues d'un instrument?

Which instrument do you like best?
Quel instrument tu préfères?

I play the guitar.
Je joue de la guitare.

I play in a band.
Je joue dans un groupe.

I'm learning the drums.
J'apprends la batterie.

I sing in a band.
Je chante dans un groupe.

Quel genre de musique tu aimes?
What kind of music do you like?

Tu as écouté le dernier album?
Have you heard the latest album?

Ils sont nuls.
They're useless.

Je peux emprunter l'album?
Can I borrow the album?

Il est génial.
It's brilliant.

†Pronounced *say-day*.

music	la musique
music shop	un magasin de disques, un disquaire
radio	la radio
(radio) station	une station
CD	un CD
CD-radio-cassette player	un lecteur CD-radio-cassette
personal CD player	un lecteur CD portable
personal stereo	un baladeur
hi-fi	une chaîne hi-fi
headphones	des écouteurs
single	un single
album	un album
mini disc	un mini-disc
a blank tape	une cassette vierge
music/pop video	un clip
track	un morceau
song	une chanson
lyrics	les paroles
tune, melody	un air
rhythm, beat	le rythme
live	en direct
group, band	un groupe
orchestra	un orchestre
solo	en solo
singer	un chanteur/une chanteuse
accompaniment	l'accompagnement
fan	un fan
tour	une tournée
concert, gig	un concert
charts	le hit-parade
the Top 50	le Top 50 (cinquante)
number one	le numéro un
hit	un tube
latest	dernier/dernière
new	nouveau/nouvelle
piano	le piano
keyboards	le clavier
synthesizer	le synthétiseur
electric guitar	la guitare électrique
bass guitar	la guitare basse
acoustic guitar	la guitare acoustique
saxophone	le saxophone
trumpet	la trompette
accordion	l'accordéon
violin	le violon
flute	la flûte

Types of music

This list includes music you're likely to hear in France. For other types of music, try using the English word as the names are often the same.

house music	la house music
heavy metal	le heavy metal
rock	le rock
rap	le rap
hip-hop	le hip-hop
techno	la techno
reggae	le reggae
funk	la musique funk
soul	la musique soul
African music	la musique africaine
rock & roll	le rock'n'roll
jazz	le jazz
blues	le blues
folk	le folk
pop	la musique pop
dance, disco	le disco
70's music	la musique des années 70 (soixante-dix)
retro	rétro
classical	la musique classique

Alors, qu'est-ce qu'on fait?
What are we doing?

Tu as une idée?
Have you got any ideas?

On fait quelque chose ce soir?
Shall we do something tonight?

Non, je ne peux pas.
No, I can't.

A quelle heure?
What time?

Où est-ce qu'on se retrouve?
Where shall we meet?

On se voit devant la fontaine.
See you at the fountain.

What is there to see here?	Qu'est-ce qu'il y a à voir ici?
Is there an admission charge?	Il faut payer l'entrée?
Is there a reduction for students?	Il y a une réduction pour les étudiants?
Can I get a ticket in advance?	Je peux prendre un billet à l'avance?
Do you know a good place to ...	Tu connais un endroit bien pour ...
go dancing?	aller danser?
listen to music?	écouter de la musique?
eat?	aller manger?
go for a drink?	aller prendre un pot*?
I'm busy tonight.	Je suis pris/prise ce soir.
What time does it ...	A quelle heure ça ...
start?	commence?
finish?	finit?
open?	ouvre?
close?	ferme?
today	aujourd'hui
tomorrow	demain
day after tomorrow	après-demain
(in the) morning	le matin
(in the) afternoon	l'après-midi
(in the) evening	le soir
this week	cette semaine
next week	la semaine prochaine
no performance tonight	ce soir, relâche
entertainment guide, listing	un programme des spectacles
club, nightclub	une boîte (de nuit)
disco	une boîte, une discothèque
rave	une rave
party	une fête, une boum
picnic	un pique-nique
show, entertainment	un spectacle
(to the) cinema	(au) cinéma
(to the) theatre	(au) théâtre
ballet	un ballet
opera	un opéra
ticket office	le guichet
student ticket	un billet étudiant
performance, film showing	une séance
guide book	un guide

Fact file

To find out what to visit, go to the tourist office (see page 6). You will get free information, leaflets and maps.

For what's on in Paris, look at *Pariscope* or *L'officiel des spectacles* (listings magazines), any daily newspaper, or local English magazines. Elsewhere, look at the local newspaper. Films are often in *version originale* or *vo* (original language) with subtitles. *Version française* or *vf* (French version) means a film has been dubbed into French. Student discounts are common.

tour	une visite	**church**	une église
region	la région	**castle**	un château
countryside	la campagne	**tower**	une tour
mountains	la montagne	**city walls**	les remparts
lake	le lac	**ruins**	des ruines
river	la rivière	**caves**	des grottes
coast	la côte	**amusement arcade**	une galerie de jeux
on the beach	à la plage	**theme park**	un parc d'attractions
in town	en ville	**festival**	une fête, un festival
at X's place	chez X	**fireworks**	un feu d'artifice
museum	un musée	**sound and light show**	un spectacle son et lumière
art gallery	un musée d'art	**wine tasting**	une dégustation de vin
exhibition	une exposition	**interesting**	intéressant/intéressante
craft exhibition	une exposition artisanale	**dull, boring**	ennuyeux/ennuyeuse
the old town	la vieille ville	**beautiful**	beau/belle
cathedral	la cathédrale		

cinema	le cinéma	**author**	l'auteur
film society/club	un ciné-club, une	**director (film)**	le réalisateur/la réalisatrice
	cinémathèque	**cast**	les acteurs
theatre	le théâtre	**actor/actress**	l'acteur/l'actrice
library	une bibliothèque	**film buff**	un mordu/une mordue*
film, movie	un film		du cinéma
play	une pièce	**production**	une réalisation
book	un livre, un bouquin	**plot**	l'intrigue
magazine	un magazine, une revue	**story**	l'histoire
comic	une BD, une bande	**set**	le décor
	dessinée	**special effects**	les effets spéciaux
novel	un roman	**photography**	la photographie
poetry	la poésie	**TV, telly**	la télé*

cable TV	la télé* câblée	adventure story	une histoire d'aventure
satellite TV	la télé* par satellite		
digital TV	la télé* numérique	war film	un film de guerre
programme	le programme	detective film	un film policier
channel	la chaîne	sci-fi	la science-fiction
news	les informations, les actualités, le journal	suspense	le suspense
		sex	le sexe
weather	la météo	violence	la violence
documentary	un documentaire	political	politique
cartoons	des dessins animés	satirical	satirique
game show	un jeu télévisé	serious	sérieux/sérieuse
serial	un feuilleton	offbeat	original/originale
soap	un mélo*	commercial	commercial/commerciale
ads	la pub*	exciting, gripping	passionnant/passionnante
dubbed	doublé/doublée	over the top	exagéré/exagérée
in English	en anglais	good	bon/bonne
with subtitles	sous-titré/titrée	OK, not bad	pas mauvais/pas mauvaise
well known	très connu/connue	bad, lousy	mauvais/mauvaise
award-winning	primé/primée	silly	bête
fringe	d'avant-garde, expérimental	funny	drôle
		fun	marrant/marrante*
block buster	une superproduction	sad	triste
a classic	un classique	It's scary.	Ça fait peur.
comedy	une comédie	Where can I hire a video?	Où est-ce que je peux louer une vidéo?
thriller	un thriller		
musical	une comédie musicale	Do I have to be a member?	Je dois être adhérent/adhérente?
horror film	un film d'épouvante		

Je peux emprunter quelque chose à lire?
Can I borrow something to read?

Ça parle de quoi?
What's it about?

J'ai étudié ce bouquin* à l'école.
I did that book at school.

C'est génial.
It's brilliant.

Tu as lu ça?
Have you read this?

C'est rasoir.*
It's so boring.

C'est de qui?
Who's it by?

Tu es toute seule?
Are you alone?

Tu as des soeurs?
Have you got any sisters?

Où est-ce que tu loges?
Where are you staying?

Non, je voyage avec des amis.
No, I'm travelling with friends.

I'm English.
Je suis anglais/anglaise.

My family is from ...
Ma famille vient de ...

I've been here for two weeks.
Je suis ici depuis deux semaines.

I'm on an exchange.
J'ai fait un échange.

I'm on holiday.
Je suis en vacances.

I'm staying with friends.
Je suis chez des amis.

I am a friend of ...
Je suis un ami/une amie de ...

I'm studying French.
J'étudie le français.

I'm travelling around.
Je voyage.

My parents are divorced.
Mes parents sont divorcés.

My birthday is on the ...
Mon anniversaire est le ...

I'm an only child.
Je suis fils/fille unique.

My name is ...	Je m'appelle ...
I live ...	J'habite ...
in the country	à la campagne
in a town	en ville
in the suburbs	en banlieue
by the sea	au bord de la mer
in a house	dans une maison
in a flat	dans un appartement
I live with ...	J'habite chez ...
I don't live with ...	Je n'habite pas chez ...
my	mon (m), ma (f), mes (plural)
your	ton (m), ta (f), tes (plural)
family	la famille
parents	les parents
father/mother	le père/la mère
stepfather	le beau-père
stepmother	la belle-mère
husband/wife	le mari/la femme
boyfriend	le petit ami
girlfriend	la petite amie
brother/sister	le frère/la soeur
step/half brother	le demi-frère
step/half sister	la demi-soeur
alone	seul/seule
single	célibataire
married	marié/mariée
surname	le nom de famille
nickname	le surnom
my address	mon adresse
my e-mail address	mon adresse e-mail

Other people

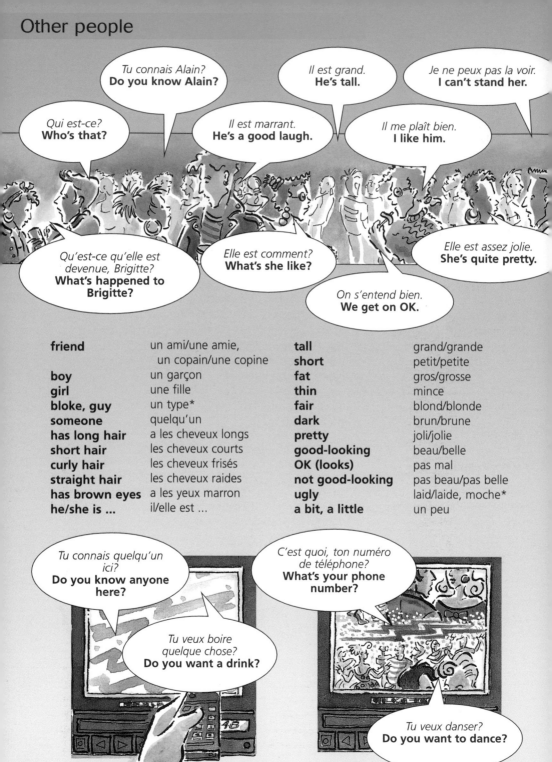

Tu connais Alain?
Do you know Alain?

Il est grand.
He's tall.

Je ne peux pas la voir.
I can't stand her.

Qui est-ce?
Who's that?

Il est marrant.
He's a good laugh.

Il me plaît bien.
I like him.

Qu'est-ce qu'elle est devenue, Brigitte?
What's happened to Brigitte?

Elle est comment?
What's she like?

Elle est assez jolie.
She's quite pretty.

On s'entend bien.
We get on OK.

friend	un ami/une amie, un copain/une copine	**tall**	grand/grande
boy	un garçon	**short**	petit/petite
girl	une fille	**fat**	gros/grosse
bloke, guy	un type*	**thin**	mince
someone	quelqu'un	**fair**	blond/blonde
has long hair	a les cheveux longs	**dark**	brun/brune
short hair	les cheveux courts	**pretty**	joli/jolie
curly hair	les cheveux frisés	**good-looking**	beau/belle
straight hair	les cheveux raides	**OK (looks)**	pas mal
has brown eyes	a les yeux marron	**not good-looking**	pas beau/pas belle
he/she is ...	il/elle est ...	**ugly**	laid/laide, moche*
		a bit, a little	un peu

Tu connais quelqu'un ici?
Do you know anyone here?

C'est quoi, ton numéro de téléphone?
What's your phone number?

Tu veux boire quelque chose?
Do you want a drink?

Tu veux danser?
Do you want to dance?

very	très, vachement**	**a creep**	un minable, un pauvre type
so	tellement		
really	vraiment	**an idiot, a prat**	un crétin/une crétine*
completely	complètement	**in a bad mood**	de mauvaise humeur
nice, OK	sympa*	**in a good mood**	de bonne humeur
not nice, horrible	pas sympa*	**angry, annoyed**	fâché/fâchée
horrible, nasty	mauvais/mauvaise, vache**	**depressed**	déprimé/déprimée
		happy	heureux/heureuse
cool, trendy, hip	branché/branchée*		
old-fashioned	ringard/ringarde*	**Have you heard that ... ?**	
clever	doué/douée	Tu sais que ... ?	
thick	bête		
boring	rasoir*	**Brigitte is going out with Alain.**	
shy	timide	Brigitte sort avec Alain.	
mad, crazy	fou/folle, dingue*		
weird	bizarre	**Luc got off with Sylvie.**	
lazy	paresseux/paresseuse	Luc a une touche avec Sylvie.	
laid back	relax*, relaxe*		
up-tight	coincé/coincée	**He/She kissed me.**	
mixed up, untogether	compliqué/compliquée	Il/Elle m'a embrassé/embrassée.	
selfish	égoïste	**They split up.**	
jealous	jaloux/jalouse	Ils ont cassé.	
rude	grossier/grossière		
macho	macho	**We had a row.**	
stuck up	snob	On s'est disputé.	
sloaney, yuppie	BCBG (bon chic, bon genre), yuppie		
		Leave me alone.	
loaded, rich	friqué/friquée*	Laissez-moi tranquille.	
cool	cool*	Laisse-moi tranquille.	

On peut se revoir?
Can I see you again?

Je peux venir aussi?
Can I come too?

Désolé, je ne peux pas.
Sorry I can't.

Tu veux venir?
Want to come?

Peut-être une autre fois.
Maybe some other time.

Tu fais du sport?
Do you do any sport?

Tu fais du jogging?
Do you go jogging?

Je ne suis vraiment pas en forme.
I'm really unfit.

Je joue au rugby.
I play rugby.

Je ne joue pas au squash.
I don't play squash.

Tu joues au tennis?
Do you play tennis?

Tous les combien?
How often?

Tu veux faire une partie de badminton?
Do you want a game of badminton?

Je n'ai pas de raquette.
I haven't got a racket.

Je fais du jogging tous les matins.
I go jogging every morning.

Catch!
Attrape!

In!/Out!
In!/Out!

Throw it to me.
Lance-le moi.

Who won?
Qui a gagné?

You're cheating!
Tu triches!

How do you play this?
Comment on joue à ça?

What are the rules?
Quelles sont les règles?

What team do you support?
Tu es pour quelle équipe?

Is there a match we could go to?
Il y a un match qu'on pourrait aller voir?

Fact file

Football, tennis, basketball and volleyball are popular games. Rugby is played a lot in the south and south west. Cycling is very popular, and the biggest spectator event is the annual *Tour de France*, a three week cycle race. In the south particularly, people of all ages play *boules* or *pétanque* (both played with metal balls, often on a patch of ground in the town square). Winter sports are very popular, with downhill skiing in the Alps and Pyrenees, but also cross-country in the Jura, Vosges and Massif Central.

sport	un sport	**sports clothes**	les vêtements de sport
match	un match		
a game (of)	une partie (de)	**once a week**	une fois par semaine
doubles	double	**twice a week**	deux fois par semaine
singles	simple		
race	une course	**I play ...**	Je joue au ...
marathon	un marathon	**I don't play ...**	Je ne joue pas au ...
championships	les championnats	**tennis**	tennis
Olympics	les Jeux Olympiques	**squash**	squash
World Cup	la Coupe du Monde	**badminton**	badminton
club	un club	**football**	foot(ball)
team	une équipe	**American football**	football américain
referee	un arbitre	**basketball**	basket
supporter	un supporter	**volleyball**	volley
training, practice	l'entraînement	**table tennis**	tennis de table
a goal	un but	**baseball**	base-ball
to lose	perdre	**I do, I go ...**	Je fais ...
a draw	match nul	**judo**	du judo
sports centre	le centre sportif	**karate**	du karaté
stadium	le stade	**jogging**	du jogging
gym	le gymnase	**running**	de la course à pied
court	le court	**aerobics**	de l'aérobic
indoor	couvert/couverte	**weight-training**	des poids et haltères
outdoor	en plein air	**body-building**	de la musculation
ball (small)	la balle	**keep-fit, gym**	de la gym
ball (large)	le ballon	**bowling**	du bowling
net	le filet	**dancing**	de la danse
trainers	des chaussures de sport	**yoga**	du yoga
tennis shoes	des tennis	**I don't do, go ...**	Je ne fais pas de† ...

†When saying *Je ne fais pas*, don't use *du, de la, de l'* or *des*. Use *de* instead, e.g. *Je ne fais pas de judo.*

I like ...	J'aime ...
I don't like ...	Je n'aime pas ...
I love ...	J'adore ...
I prefer ...	Je préfère ...
swimming	la natation
(scuba) diving	la plongée (sous-marine)
sailing	faire de la voile
surfing	le surf
canoeing	faire du canoë
rowing	faire de l'aviron
sunbathing	me faire bronzer
boat	un bateau
sail	la voile
surfboard	une planche de surf
windsurfer	une planche à voile
sea	la mer
beach	la plage
swimming pool	la piscine
in the sun	au soleil
in the shade	à l'ombre
mask	un masque
snorkel	un tuba
flippers	des palmes
wetsuit	une combinaison de plongée
life jacket	un gilet de sauvetage
fishing	la pêche
fishing rod	la canne à pêche

cycling	le cyclisme
racing bike	un vélo de course
mountain bike	un vélo tout terrain, un VTT
touring bike	un vélo de randonnée
BMX	un BMX
horse riding	l'équitation
horse	un cheval
walking, hiking	la marche à pied
footpath	un chemin (de randonnée)
skateboarding	faire du skateboard
roller skating	faire des rollers
ice rink	une patinoire
skates	des patins
skiing	faire du ski
cross-country skiing	le ski de fond
snowboarding	le surf des neiges
ski run	une piste de ski
ski pass	un forfait
ski lifts	les remontées mécaniques
chair lift	le télésiège
drag lift	le téléski, le tire-fesses*
skis	des skis
ski boots	des chaussures de ski
ski goggles	des lunettes de ski
snow	la neige

43

Qu'est-ce que tu fais?
What do you do?

Où est-ce que tu fais tes études?
Where are you studying?

C'est quel genre de lycée?
What sort of college is it?

A quelle heure tu sors?
What time do you finish?

Tu as beaucoup de travail?
Do you have a lot of work?

Oui, plein.
Yes, loads.

I do ...	Je fais ...
computer studies	de l'informatique
maths	des maths
physics	de la physique
chemistry	de la chimie
biology	de la biologie
natural sciences	des sciences naturelles, des sciences nat
geography	de la géographie
history	de l'histoire
economics	de l'économie
business studies	des études commerciales
languages	des langues
French	du français
English	de l'anglais
Spanish	de l'espagnol
German	de l'allemand
literature	de la littérature
philosophy	de la philosophie, de la philo
sociology	de la sociologie, de la socio
psychology	de la psychologie, de la psycho
religious studies	de l'instruction religieuse
general studies	de l'éducation civique
design and technology	du dessin industriel et de la techno
art	du dessin, des arts plastiques
drama	du théâtre
music	de la musique
PE	de la gym
school	une école, un bahut*
mixed	mixte
boarding school	un internat
private school	un collège privé
term	un trimestre
holidays	les vacances
beginning of term	la rentrée
uniform	un uniforme

school club	un club, un foyer
class representative	le délégué/la déléguée de classe
lesson, lecture	un cours
tuition, coaching, private lessons	des cours particuliers, du soutien
homework	des devoirs
essay	une dissertation
translation	une traduction
project	un projet
coursework, presentation	un exposé
revision	la révision
test	un contrôle
oral	oral/orale
written	écrit/écrite
continuous assessment	le contrôle continu
mark, grade	la note
teacher, lecturer	le professeur, le/la prof
(language) assistant	l'assistant/l'assistante
good	bon/bonne
bad	mauvais/mauvaise
strict	strict/stricte, sévère
easy going	pas strict/stricte, sympa
discipline	la discipline
to repeat (a year)	redoubler
suspended	renvoyé/renvoyée temporairement
expelled	renvoyé/renvoyée
to skip a lesson	sauter un cours
a grant	une bourse

I'm a student.
Je suis étudiant/ étudiante.

I'm still at school.
Je vais encore à l'école.

I want to do ...
J'aimerais faire ...

He is skiving, bunking off.
Il fait l'école buissonnière.

Fact file

Types of schools and colleges include *un collège* (comprehensive-type school for the first four years of secondary school), *un lycée d'enseignement professionnel* (secondary school with vocational bias), *un lycée* (similar to a grammar school), *un IUT* or *institut universitaire de technologie* (polytechnic), *une université* or *une faculté*, often shortened to *fac* (university), and *une haute école* (élite university with entry by *concours* (competitive exam)).

Most schools are mixed and uniform is rare. Summer holidays run from late June to early September. Schools employ *surveillants* or *pions** to keep discipline.

Secondary school starts at about age 11 with *sixième* form and goes up to *première* and finally *terminale*. At about 16, most pupils get the *brevet* certificate, based on average marks. Many pupils go on to take the *CAP* or *BEP* (vocational exams), the *HT* (more technological), or *bac* – short for *baccalauréat* – which gives access to universities. School is compulsory until age 16.

Tu veux faire quoi après le lycée?
What do you want to do when you finish college?

Tu études quelles matières?
What subjects are you doing?

Tu es en quelle classe?
What year are you in?

Quand est-ce que tu passes tes examens?
When are your exams?

Qu'est-ce que tu préfères?
What do you like best?

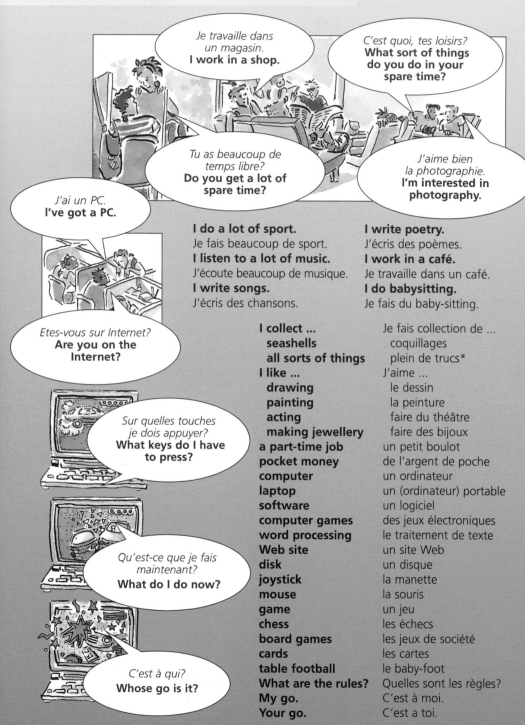

Je travaille dans un magasin.
I work in a shop.

C'est quoi, tes loisirs?
What sort of things do you do in your spare time?

Tu as beaucoup de temps libre?
Do you get a lot of spare time?

J'aime bien la photographie.
I'm interested in photography.

J'ai un PC.
I've got a PC.

Etes-vous sur Internet?
Are you on the Internet?

Sur quelles touches je dois appuyer?
What keys do I have to press?

Qu'est-ce que je fais maintenant?
What do I do now?

C'est à qui?
Whose go is it?

I do a lot of sport.
Je fais beaucoup de sport.
I listen to a lot of music.
J'écoute beaucoup de musique.
I write songs.
J'écris des chansons.

I write poetry.
J'écris des poèmes.
I work in a café.
Je travaille dans un café.
I do babysitting.
Je fais du baby-sitting.

I collect ...	Je fais collection de ...
seashells	coquillages
all sorts of things	plein de trucs*
I like ...	J'aime ...
drawing	le dessin
painting	la peinture
acting	faire du théâtre
making jewellery	faire des bijoux
a part-time job	un petit boulot
pocket money	de l'argent de poche
computer	un ordinateur
laptop	un (ordinateur) portable
software	un logiciel
computer games	des jeux électroniques
word processing	le traitement de texte
Web site	un site Web
disk	un disque
joystick	la manette
mouse	la souris
game	un jeu
chess	les échecs
board games	les jeux de société
cards	les cartes
table football	le baby-foot
What are the rules?	Quelles sont les règles?
My go.	C'est à moi.
Your go.	C'est a toi.

What do you want to do later?
Tu veux faire quoi, plus tard?
When I finish ...
Quand j'aurai fini ...
One day ...
Un jour ...
I want to be a ...
Je voudrais être ...

I want ...
to live/work abroad
to travel
to have a career
to get a good job
to get my
qualifications
to carry on studying

Je voudrais ...
habiter/travailler à l'étranger
voyager
faire une carrière
trouver un bon boulot
obtenir mes diplômes

poursuivre mes études

What do you think about ...?
Qu'est-ce que tu penses de ...?
I don't know much about ...
Je ne sais pas grand-chose sur ...
Can you explain ...?
Tu peux/Vous pouvez expliquer ...?
I feel angry about (pollution).
(La pollution), ça me met en colère.

I think ...
Je pense ...
I belong to ...
J'appartiens à ...
I believe in ...
Je crois à ...
I don't believe in ...
Je ne crois pas à ...

You're right.
Tu as raison.
I don't agree.
Je ne suis pas d'accord.
I'm for, I support ...
Je suis pour ...
I'm against ...
Je suis contre ...

the future	l'avenir	**ozone layer**	la couche d'ozone
(in) the past	(dans) le passé	**deforestation**	le déboisement
now, nowadays	de nos jours, maintenant	**nuclear power**	l'énergie nucléaire
religion	la religion	**recycling**	le recyclage
god	dieu	**politics**	la politique
human rights	les droits de l'homme	**government**	le gouvernement
gay	gay, homo	**democratic**	démocratique
feminist	féministe	**elections**	des élections
abortion	l'avortement	**party**	un parti
drugs	les drogues	**revolution**	une révolution
drug addict	un drogué/une droguée	**the left**	la gauche
HIV positive	séropositif/séropositive	**the right**	la droite
Aids	le Sida	**fascist**	fasciste
unemployment	le chômage	**communist**	communiste
Third World	le Tiers-Monde	**socialist**	socialiste
peace	la paix	**greens, green**	les verts, les
war	la guerre	**movement**	écologistes
terrorism	le terrorisme	**conservative**	conservateur/
environment	l'environnement		conservatrice
pollution	la pollution	**reactionary**	réactionnaire, réac*
conservation	la conservation	**politically active,**	engagé/engagée
global warming	le réchauffement de la	**committed**	
	planète	**march, demo**	une manifestation,
greenhouse effect	l'effet de serre		une manif*

Illness, problems, emergencies

I am ill.	Je suis malade.
It hurts.	Ça fait mal.
It hurts a lot.	Ça fait très mal.
It hurts a little.	Ça fait un peu mal.
It itches.	Ça me démange.
I've cut myself.	Je me suis coupé/coupée.
I think I've broken my ...	Je crois que je me suis cassé...
I've been stung by a wasp.	J'ai été piqué/piquée par une guêpe.
I've got mosquito bites.	J'ai été piqué/piquée par des moustiques.
He/She's had too much to drink.	Il/Elle a trop bu.
I feel dizzy.	J'ai la tête qui tourne.
I'm constipated.	Je suis constipé/constipée.
I'm on medication for ...	Je prends des médicaments pour ...
I'm allergic ...	Je suis allergique ...
to antibiotics	aux antibiotiques
to some medicines	à certains médicaments
I have ...	J'ai ...
food poisoning	un empoisonnement alimentaire
diarrhoea	la diarrhée
sunstroke	un coup de soleil
a headache	mal à la tête
a stomach ache	mal au ventre
my period	mes règles
an infection	une infection
a sore throat	mal à la gorge
a cold	un rhume
flu	la grippe
a cough	une toux
hayfever	le rhume des foins
asthma	de l'asthme
a toothache	mal aux dents
a temperature	de la température
the shivers	des frissons
a hangover	la gueule de bois*
doctor	le médecin, le docteur
female doctor	une femme médecin
dentist	le/la dentiste
optician	l'opticien/l'opticienne
chemist's, pharmacist's	la pharmacie
pill	un cachet, une pilule
suppository	un suppositoire
injection	une piqûre

Je ne me sens pas bien.
I don't feel well.

Qu'est-ce qui ne va pas?
What's wrong?

Je vais vomir.
I'm going to be sick.

Je suis vraiment désolé.
I'm really sorry about this.

Il faut que je voie un médecin.
I need to see a doctor.

Il y a une pharmacie ouverte près d'ici?
Is there a chemist open around here?

Vous pouvez me donner quelque chose pour le rhume des foins?
Can you give me something for hayfever?

> J'ai perdu une lentille.
> **I've lost my contact lens.**

> J'ai cassé mes lunettes.
> **I've broken my glasses.**

> On m'a volé mes affaires.
> **Someone's stolen my things.**

> Je n'ai pas vu ce qui s'est passé.
> **I didn't see what happened.**

Fact file

In France everyone has to carry their identity card, so keep your passport with you. Don't be surprised if you are asked to show your *papiers* (documents, ID).

If you have to see a doctor or go to the *service des urgences* (casualty department) of the local *hôpital* (hospital), expect to pay, though not upfront in an emergency. You should be able to claim back expenses on insurance, but hang on to all the paperwork.

Emergencies

Emergency phone numbers: police 17; fire 18; ambulance 15. For very serious problems, contact the closest *consulat britannique* (British consulate).

There's been an accident.	Il vient d'y avoir un accident.
Help!	Au secours!
Fire!	Au feu!
Stop thief!	Au voleur!
Please call ...	S'il vous plaît, appelez...
an ambulance	une ambulance
the police	la police
the fire brigade	les pompiers
the lifeguard	le maître-nageur

wallet	mon portefeuille
(hand)bag	mon sac (à main)
my things	mes affaires
my papers	mes papiers
my passport	mon passeport
my key	ma clé
my mobile	mon portable
all my money	tout mon argent
lost property	objets perdus
I'm lost.	Je suis perdu/perdue.
I'm scared.	J'ai peur.
I'm in trouble.	J'ai des ennuis.

I need to talk to someone.
Il faut que je parle à quelqu'un.

I don't know what to do.
Je ne sais pas quoi faire.

I don't want to cause trouble, but ...
Je ne veux pas faire d'ennuis, mais ...

A man's following me.
Il y a un homme qui me suit.

Can you keep an eye on my things?
Vous pouvez surveiller mes affaires?

Has anyone seen ...?
Quelqu'un a vu ...?

Please don't smoke.
Ça vous ennuierait de ne pas fumer?

It doesn't work.
Ça ne marche pas.

There's no water/power.
Il n'y a pas d'eau/de courant.

Slang and everyday French

This book has included informal French and slang where appropriate, but these two pages list a few of the most common words and phrases. When using slang it is easy to sound off-hand or rude without meaning to. Here, as in the rest of the book, a single asterisk after a word shows it is mild slang, but two asterisks show it can be quite rude and it may be safest to avoid using it. You will find more slang in the dictionary.

Alternative pronunciations

I don't know	j'sais pas* (je ne sais pas)
I haven't	j'ai pas* (je n'ai pas)
you have	t'as* (tu as)
you are	t'es* (tu es)
there is/are	y a*(il y a)
yes	ouais* (oui)
well	ben* (bien)
nice, friendly	sympa (sympathique)

Abbreviations

mad, crazy, keen	fana (fanatique)
ecologist	un écolo (écologiste)
intellectual	un intello (intellectuel)
teacher	un prof (professeur)
in the morning	du mat (du matin)
cinema	le ciné (cinéma)
test	une interro (interrogation)
flat	un appart (appartement)

Fillers and exclamations

OK	OK, bien, d'acc
right	bon, alors
well	eh bien
actually, in fact	en fait
by the way	au fait
damn	mince*, zut*, flûte*

American and English imports

le boss; cool; flipper **(to flip)**; un job; le look; non-stop; un scoop; sexy; le show-biz; un spot **(a commercial, an ad)**; le stress

very	hyper, super, vachement**
great, fab, cool	génial/géniale, chouette, super*, terrible, d'enfer*
rubbish, bad, disgusting	moche*, infect/infecte, nul, dégueulasse**
boring	emmerdant/emmerdante**
irritating, annoying	énervant/énervante
funny	marrant/marrante*
crazy, mad	dingue*, cinglé/cinglée*
lucky	verni/vernie*
broke	fauché/fauchée, à sec*
guy, bloke	un type*, un mec*, un gars*
friend, mate	un pote*
kid	un/une gosse*, un/une môme*
policeman	un flic*
money, dosh	les sous, le fric*, le blé*, les ronds*, l'oseille
francs	balles*, e.g. 100 balles*, sacs e.g. 100 sacs
clothes	les fringues*
car	la bagnole*, la tire*, la caisse*
food, grub	la bouffe**
school	le bahut*
school, company	la boîte*
room	la piaule*
problem	un pépin*, un 'blem*
to have fun	se marrer*
to understand, get it	piger*, capter*
to talk rubbish	baratiner*
to chat up	baratiner*, draguer** brancher**
to steal, nick	piquer*, faucher
to chuck out, sack	virer
to crack up, lose it	craquer*
to fail, fall through	foirer*
to be careful	faire gaffe*
to be on good form	avoir une pêche d'enfer*
to be full of beans	avoir la frite*, avoir la pêche*
to work	bosser*
It's a turn-on.	C'est le pied.*
You're getting on my nerves.	Tu m'énerves. Tu me gonfles.*
Leave me alone.	Fous-moi la paix.** Lâche-moi les baskets.**
I don't care.	Je m'en fous.*

Countries, nationalities, faiths

Countries

country	le pays	**continent**	le continent
north	le nord	**south**	le sud
east	l'est	**west**	l'ouest
Africa	l'Afrique (f)		
Algeria	l'Algérie (f)		
Asia	l'Asie (f)		
Australia	l'Australie (f)		
Austria	l'Autriche (f)		
Bangladesh	le Bangladesh		
Belgium	la Belgique		
Canada	le Canada		
Caribbean Islands	les Petites Antilles (f)		
Central America	l'Amérique Centrale (f)		
China	la Chine		
Corsica	la Corse		
England	l'Angleterre (f)		
Europe	l'Europe (f)		
France	la France		
Germany	l'Allemagne (f)		
Great Britain	la Grande-Bretagne		
Greece	la Grèce		
Hungary	la Hongrie		
India	l'Inde (f)		
Ireland	l'Irlande (f)		
Israel	Israël (m)		
Italy	l'Italie (f)		
Jamaica	la Jamaïque		
Japan	le Japon		
Martinique	la Martinique		
Middle East	le Moyen-Orient		
Morocco	le Maroc		
Netherlands	les Pays-Bas		
New Zealand	la Nouvelle-Zélande		
North Africa	l'Afrique du Nord		
Pakistan	le Pakistan		
Poland	la Pologne		
Russia	la Russie		
Scotland	l'Écosse (f)		
South America	l'Amérique du Sud (f)		
Spain	l'Espagne (f)		
Switzerland	la Suisse		
Tunisia	la Tunisie		
Turkey	la Turquie		
United States	les Etats-Unis		
Vietnam	le Viêt-Nam		
Wales	le pays de Galles		

Nationalities

You can say "I come from" + country:

Je viens du + (m) name e.g. *Je viens du Japon*
Je viens de la + (f) name e.g. *Je viens de la Suisse*
Je viens d' + names that start with a vowel e.g. *Je viens d'Angleterre*
Je viens des + plural names e.g. *Je viens des Etats-Unis.*

Or you can say "I am ..." + adjective for nationality, e.g. *Je suis:*

Algerian	algérien/algérienne
American	américain/américaine
Australian	australien/australienne
Austrian	autrichien/autrichienne
Belgian	belge
Canadian	canadien/canadienne
Dutch	néerlandais/néerlandaise
English	anglais/anglaise
French	français/française
German	allemand/allemande
Indian	indien/indienne
Irish	irlandais/irlandaise
Italian	italien/italienne
Moroccan	marocain/marocaine
Pakistani	pakistanais/pakistanaise
Scottish	écossais/écossaise
Spanish	espagnol/espagnole
Swiss	suisse
Welsh	gallois/galloise

Faiths

agnostic	un/une agnostique
atheist	un/une athée
Buddhist	bouddhiste
Catholic	catholique
Christian	chrétien/chrétienne
Hindu	hindou/hindoue
Jewish	juif/juive
Muslim	musulman/musulmane
Protestant	protestant/protestante
Sikh	sikh

Numbers, colours, days, dates

Numbers

0 zéro	**31** trente et un
1 un	**40** quarante
2 deux	**50** cinquante
3 trois	**60** soixante
4 quatre	**70** soixante-dix
5 cinq	**71** soixante et onze
6 six	**72** soixante-douze
7 sept	**80** quatre-vingts
8 huit	**81** quatre-vingt-un
9 neuf	**82** quatre-vingt-deux
10 dix	**90** quatre-vingt-dix
11 onze	**91** quatre-vingt-onze
12 douze	**92** quatre-vingt-douze
13 treize	**100** cent
14 quatorze	**101** cent un
15 quinze	**200** deux cents
16 seize	**300** trois cents
17 dix-sept	**1,000** mille
18 dix-huit	**1,100** mille cent
19 dix-neuf	**1,200** mille deux cents
20 vingt	**2,000** deux mille
21 vingt et un	**2,100** deux mille cent
22 vingt-deux	**10,000** dix mille
23 vingt-trois	**100,000** cent mille
30 trente	**1,000,000** un million

Colours

colour	la couleur
light	clair/claire
dark	foncé/foncée
blue	bleu/bleue
navy	bleu marine
green	vert/verte
yellow	jaune
orange	orange
purple	mauve, violet/violette
pink	rose
red	rouge
white	blanc/blanche
grey	gris/grise
brown	marron, brun/brune
black	noir/noire

Days and dates

Monday	lundi
Tuesday	mardi
Wednesday	mercredi
Thursday	jeudi
Friday	vendredi
Saturday	samedi
Sunday	dimanche
January	janvier
February	février
March	mars
April	avril
May	mai
June	juin
July	juillet
August	août
September	septembre
October	octobre
November	novembre
December	décembre
day	le jour
week	la semaine
month	le mois
year	l'année, l'an
diary	un agenda
calendar	un calendrier
yesterday	hier
the day before yesterday	avant-hier
today	aujourd'hui
the next day	le lendemain
tomorrow	demain
the day after tomorrow	après-demain
last week	la semaine dernière
this week	cette semaine
next week	la semaine prochaine
What's the date?	Quelle est la date?
on Mondays	le lundi
in August	en août
(on) 1st April	le premier avril
(on) 2nd January	le deux janvier
in the year 2000	en l'an deux mille
in 2005	en deux mille cinq
2010	deux mille dix

Time

hour	l'heure
What time is it?	Quelle heure est-il?
It's 1 o'clock.	Il est une heure.
2 o'clock	deux heures
minute	la minute
morning	le matin
afternoon	l'après-midi
evening	le soir
midday	midi
midnight	minuit
quarter past two	deux heures et quart
half past two	deux heures et demie
quarter to two	deux heures moins le quart
five past two	deux heures cinq
ten to two	deux heures moins dix
What time ... ?	A quelle heure ... ?
in ten minutes	dans dix minutes
half an hour ago	il y a une demi-heure
at 09.00	à neuf heures
at 13.17	à treize heures dix-sept
at 9am	à neuf heures du matin
at 3pm	à trois heures de l'après-midi
at 9 in the evening	à neuf heures du soir

Seasons and weather

season	la saison	**sky**	le ciel
spring	le printemps	**sun**	le soleil
summer	l'été	**clouds**	les nuages
autumn	l'automne	**rain**	la pluie
winter	l'hiver	**snow**	la neige

It's fine.	Il fait beau.
It's sunny.	Il fait soleil.
It's hot.	Il fait chaud.
It's windy.	Il fait du vent.
It's raining.	Il pleut.
It's foggy.	Il y a du brouillard.
It's snowing.	Il neige.
It's icy.	Il y a du verglas.
It's cold.	Il fait froid.
It's freezing.	Il gèle.
It's horrible.	Il fait mauvais.
What's the weather like?	
Quel temps fait-il?	

The fact files below focus on essential, practical information which is different from that given for France.

Fact file: Belgium

Languages – French is mostly spoken in the south, Flemish in the north. **Travel** – For under 26s, cheap deals include the *Go Pass* and the *Tourrail* card, both valid on the *SNCB* (Belgian railways). Taxis take up to four passengers but can be expensive. Mopeds can be ridden from age 16. **Banks and phones** – Currency is the Belgian *franc* (F or BEF) or, from 2002, the euro. Banking hours are usually 9am-4pm with an hour's closure for lunch. In cities, some banks are open at lunchtime and on Saturday morning. Phones are either coin or card operated. **Shopping** – Opening times are 9am-6pm, or later on Friday. Shops close on Sunday and one other day. **Emergency phone numbers** – Police 101, fire and ambulance 100.

Fact file: Switzerland

Languages – The three official languages are French, German and Italian. **Travel** – Cheap deals include the *Swiss Pass, Swiss Flexi Pass* and *Half Fare Travel Card,* valid on trains, and most bus and lake steamer services. There are also various regional travel passes. The *PTT* (post office) runs bus services to remote areas. To hire bikes from stations you must book the day before. You have to be 18 to ride a moped. **Banks and phones** – Currency is the Swiss *franc* (SF). In cities banks open 8.30am-4.30pm on weekdays; elsewhere they close for lunch from 12 noon-2pm. Train stations and chain stores often change money. Phone boxes mainly take *taxcards* (phonecards). **Shopping** – Opening times vary a lot. Some shops are closed on Monday mornings. **Emergencies** – There is no national health service so make sure you are insured. Phone numbers – police 117; fire 118; ambulance 144.

To pronounce French well, you need the help of a French speaker or some language tapes, but these general points will help you to make yourself understood. Bear in mind that there are exceptions and regional variations.

Vowel sounds

a sounds like "a" in cat.

e, *eu* and *oe* sound a bit like "u" in "fur". At the end of a word, *e* is silent.

é sounds like "a" in "late", but a bit clipped.

è, *ê* and *ai* sound like "ai" in "air".

i sounds like "i" in machine but clipped.

o sounds like "o" in soft.

ô, *au*, and *eau* sound like "au" in "autumn".

u is a sharp "u" sound. Round your lips to say "oo", then try to say "ee", and you will be close.

oi sounds like "wa" in "wagon".

ou sounds like "oo" in "moody".

ui sounds like "wee" in "week".

Nasal sounds

French has some slightly nasal sounds in which the *n* or *m* are barely sounded:

an and *en* are a bit like "aun" in "aunt".

am and *em* (when they precede *p* or *b*) sound like *an/en* but with a hint of an "m".

in (when it precedes a consonant or is at the end of a word) and *ain* sound a bit like "an" in "can".

im (when it precedes *p* or *b*) sounds like *in/ain* but with a hint of an "m".

on is a bit like "on" in "song".

un (at the end of a word or before a consonant) is a bit like "an" in "an apple".

Consonants

c is hard as in "cat", except before *i* or *e*, or with a cedilla: *ç*. Then it is like "s" in "sun".

ch sounds like "sh" in "shoe".

g is like "g" in "go" except before *e* or *i*. Then it is soft like the "j" sound in "measure".

gn is like the "nio" sound in "onion".

h is never pronounced.

j is like the "j" sound in "measure".

ll when it follows *i* is like "y" in "young".

ail on the end of a word is like "y" in "sky".

qu is the same as a hard *c* (the "u" is silent).

r is made in the back of the throat.

s is like "z" in "zoo", and *ss* or *s* at the start of a word is like "s" in "soap".

Consonants at ends of words are usually silent unless an *e* comes after. At ends of words *er*, *et* and *ez* usually sound like *é*.

French alphabet

Applying the points above, this is how you say the alphabet: A, Bé, Çé, Dé, Eu, èFe, G = jé, acHe, I, Ji, Ka, èLe, èMe, èNe, O, Pé, Quu, èRe, èSse, Té, U, Vé, W = double-vé, iXe, Y = i-grèque, Zède.

How French works

Nouns

All French nouns are either masculine (m) or feminine (f).

For a few nouns the gender is obvious, e.g. *le garçon* (boy) is masculine and *la fille* (girl) is feminine. For most nouns the gender seems random, e.g. *le tronc* (trunk) is masculine and *la branche* (branch) is feminine. Some nouns can be either gender, e.g. *le/la touriste* (tourist m/f) and some have two forms, e.g. *l'étudiant/l'étudiante* (student m/f).

The article (the word for "the" or "a") shows the gender of the noun: with masculine nouns "the" is *le*, e.g. *le train* (the train) and "a" is *un*, e.g. *un train* (a train); with feminine nouns, "the" is *la*, e.g. *la boîte* (the box) and "a" is *une*, e.g. *une boîte* (a box); with nouns that begin with a vowel and some nouns beginning with *h*, "the" is *l'*, e.g. *l'avion* (the plane) or *l'heure* (the hour). "A" is still *un* or *une*, e.g. *un avion* (a plane) or *une heure* (an hour).

Sometimes French uses an article where English doesn't, e.g. *J'aime le thé* (I like tea).

To help you get articles right, this phrasebook gives nouns with the article most likely to be useful, and the dictionary makes genders clear by listing nouns with *le* or *la*, or adding (m) or (f) after those that begin with a vowel.

Don't worry if you muddle up *le* and *la*; you will still be understood. It is worth knowing the gender of nouns, though, since other words, especially adjectives, change to match them. Always learn a noun with *le* or *la* – or *un* or *une* for nouns beginning with a vowel. Many nouns ending in *e* are feminine.

Plurals

In the plural, the French for "the" is *les*, e.g. *les trains* (the trains).

In English "some" (the plural for "a") is often left out. In French *un* or *une* becomes *des* in the plural and is always used, e.g. *Il y a des types qui ...* (There are blokes who ...)

To make a noun plural, add *s*, e.g. *deux trains* (two trains). For some nouns you add *x*, e.g. *deux gâteaux* (two cakes).

De, du, de la, de l', des (any, some)

When talking about things like butter or water, English uses "any", "some" or no article, e.g. Is there any butter left? I want some butter. There's water in the jug.

French has a special article that is always used in these cases, *de* + "the"; but *de* + *le* become *du*, and *de* + *les* become *des*, so:
du + (m) noun, e.g. *Tu veux du café?* (Would you like some coffee?);
de la + (f) noun, e.g. *Tu as de la musique rock?* (Do you have any rock music?);
de l' + nouns beginning with a vowel, e.g. *Tu veux de l'eau gazeuse?* (Do you want any fizzy water?);
des + plural nouns, e.g. *Tu veux des frites?* (Do you want some chips?)
In negative sentences simply use *de* + noun, or *d'* before a vowel, e.g. *Je ne veux pas de café/d'eau* (I don't want any coffee/water).

De (of)

In French "of" is *de*. It works in the same way as *de* meaning "any, some": with (m) nouns use *du*, e.g. *la couleur du mur* (the colour of the wall), and so on.

French uses "of" to show possession where English doesn't, e.g. *le pull de Paul* (Paul's jumper, literally "the jumper of Paul").

Au, à la, à l', aux (to, at)

The French for "to" and "at" is *à*. With *le* and *les*, *à* becomes *au* and *aux*, so use:
au + (m) nouns, e.g. *Je vais au ciné* (I'm going to the cinema);
à la + (f) nouns, e.g. *Je suis à la gare* (I'm at the station);
à l' + nouns that begin with a vowel, e.g. *Je suis à l'aéroport* (I'm at the airport);
aux + plural nouns, e.g. *Je vais aux Etats-Unis* (I'm going to the States).

Ceci, cela, ça, (this, that)

"This" is *ceci*, "that" is *cela*, but both are shortened to *ça* in everyday French, e.g. *Je voudrais ça* (I'd like this/that).

Celui-ci and *celle-ci* are the (m) and (f) forms for "this one". *Celui-là* and *celle-là* are the (m) and (f) forms for "that one".

Ce, cette, cet, ces (this, that)

Used as an adjective, "this" and "that" are:
ce + (m) nouns, e.g. *ce type* (this bloke);
cette + (f) nouns, e.g. *cette fille* (this girl);
cet + nouns beginning with a vowel, e.g. *cet idiot* (that idiot); *ces* + plural nouns, e.g. *ces filles* (those girls).

Adjectives

In French, many adjectives agree with the noun they refer to; this means they change when used with a feminine or plural noun.

Many add an *e* on the end when used with a (f) noun. The *e* also changes the sound of the word as it means you pronounce the consonant, e.g. *vert* (green) with a silent *t* becomes *verte* with a voiced *t*: *un pull vert* (a green jumper), *une porte verte* (a green door). Most adjectives ending in a vowel add an extra *e* but sound the same, e.g. *bleu/bleue*.

In this book, adjectives that change are either given twice: (m) form followed by (f) form, e.g. *vert/verte* (green), or the (f) form is given in brackets after the (m), e.g. *vert(e)*.

Some adjectives don't change, e.g. any that end in *e* like *sympathique* (nice).

In the plural, most adjectives add an *s*, e.g. *des pulls verts* (green jumpers), *des portes vertes* (green doors).

Most adjectives follow the noun but some common ones usually come before, e.g.:

beautiful *beau/belle*	young *jeune*
nice, kind *gentil/gentille*	pretty *joli/jolie*
bad *mauvais/mauvaise*	good *bon/bonne*
big, tall *grand/grande*	long *long/longue*
small, short *petit/petite*	old *vieux/vieille*
fat, big *gros/grosse*	

Making comparisons

To make a comparison, put the following words in front of the adjective:
plus (more, ...er), e.g. *plus important* (more important), *plus gros* (fatter);
moins (less), e.g. *moins gros* (less fat);
aussi (as), e.g *aussi gros* (as fat);
le plus/la plus (the most, the ...est), e.g. *le plus important* (the most important).

plus ... que (more ... than, ...er than), e.g. *Il est plus grand que Joe* (He's taller than Joe);
moins que (less ... than), e.g. *Elle est moins grande que lui* (She's less tall than him);
aussi ... que (as ... as), e.g. *Il est aussi maigre qu'elle* (He's as thin as her).
Que shortens to *qu'* in front of a vowel.

There are some exceptions, e.g. *bon/bonne* (good), *meilleur/meilleure* (better), *le meilleur/la meilleure* (the best), *mauvais/mauvaise* (bad), *pire* (worse), *le pire/la pire* (the worst).

How French works

My, your, his, her etc.

These words agree with their noun, e.g. *mon frère* (my brother), *ma soeur* (my sister), *mes parents* (my parents).

In front of	(m) noun	(f) noun	plural noun
my	*mon*	*ma*	*mes*
your	*ton*	*ta*	*tes*
his/her	*son*	*sa*	*ses*
our	*notre*	*notre*	*nos*
your	votre	*votre*	*vos*
their	*leur*	*leur*	*leurs*

Before a vowel or *h*, use the (m) form, e.g. *mon écharpe* (my scarf) even though *écharpe* is (f).

I, you, he, she etc.

I *je* or *j'*
Je shortens to *j'* in front of vowels, e.g. *j'aime* (I like).

you *tu* or *vous*
Say *tu* to a friend, or someone of your own age or younger. Use *vous* when you talk to an adult. If in doubt, use *vous*. *Vous* is also the plural form. Use it when speaking to more than one person.

he *il*   she *elle*   it *il* or *elle*
There is no special word for "it". Since nouns are (m) or (f), you use "he" to refer to a male or (m) thing and "she" to refer to a female or (f) thing, e.g. *Le train? Il est en retard* (The train? It's late) or *La gare? Elle est là-bas* (The station? It's over there)

we *nous* or *on*
Nous means "we", e.g. *Nous sommes en retard* (We are late). However, *nous* sounds formal, so people often use the more colloquial word *on* instead. Like "one" in English, *on* takes the he/she form of the verb: *On est en retard* (We're late)

they *ils* or *elles*
Ils is used for males and (m) things, and *elles* for females and (f) things.

Me, you, him etc.

me *me*	us *nous*		
you *te*	you *vous*		
him/it *le*	her/it *la*	them *les*	

In French these come before the verb, e.g. *Je le veux* (I want it).

Verbs

French verbs have more tenses (present, future etc.) than English verbs, but there are simple ways of getting by which are explained here.

Present tense

In dictionaries and indexes, verbs are listed in the infinitive form, e.g. "to read", "to like". Many French infinitives end in *er* e.g. *regarder* (to watch) and follow the same pattern. Drop *er* and replace it with the ending you need:

regarder

I watch	*je regard e*
you watch	*tu regard es*
he/she/it/watches	*il/elle regard e*
we watch	*nous regard ons*
you watch	*vous regard ez*
they watch	*ils/elles regard ent*

French doesn't distinguish between the two English present tenses, e.g. "I watch" or "I'm watching", so *je regarde* can mean either. Another tip is that verbs are generally easier than they look: many forms sound the same even though the spelling changes, e.g. *aime*, *aimes* and *aiment* all sound alike.

Useful irregular verbs

to be	être
I am	je suis
you are	tu es
he/she/it is	il/elle est
we are	nous sommes
you are	vous êtes
they are	ils/elles sont

to have (got)	avoir
I have	j'ai
you have	tu as
he/she/it has	il/elle a
we have	nous avons
you have	vous avez
they have	ils/elles ont

to go	aller
I go	je vais
you go	tu vas
he/she/it goes	il/elle va
we go	nous allons
you go	vous allez
they go	ils/elles vont

to come	venir
I come	je viens
you come	tu viens
he/she/it comes	il/elle vient
we come	nous venons
you come	vous venez
they come	ils/elles viennent

to make, do	faire
I make, do	je fais
you make, do	tu fais
he/she/it makes, does	il/elle fait
we make, do	nous faisons
you make, do	vous faites
they make, do	ils/elles font

to want (to)	vouloir
I want	je veux
you want	tu veux
he/she/it wants	il/elle veut
we want	nous voulons
you want	vous voulez
they want	ils/elles veulent

to be able to	pouvoir
I can	je peux
you can	tu peux
he/she/it can	il/elle peut
we can	nous pouvons
you can	vous pouvez
they can	ils/elles peuvent

to have to/must	devoir
I have to/must	je dois
you have to/must	tu dois
he/she/it has to/must	il/elle doit
we have to/must	nous devons
you have to/must	vous devez
they have to/must	ils/elles doivent

The last three verbs are handy for making sentences like:
Je veux manger (I want to eat);
Je peux venir avec toi (I can come with you);
Je dois regarder la télé (I must watch TV).
The second verb is in the infinitive (see page 58).

Talking about the future

There is a future tense in French, e.g.
Je regarderai la télé (I shall watch TV) but it is easier to use the "going to" future:
Je vais regarder la télé (I'm going to watch TV). For everyday use, this form is also more common. As in English, simply use the present of *aller* (to go) + an infinitive (see page 58).

How French works

Talking about the past

The easiest way is to use the perfect tense, e.g. *J'ai regardé* which can mean "I watched" or "I have watched". You make the perfect with the present of *avoir* (to have) + something called the past participle of the verb:
er verbs change their ending to *é* to make the past participle, e.g. *regarder* becomes *regardé* (they sound just the same);
most verbs ending in *ir* in the infinitive change to *i*, e.g. *dormir* becomes *dormi*: *il a dormi* (he slept/has slept).

Some verbs form the perfect tense with *être* (to be) instead of *avoir*, e.g. *Il est allé* (he went/has been). Below are the most useful of these (past participles are also shown if they are not regular *er* or *ir* verbs):

to go *aller*	to stay *rester*
to arrive *arriver*	to come *venir, venu*
to go in *entrer*	to go out *sortir*
to leave *partir*	to go up *monter*
to go home *rentrer*	to fall *tomber*
to go back *retourner*	
to go down *descendre, descendu*	
to become *devenir, devenu*	

The imperfect, or past, tense of "to be" and "to have" is also useful for talking about the past:

I was	*j'étais*
you were	*tu étais*
he/she/it was	*il/elle était*
we were	*nous étions*
you were	*vous étiez*
they were	*ils/elles étaient*

I had	*j'avais*
you had	*tu avais*
he/she/it had	*il/elle avait*
we had	*nous avions*
you had	*vous aviez*
they had	*ils/elles avaient*

Negatives

To make a sentence negative, put *ne* and *pas* on either side of the verb, e.g. *je veux* (I want), *je ne veux pas* (I don't want) or *j'aime danser* (I like dancing), *je n'aime pas danser* (I don't like dancing). In spoken French it is common to drop the *ne*, e.g. *Je veux pas* (I don't want).

Other useful negative words:
ne ... jamais (never), e.g.
Il ne veut jamais (He never wants);
ne ... personne (nobody), e.g.
Je n'aime personne (I don't like anybody);
ne ... rien (nothing), e.g.
Je ne veux rien (I don't want anything).

Making questions

The simplest way to make a question is to give a sentence the intonation of a question – raise your voice at the end, e.g. *Il aime Anne* (He likes Anne) becomes *Il aime Anne?* (Does he like Anne?) Another way is to put *Est-ce que ... ?* at the beginning of the sentence, e.g. *Est-ce qu'il aime Anne?* (Does he like Anne?)

In formal, polite French, you change the order of the words, e.g. *Voulez-vous du café?* (Would you like some coffee?)

As in English, many questions are formed using a word like *pourquoi* (why?). The question is made in one of the usual ways: with no change to the sentence: *Pourquoi tu veux ça?* (Why do you want that?); with *est-ce que*: *Pourquoi est-ce que tu veux ça?*; with a change of order: *Pourquoi veux-tu ça?*

These words can be used in the same way:

who? *qui?*	where? *où?*
what *quoi?*	when? *quand?*
which? *quel?*	how? *comment?*
how much? *combien?*	

This dictionary lists essential words. If the word you want is missing, try to think of a different one that you could use instead. In the English to French list (pages 62-103), illustrations with labels provide lots of extra words. Below are some tips on using the dictionary.

A typical entry in the English to French list looks like this:

This is the word you looked up.

This is the French translation.

red **rouge** *rooj*

This is the French pronunciation hint. Read it as if it were an English word and you will be close to the French.

"or" introduces an extra French translation. Words in brackets after "or" hint at the difference in meaning:

ball **la balle** *bal*, or (large) **le ballon** *ba-lon*

le/la Most French nouns (see page 56) are masculine or feminine. So that you know which each is, they are listed with the French for "the" - usually *le* for masculine nouns and *la* for feminine nouns. Nouns that can be either are listed with *le/la*:

cinema **le cinéma** *see-naima*
station **la gare** *gar*
tourist **le/la touriste** *tooreest*

[m] stands for masculine
[f] stands for feminine

For nouns that begin with a vowel (or sometimes *h*), "the" is *l'*; for plural nouns it is *les*. So that you know if these are masculine or feminine, they are followed by **[m]** or **[f]** - or **[m/f]** if they can be either.

(e) Most French adjectives (see page 57), and a few nouns, have two forms: masculine and feminine. The feminine is often made by adding an *e* (or another letter and *e*) to the masculine. Often both forms are said the same way. In this case, you will see the masculine, a bracket showing the letters you add for the feminine, and then the pronunciation:

pretty **joli(e)** *jolee*

f: The extra letters can make the feminine sound different from the masculine. If so, you will see *f:* with a second pronunciation:

grey **gris(e)** *gree f: greez*

If the feminine word is very different, you will see *f:* followed by the feminine word spelled out in full, and its pronunciation:

fresh **frais** *frai* **f: fraîche** *fraish*

pl: introduces any unusual plural you need to know about:

eye **l'oeil [m]** *uh-yuh* **pl: les yeux** *yuh*

* indicates that words are familiar or mild slang, and are best avoided in formal situations:

chaos **la pagaille*** *pag-eye*

** indicates words that are very familiar or slangy, or that would be offensive if used in the wrong situation. It is safest to avoid them altogether or at least use them only with friends of your own age:

to chat up **draguer**** *dragai*

Verbs (see page 58) are listed in the infinitive form, e.g. "to eat", but you will find them listed under "e" for eat, etc.

a, an *un un* **f: une** *ewnn*
about (approximately)
environ *onveeron;* what's
it about? (film, book)
de quoi ça parle? *duh
kwa sa parl*
above au-dessus de
o-duhssew-duh
abroad à l'étranger
a-lai-tron-jai
accent l'accent [m] *akson*
to accept accepter *akseptai*
accident l'accident [m]
akseedon
accommodation (places to
stay) **le logement** *lojmon*
to ache (or to have a
head/back etc. ache) **avoir
mal à** *avwar mal a* (see
Useful irregular verbs p. 59,
Au, à la, à l', aux p. 57 and
pictures on this page)
to act (theatre) **jouer**
joo-ai
actor l'acteur [m]
aktuhr
actress l'actrice [f]
aktreess
to add ajouter *ajootai*
address l'adresse [f] *adress*
adopted adoptif *adopteef*
f: adoptive *adopteev*
adult l'adulte [m/f] *adewlt*
advantage l'avantage [m]
avontaj; to take advantage
of **profiter de** *profeetai duh*
adventurous aventureux
avon-tewruh
f: aventureuse
avon-tewrurz
advertisement (in paper)
l'annonce [f] *annonss,* or
(at cinema, on TV) **la pub***
pewb; classified ads **les
petites annonces**
puhteet-zannonss
advice le conseil
konssaiy

aerobics l'aérobic [f]
a-airobeek
Africa l'Afrique [f] *afreek*
after après *aprai*
**afternoon l'après-midi
[m/f]** *aprai-meedee*
again de nouveau *duh
noovo,* or **encore** *onkor*
against contre *kontr*
age l'âge [m] *aj;*
underage **mineur(e)**
mee-nuhr

to ache *avoir mal à*

J'ai mal à la tête.
jai mal a la tett

J'ai
mal aux dents.
jai mal o don

J'ai mal à l'oreille.
jai mal a loraiy

J'ai mal au ventre.
jai mal o vontr

J'ai mal aux reins.
jai mal o ran

ago il y a *eel-ee-a,* e.g. ten
days ago **il y a dix jours**
to agree être d'accord
etr dakor
aid l'aide [f] *ed*
AIDS le SIDA *seeda*
air l'air [m] *air;*
air-conditioned **air
conditionné** *air kondeess-
yonnai*
**airline la compagnie
aérienne** *kompannee
a-airee-yenn*
airmail par avion *par
av-yon*
airport l'aéroport [m]
a-airopor
alarm clock le réveil
rev-aiy
album l'album [m] *albom*
alcohol l'alcool [m] *alkol*
alcoholic alcoolisé(e)
alkoleezai; non-alcoholic
sans alcool *son-zalkol*
all tout(e) *too* **f: toot,
pl: tous** *(too)* **f: toutes**
toot; all right (I agree)
d'accord *dakor,* or
(it's OK) **ça va** *sa-va*
allergy l'allergie [f]
alairjee
almost presque *pressk*
alone seul(e) *surl*
already déjà *dai-ja*
also aussi *o-see*
alternative (not
conventional) **original(e)**
oreejeennal
always toujours *toojoor*
amazing (unbelievable)
incroyable *ankr-wa-
yabl,* or (fab, great)
génial(e) *jainn-yal*
**ambulance
l'ambulance [f]**
ombewlonss
America l'Amérique [f]
ammaireek

American **américain(e)**
ammaireekan
f: ammaireekenn
and **et** *ai*
angry **en colère** *on kolair*
animal **l'animal [m]**
annee-mal
ankle **la cheville** *shuh-veey*
to annoy **énerver**
ainnairvai, or **agacer**
agassai; to get annoyed
s'énerver *sainnairvai*
annoying (slightly)
embêtant(e) *ombetton*
f: ombettont, or (very)
énervant(e) *ainnairvon*
f: ainnairvont
answer **la réponse**
raiponss
to answer **répondre**
raipondr
answering machine
le répondeur *raiponduhr*
antibiotic **l'antibiotique**
[m] *ontee-beeo-teek*
antiseptic **antiseptique**
ontee-septeek
any (as in "do you have any
matches?") **de** *duh* or **du**
dew or **de la** *duh la* or
de l' *duhl* or **des** *dai* (see
p. 56), or (as in "any old
thing") **n'importe quel(le)**
namport kel
anyone **quelqu'un** *kelkun*,
or (as in "anyone can do it")
n'importe qui *namport kee*
(see also 'nobody')
anything **quelque chose**
kelkuh shoze, or (as in
"anything will do")
n'importe quoi *namport
kwa* (see also 'nothing')
anywhere **quelque part**
kelkuh par, or (as in "just
anywhere") **n'importe où**
nampor-too (see also
'nowhere')

apple **la pomme** *pomm*
(see also picture right);
apple pie **la tarte aux
pommes** *tart-o-pomm;*
apple turnover **le chausson
aux pommes** *shosson o
pomm*
appointment **le rendez-
vous** *rondai-voo*
apricot **l'abricot [m]**
abreeko
April **avril** *avreel*
Arab **arabe** *a-rab*
arcade (amusement)
la galerie de jeux
galree duh juh
archaeology **l'archéologie
[f]** *arkai-olojee*
architecture **l'architecture
[f]** *arshee-tektewr*
area (region) **la région**
raij-yon, or (part of town)
le quartier *kart-yai*
argument **la dispute**
deespewt; to have an
argument **se disputer**
suh deespewtai
arm **le bras** *bra*
around **autour de** *otoor
duh*
to arrive **arriver** *areevai*
art **l'art [m]** *ar*, or (school
subject) **le dessin** *dessan;*
art school **l'école des
beaux-arts [f]** *aikol dai
bo-zar*
artist **l'artiste [m/f]** *arteest*
as (like) **comme** *komm;*
as ... as **aussi ... que**
o-see ... kuh; as usual
comme d'habitude *komm
dabeetewd*
ashtray **le cendrier**
sondree-ai
Asia **l'Asie [f]** *azee*
to ask **demander** *duh-
mondai;* to ask out **inviter**
anveetai

apple **la pomme**
la queue *kuh*
la peau *po*
le trognon
tronn-yon

le pépin *paipan*

aspirin **l'aspirine [f]**
aspeereenn; an aspirin **un
comprimé d'aspirine** *un
kompreemai daspeereenn*
assistant (in shop, store)
le vendeur *vonduhr*
f: la vendeuse *vonduhz*
asthma **l'asthme [m]**
ass-m
at (time, place) **à** *a* (see Au,
à la, à l', aux p. 57), or (at
X's place) **chez** *shai*, e.g. at
Mark's **chez Mark**
to attack **attaquer** *atakai*
attractive **séduisant(e)**
saidweezon f: *saidweezont*
audience **le public**
pewbleek
August **août** *oot*
Australia **l'Australie [f]**
osstralee
Australian **australien(ne)**
osstral-yan f: *osstral-yenn*
author **l'auteur [m/f]** *otuhr*
autumn **l'automne [m]**
otonn
avalanche **l'avalanche [f]**
avalonsh
average **moyen(ne)**
mwa-yan f: *mwa-yenn*
avocado **l'avocat [m]**
avoka
to avoid **éviter** *aiveetai*

away **à** *a*, e.g. it's 3km away **c'est à 3km**

awful **affreux** *afruh* f: **affreuse** *afruhz*

back (not front) **l'arrière [m]** *ar-yair*, or (part of body) **le dos** *do*

backpack **le sac à dos** *sak a do*

backpacker **le routard** *rootar*

bad **mauvais(e)** *movai* f: *movaiz*; not bad **pas mal** *pa mal*; really bad **nul(le)*** *newl*; too bad! **tant pis!** *ton pee*

badge **le badge** *badj*, or (small) **le pin's** *peennz*

badly **mal** *mal*

badminton **le badminton** *bad-meenntonn*

bag **le sac** *sak*

baker's **la boulangerie** *boolonj-ree*

balcony **le balcon** *balkon*

ball **la balle** *bal*, or (large) **le ballon** *ba-lon*

ballet **le ballet** *balai*

banana **la banane** *ba-nann*

band (musical) **le groupe** *groop* (see picture below)

bank (money) **la banque** *bonk*

bar **le bar** *bar*, or (counter) **le comptoir** *kontwar*

bargain **la bonne affaire** *bonn afair*

baseball **le base-ball** *baiz-bol*

basketball **le basket** *basskett*

bat (sport) **la batte** *batt*

bath **le bain** *ban*

bathroom **la salle de bain** *sal duh ban*

battery **la pile** *peel*, or (car) **la batterie** *ba-tree*

to be **être** *etr*, or (as in "to be hot/hungry/X years old") **avoir** *avwar*, or (for weather, as in "to be hot/cold") **faire** *fair* (see Useful irregular verbs p.59 and Weather p.52)

beach **la plage** *plaj*

beans **les haricots [m]** *areeko*; green beans **les haricots verts** *areeko vair*

beard **la barbe** *barb*

beat (rhythm) **le rythme** *reetm*

beautiful **beau†** *bo* f: **belle** *bel*

because **parce que** *parss-kuh*; because of **à cause de** *a koze duh*

to become **devenir** *duh-vuh-neer*

bed **le lit** *lee*; double bed **le grand lit** *gron lee*; bed and breakfast (guest house) **la chambre d'hôtes** *shombr dot*

bedroom **la chambre (à coucher)** *shombr (a kooshai)*

beetle **le scarabée** *skarabai*

beef **le boeuf** *burf*

beer **la bière** *bee-yair*, or (on tap) **la (bière) pression** *(bee-yair) press-yon*, or **le demi** *duh-mee*

before **avant** *avon*

beggar **le/la mendiant(e)** *mond-yon* f: *mond-yont*

beginner **le/la débutant(e)** *daibewton* f: *daibewtont*

beginning **le début** *daibew*

behind **derrière** *dair-yair*

Belgium **la Belgique** *beljeek*

belt **la ceinture** *santewr*

bend (in the road) **le virage** *veeraj*

best (person or thing, as in "the best film") **le/la meilleur(e)** *mai-yuhr*, or (action, as in "Sam plays best") **le/la mieux** *m-yuh*; the best (as in "it's the best!") **le top*** *top*

band **le groupe**

la guitariste *geetareest*

la batterie *ba-tree*

le batteur *batuhr*

le joueur de synthétiseur *joo-uhr duh santaiteezuhr*

la guitare *geetar*

le saxo* *sakso*

le saxophoniste *saksofonneest*

le synthé* *santai*

le micro* *meekro*

le chanteur *shontuhr*

†beau changes to **bel** *bell* in front of a [m] word beginning with a vowel, or sometimes an "h", e.g. **un bel homme**.

better (person or thing, as in "this café is better") **meilleur(e)** *mai-yuhr*, or (action, as in "Sam plays better") **mieux** *m-yuh*; to feel better **se sentir mieux** *suh sonteer m-yuh*; it is better to ... **il vaut mieux ...** *eel vo m-yuh ...*

between **entre** *ontr*

big **grand(e)** *gron* f: *grond*

bike **le vélo** *vailo*; racing bike **le vélo de course** *vailo duh koorss*; mountain bike **le vélo tout terrain** *vailo too tai-ran*, or **le VTT** *vai tai tai*; by bike **en vélo** *on vailo* (see also 'motorbike' and picture above right)

biker **le motard** *mo-tar*

bill (restaurant) **l'addition [f]** *adeess-yon*

bin (rubbish) **la poubelle** *poobell*

binoculars **les jumelles [f]** *jew-mell*

biodegradable **biodégradable** *bee-o-daigra-dabl*

bird **l'oiseau [m]** *wazo*

birthday **l'anniversaire [m]** *anneevair-sair*; happy birthday **joyeux anniversaire** *jwa-yuh-z-anneevair-sair*

biscuit **le biscuit** *beeskwee*

bit (as in "a bit of cake") **le morceau** *morso*, or (as in "a bit tired/hungry") **un peu** *un puh*

to bite **mordre** *mordr*, or (insect) **piquer** *peekai*

bitter **amer** f: **amère** *amair*

black **noir(e)** *nwar*

blanket **la couverture** *koovairtewr*

bike **le vélo**
le guidon *geedon*
la selle *sell*
le pneu *pnuh*
la roue *roo*
la chaîne *shenn*
la pédale *paidal*
la gourde *goord*
la pompe *pomp*
le frein *fran*
les vitesses [f] *veetess*

to bleed **saigner** *sainn-yai*

blind **aveugle** *avurgl*

blister **l'ampoule [f]** *ompool*

bloke **le type*** *teep*, or **le mec*** *mek*

blond **blond(e)** *blon* f: *blond*; the blond guy/girl **le/la blond(e)**

blood **le sang** *son*; blood pressure **la tension** *tonss-yon*

blue **bleu(e)** *bluh*

to boast **se vanter** *suh vontai*, or **frimer*** *free-mai*

boat (big) **le bateau** *bato*, or (small) **la barque** *bark*; to go by boat **prendre le bateau** *prondr luh bato* (see also 'sailing')

body **le corps** *kor*

boiled **bouilli(e)** *boo-yee*

bone **l'os [m]** *oss* pl: *o*, or (fish bone) **l'arête [f]** *a-rett*

book **le livre** *leevr*

to book **réserver** *raizairvai*; booked up **complet** *komplai* f: **complète** *komplett*

bookshop **la librairie** *leebrairee*

boot **la botte** *bott*, or (for climbing, skiing, walking) **la chaussure** *sho-sewr*

border (frontier) **la frontière** *frontee-air*

bored to be bored **s'ennuyer** *sonnwee-yai*

boring **ennuyeux** *onnwee-yuh* f: **ennuyeuse** *onnwee-yuhz*, or **rasoir*** *razwar*

to borrow **emprunter** *ompruntai*

boss **le/la patron(ne)** *patron* f: *patronn*, or **le boss***

both **tous les deux** *too lai duh* f: **toutes les deux** *toot lai duh*

bottle **la bouteille** *bootaiy*; bottle opener **le décapsuleur** *daikap-sewluhr*, or **l'ouvre-bouteille [m]** *oovr-bootaiy*

bottom (not top) **le bas** *ba*, or (of river, pool, glass) **le fond** *fon*, or (bum) **le derrière** *dair-yair*

bowl **le bol** *bol*

bowling (ten pin) **le bowling** *boleeng*

boxer shorts **le caleçon** *kalson*

box office **le guichet** *geeshai*

boy **le garçon** *garson*

boyfriend **le petit ami** *puhtee-tammee*

bra **le soutien-gorge** *sootee-an gorj*, or **le soutif**** *sooteef*

brakes **les freins [m]** *fran*

brave **courageux** *koorajuh* f: **courageuse** *koorajuhz*

bread **le pain** *pan*; wholemeal bread **le pain complet** *pan komplai*

to break **casser** kassai;
to break down **tomber en panne** tombai on pann;
to break up (with a person) **se séparer** suh saiparai, or **casser*** kassai
breakfast **le petit déjeuner** puhtee daijuhnai, or **le petit déj*** ptee daij
breast (bosom) **le sein** san, or (chest) **la poitrine** pwatreenn
breath **l'haleine [f]** a-lenn; out of breath **essoufflé(e)** aissooflai
to breathe **respirer** respeerai
bridge **le pont** pon
bright (clever) **doué(e)** doo-ai, or (colour) **vif** veef f: **vive** veev
brilliant (fantastic) **génial(e)** jainn-yal
to bring (person) **amener** amm-nai, or (thing) **apporter** a-portai
Britain **la Grande-Bretagne** grond-bruhtann-yuh
broke (no money) **à sec*** a sek, or **fauché(e)*** fo-shai
broken **cassé(e)** kassai
brother **le frère** frair; or **le frangin*** fronjan
brown **brun(e)** brun f: brewnn, or **marron** maron, or (tanned) **bronzé(e)** bronzai
bruise **le bleu** bluh
brush **la brosse** bross, or (paintbrush) **le pinceau** panso
bug (germ) **le microbe** meekrob, or (insect) **la bestiole** best-yol
building **le bâtiment** batee-mon
bull **le taureau** toro
bump (lump on head/ski run) **la bosse** boss

to bump into (something) **se cogner contre** suh konn-yai kontr, or (someone by chance) **tomber sur** tombai sewr
to bunk off **sécher*** saishai
to burn **brûler** brewlai
to burst (explode) **éclater** aiklatai, or (tyre, balloon) **crever** krevai
bus **le bus** bewss; bus station **la gare routière** gar root-yair; bus stop **l'arrêt de bus [m]** arai duh bewss; to take the bus **prendre le bus** prondr luh bewss
busy **occupé(e)** okewpai
but **mais** mai
butcher's **la boucherie** boosh-ree
butter **le beurre** buhr
to buy **acheter** ash-tai
by (near) **près de** prai duh, or (as in "saved by someone") **par** par; by my/your/him/herself **tout(e) seul(e)** too surl f: toot surl
bye **salut*** sa-lew; or **tchao*** tsha-o
café **le café** kafai; or **le bar** bar
cake **le gâteau** gato; cake shop **la pâtisserie** pateess-ree; it's a piece of cake **c'est du gâteau*** sai dew gato
calculator **la calculette** kalkew-lett
to call **appeler** apuhlai; to be called **s'appeler** sapuhlai
calm **calme** kalm
calorie **la calorie** kaloree; low-calorie **à basses calories** a bass kaloree

camera **l'appareil-photo**

la pellicule peleekewl
le flash flash
le zoom zoom
l'objectif [m] objekteef
le bouchon de l'objectif booshon duh lobjekteef
le pare-soleil parsolaiy

camcorder (video camera) **le caméscope** kammaiskop
camera **l'appareil-photo [m]** aparaiy foto (see also picture above)
to camp **camper** kompai; to go camping **(aller) faire du camping** (allai) fair dew kompeeng
campsite **le camping** kompeeng (see also picture below right)
can (of fruit/drink) **la boîte** bwat; can opener **l'ouvre-boîte [m]** oovr-bwat
can (to be able to) **pouvoir** poovwar (see Useful irregular verbs p. 59), or (to know how to) **savoir** savwar
Canada **le Canada** kannada
canal **le canal** kannal
to cancel **annuler** annewlai
candle **la bougie** boojee
canoe **le canoë** kanno-ai, or (kayak) **le kayak;** to go canoeing **faire du canoë/kayak**
cap (hat) **la casquette** kasskett

capital (city) *la capitale kapeetal*
captain *le capitaine kapeetenn*
car *la voiture vwa-tewr*, or *la bagnole* bann-yol;* car park *le parking parkeeng*
card *la carte kart;* credit card *la carte de crédit kart duh kraidee;* a game of cards *une partie de cartes ewnn partee duh kart*
care: I don't care! *ça m'est égal! sa mai-taigal,* or *je m'en fous!** juh mon foo*
career *la carrière kar-yair*
careful *prudent(e) prewdon f: prewdont;* to be careful *faire attention fair atonss-yon*
carnival *le carnaval kar-naval*
carrot *la carotte ka-rott*
to carry *porter portai*
cartoon *le dessin animé dessan annee-mai*
case in case *au cas où o ka oo*
cash (money) *l'argent liquide [m] arjon leekeed,* or *le liquide;* cash dispenser/cashpoint machine *le distributeur de billets dee-stree-bewtuhr duh bee-yai*

cassette *la cassette ka-sett;* cassette player *le lecteur de cassettes lektuhr duh ka-sett*
castle *le château sha-to*
casual (relaxed, informal) *décontracté(e) daikontraktai*
cat *le chat sha*
to catch *attraper atrapai*
cathedral *la cathédrale kataidral*
Catholic *catholique katoleek*
cave (small) *la caverne kavairnn,* or (large) *la grotte grott*
caving *la spéléologie spailai-olojee,* or *la spéléo*
CD *le CD saidai;* CD player *le lecteur de CD lektuhr duh sai dai*
to celebrate *fêter fettai*
cellar *la cave kav*
cemetery *le cimetière seemt-yair*
centre *le centre sontr*
century *le siècle see-aikl*
cereal *les céréales [f] sai-rai-al*
chair *la chaise shaiz,* or (with arms) *le fauteuil fotuh-y*
champion *le/la champion(ne) shomp-yon f: shomp-yonn*

championship *le championnat shomp-yonna*
chance (accident) *le hasard azar,* or (opportunity) *l'occasion [f] okaz-yon,* or (risk) *le risque reesk;* by chance *par hasard par azar*
change *le changement shonj-mon,* or (money) *la monnaie monnai*
to change *changer shonjai*
changing-room *le vestiaire vest-yair*
channel (TV) *la chaîne shenn;* the Channel *la Manche monsh;* the Channel tunnel *le tunnel sous la Manche tew-nel soo la monsh;* the Channel Islands *les îles anglo-normandes [f] eel onglo-normond*
chaos *la pagaille* pag-eye*
character (personality) *le caractère karaktair,* or (person in cartoon etc.) *le personnage pairsonnaj*
charity (organization) *l'organisme de charité [m] organneezm duh shareetai*
charter (plane, flight) *le charter shartair*
charts (top records) *le top 50 top sankont*

campsite *le camping*

le camping-car kompeeng kar
la tente tont
la caravane karavann
le hamac amak
le maillet my-ai
les poubelles[f] poobell
la gourde goord
le camping-gaz kompeeng gaz
le piquet peekai
la réception rai-sepss-yonn
les sanitaires[m] sanneetair

climbing *l'escalade [f]*
or *la grimpe**

le rocher
roshai

le mousqueton
moosk-ton

le grimpeur
grampuhr

le casque
kask

la sangle
sangl

la magnésie
mann-yaizee

le sac à magnésie
sak a mann-yaizee

le baudrier
bodree-ai

le chausson d'escalade
shosson deskalad

la corde
kord

to chat *bavarder* *bavardai;*
to chat up **draguer****
dragai, or **brancher****
bronshai
cheap **pas cher** f: **pas chère**
pa shair, or **bon marché**
bon marshai
cheaper **moins cher**
f: **moins chère** *mwan chair*
to cheat (at cards etc.)
tricher *treeshai*
to check (a fact, date)
vérifier *vaireef-yai,* or
(a passport, ticket)
contrôler *kontrolai;*
to check in (luggage)
enregistrer *onruh-jeess-trai*
check-in (at airport)
l'enregistrement [m]
onruh-jeess-truhmon
check-out (cash register)
la caisse *kess*
cheeky **gonflé(e)*** *gonflai*
cheers (à ta/votre) **santé**
(a ta/votr) sontai, or **à la**
tienne/vôtre *a la tee-enn/*
votr
cheer up! **courage!** *kooraj*
cheese **le fromage** *fromaj*
chemist's **la pharmacie**
farmassee
cheque **le chèque** *shek;*
cheque-book **le chéquier**
shaik-yai
cherry **la cerise** *suhreez*
chess **les échecs [m]** *aishek*
chest (part of body)
la poitrine *pwatreenn*
chewing gum **le chewing-gum** *shweeng-gomm*
chicken **le poulet** *poolai*
child *l'enfant [m/f]* *onfon*
chips **les frites [f]** *freet*
chocolate **le chocolat**
shokola; hot chocolate **le**
chocolat chaud *shokola sho*
choice **le choix** *shwa*

choir **le choeur** *kuhr*
to choose **choisir** *shwazeer*
chop (e.g. pork/lamb)
la côtelette *kotlett*
Christian **chrétien(ne)**
krait-yan f: *krait-yenn*
Christmas **Noël** *no-ell*
to chuck (throw) **balancer***
balonssai, or (finish with a
boy/girlfriend) **laisser**
tomber *laissai tombai,* or
plaquer** *plakai*
church *l'église [f]* *aigleez*
cider **le cidre** *seedr*
cigarette **la cigarette**
seegarett, or **la clope**** *klop*
cinema **le cinéma** *see-naima,* or **le ciné*,** or
le cinoche* *see-nosh*
circus **le cirque** *seerk*
city **la ville** *veel*
classical **classique** *klasseek*
clean **propre** *propr*
clever **intelligent(e)**
anteleejon f: *anteleejont,*
or (cunning) **malin** *malan*
f: **maligne** *maleenn,* or
(gifted) **doué(e)** *doo-ai*
cliff **la falaise** *falaiz*
to climb **grimper** *grampai*
climber **le grimpeur**
grampuhr f: **la grimpeuse**
grampurz
climbing *l'escalade [f]*
eskalad, or **la grimpe***
gramp, or (mountain-climbing) *l'alpinisme [m]*
alpee-neezm, or (rock-climbing on boulders)
la varappe *varap*
(see also picture on left)
cloakroom **le vestiare**
vest-yair
close **près de** *prai duh,* or
(feeling) **proche** *prosh;*
close by **tout près** *too prai*
to close **fermer** *fairmai*
closed **fermé(e)** *fairmai*

clothes **les vêtements [m]** vetmon, or **les fringues* [f]** frang
cloud **le nuage** new-aj
club **le club** klerb, or (night-club) **la boîte* (de nuit)** bwat (duh nwee)
clubbing: to go clubbing **aller en boîte*** allai on bwat
coach (bus) **le car** kar, or (trainer) **l'entraîneur [m/f]** ontrai-nuhr
coast **la côte** kote
coat **le manteau** monto
code (post/entry code) **le code** kod, or (for phoning) **l'indicatif [m]** andeekateef
co-ed (school) **mixte** meekst
coffee **le café** kafai; a black coffee **un café (noir)** un kafai (nwar); a coffee with milk/cream **un (café-)crème** kremm; a decaffeinated coffee **un déca** daika
coin **la pièce** pee-ess
coincidence **la coïncidence** ko-ansseedonss
cold **froid(e)** frwa f: frwad, or (chilled) **frais** frai f: **fraîche** fraish; to be cold (person) **avoir froid** avwar frwa, or (weather) it is cold **il fait froid** eel fai frwa; to have cold feet (about something) **avoir la trouille**** avwar la troo-yuh
cold (illness) **le rhume** rewmm; to have a cold **être enrhumé(e)** etr onrew-mai
to collect (stamps etc.) **collectionner** koleks-yonnai
colour **la couleur** kooluhr
comb **le peigne** penn-yuh
to come **venir** vuh-neer; to come back **revenir** ruh-vuh-neer; to come in **entrer** ontrai

comfortable **confortable** konfortabl; to be/feel comfortable **être à l'aise** etr a laiz
comic book **la bande dessinée** bond desseennai, or **la BD** bai dai
common **courant(e)** kooron f: kooront; common sense **le bon sens** bon sonss
compass (small) **la boussole** boossol or (large) **le compas** kompa
competition **le concours** konkoor, or (people you are up against) **la concurrence** konkew-ronss
to complain **se plaindre** suh plandr
completely **complètement** komplaitmon
compulsory **obligatoire** oblee-ga-twar
computer **l'ordinateur [m]** ordee-natuhr; computer studies **l'informatique [f]** anfor-mateek
concert **le concert** konssair
condom **le préservatif** praizairvateef, or **la capote**** kapott
to confuse **confondre** konfondr
congratulations **félicitations** faileesseetass-yon
connection (plane, train) **la correspondance** korespondonss
conservation **la défense de l'environnement** daifonss duh lonveeronn-mon
constipated **constipé(e)** konsteepai
consulate **le consulat** konssewla

to contact **contacter** kontaktai
contact lens **la lentille (de contact)** lonteey (duh kontakt); soft/hard lens **la lentille souple/dure** lonteey soopl/dewr; cleansing/rinsing solution **la solution de décontamination/neutralisation** solewss-yon duh dai-konta-mee-nass-yon/nuh-tralee-zass-yon
contagious **contagieux** kontaj-yuh f: **contagieuse** kontaj-yurz
contemporary **contemporain(e)** kontomporan f: kontemporenn
to continue **continuer** kontee-newai
contraceptive **le contraceptif** kontrassepteef
conversation **la conversation** konvairsass-yon
to cook **faire de la cuisine** fair duh la kweezeenn
cool (trendy, relaxed) **cool***
to cope **se débrouiller** suh daibroo-yai, or (to face up to) **faire face à** fair fass a
to copy **copier** kop-yai
cork **le bouchon** booshon
corkscrew **le tire-bouchon** teer-booshon
corner **le coin** kwan
correct **correct(e)** korekt
Corsica **la Corse** korss
cosmopolitan **cosmopolite** kozmopoleet
to cost **coûter** kootai
cotton (material) **le coton** koton; cotton wool **le coton**
country (nation) **le pays** pai-ee, or (countryside) **la campagne** kompann-yuh

course (series of lessons) **le cours** *koor,* or (meal) **le plat** *pla;* first course **l'entrée [f]** *ontrai;* of course **bien sûr** *bee-an sewr*

court (tennis, squash) **le court** *koor,* or (basketball, volleyball) **le terrain** *tairan*

cousin **le/la cousin(e)** *koozan f: koozeenn*

to cover **couvrir** *koovreer*

cow **la vache** *vash*

coward **le lâche** *lash*

to crack (lose control, give in) **craquer** *krakai;* to crack a joke **sortir une blague** *sorteer ewnn blag;* to crack up (laugh) **être écroulé(e)* (de rire)** *etr aikroolai (duh reer)*

cramp **la crampe** *kromp*

crazy **fou** *foo* **f: folle** *fol,* or **cinglé(e)*** *sanglai,* or **dingue*** *dang;* to drive crazy **rendre fou/dingue*** *rondr foo/dang;* to be crazy about (a person) **être fou de** *etr foo duh,* or (a thing) **adorer** *adorai;* you must be crazy! **ça va pas la tête?**** *sa va pa la tet*

credit card (see 'card')

creepy **qui donne la chair de poule** *kee donn la shair duh pooll*

cricket (sport) **le cricket** *cricket,* or (insect) **le grillon** *gree-yon*

crime **le crime** *kreemm*

crisis **la crise** *kreez*

crisps **les chips [f]** *sheeps*

to criticize **critiquer** *kreeteekai*

cross (angry) **fâché(e)** *fashai,* or (sign) **la croix** *krwa*

to cross **traverser** *travairsai*

crossing (by ferry etc.) **la traversée** *travairsai* (see also 'pedestrian')

crossroads **le carrefour** *karfoor*

crossword **les mots croisés [m]** *mo krwazai*

cruel **cruel(le)** *krew-ell*

crush: I've got a crush on him/her **il/elle me fait craquer**** *eel/ell muh fai krakai*

to cry (weep) **pleurer** *pluhrai*

cucumber **le concombre** *konkombr*

cult **le culte** *kewlt*

cultural **culturel(le)** *kewltewrell*

culture **la culture** *kewltewr*

cup **la tasse** *tass*

cupboard **le placard** *plakar*

curious **curieux** *kewr-yuh* **f: curieuse** *kewr-yuhz*

custom **la coutume** *kootewmm*

customer **le/la client(e)** *klee-on f: klee-ont*

customs **la douane** *dwann*

to cut **couper** *koopai*

damn **zut*** *zewt,* or **mince*** *manss*

to dance **dancer** *donsai*

dancer **le danseur** *dansuhr* **f: la danseuse** *dansuhz*

dangerous **dangereux** *donj-ruh* **f: dangereuse** *donj-ruhz*

to dare (risk) **oser** *ozai,* or (challenge) **défier** *daifee-ai*

dark **sombre** *sombr,* or (colour) **foncé(e)** *fonsai* (see also 'hair' picture); it is dark **il fait noir** *eel fai nwar*

dart **la fléchette** *flaishett*

date **la date** *dat,* or (meeting with boy/girlfriend) **le rendez-vous** *rondai-voo,* or **le rancard**** *ronkar;* date of birth **la date de naissance** *dat duh naissonss;* up to date (current) **à jour** *a joor;* out of date (no longer valid) **périmé(e)** *paireemai*

day **le jour** *joor;* the next day **le lendemain** *lond-man;* the day before **la veille** *vaiy;* day off **le jour de congé** *joor duh konjai*

dead **mort(e)** *mor f: mort*

deaf **sourd(e)** *soor f: soord*

dear **cher f: chère** *shair*

decaffeinated **décaféiné(e)** *dai-kafai-eennai*

December **décembre** *daissombr*

to decide **décider** *daisseedai*

deck (on boat) **le pont** *pon;* deck chair **la chaise longue** *shaiz long,* or **le transat*** *tronzat*

deep **profond(e)** *profon f: profond*

degree (as in "90°") **le degré** *duhgrai,* or (university) **la licence** *leessonss*

delay **le retard** *ruhtar*

delicatessen (for ready-made dishes) **le traiteur** *traituhr,* or (for salami, pâté, etc.) **la charcuterie** *sharkewtree*

delicious **délicieux** *daileess-yuh* **f: délicieuse** *daileess-yuhz*

democracy **la démocratie** *dai-mokrassee*

demonstration **la manifestation** *manneefestass-yon,* or (demo) **la manif***

denim (made of denim) **en jean** *on djeenn*
dentist **le/la dentiste** *donteest*
deodorant **le déodorant** *dai-odoron*
department store **le grand magasin** *gron magazan*
departure **le départ** *daipar;* departure lounge **la salle d'embarquement** *sal dombark-mon*
to depend **dépendre** *daipondr*
deposit (money left as guarantee) **la caution** *koss-yon,* or (money given in advance) **les arrhes [f]** *ar*
depressing **déprimant(e)** *daipreemon f: daipreemont*
to describe **décrire** *daikreer*
desk **le bureau** *bewro*
dessert **le dessert** *daissair*
detail **le détail** *dai-tie*
detour **le détour** *daitoor*
diabetic **diabétique** *dee-abaiteek*
dialect **le dialecte** *dee alekt*
dialling tone **la tonalité** *tonnaleetai* (see also 'code')
diarrhoea **la diarrhée** *dee-arai*
diary **l'agenda [m]** *ajenda,* or (private book) **le journal** *joor-nal*
dice **le dé** *dai*
dictionary **le dictionnaire** *deeksee-onnair,* or **le dico*** *deeko*
diesel (fuel) **le gazole** *ga-zol*
diet **le régime** *raijeemm;* to go on a diet **se mettre au régime** *suh metr o raijeemm*
different **différent(e)** *deefairon f: deefairont*
difficult **difficile** *deefeesseel*

dining room **la salle à manger** *sal a monjai*
dinner (evening) **le dîner** *dee-nai,* or (midday) **le déjeuner** *daijuh-nai*
direction **la direction** *deereks-yon*
director (of film) **le metteur en scène** *metuhr on senn*
dirty **sale** *sal,* or (rude) **grossier** *gross-yai* **f: grossière** *gross-yair;* to get dirty **se salir** *suh saleer;* to have a dirty mind **avoir l'esprit mal tourné** *avwar lesspree mal toor-nai*
disabled **handicapé(e)** *ondeekapai*
disadvantage (drawback) **l'inconvénient [m]** *ankonvenn-yon*
disappointed **déçu(e)** *daissew*
disaster **la catastrophe** *katastrof*
disc jockey **le disc-jockey** *deesk jokai*

diving **la plongée**

disco **la discothèque** *deeskotek,* or **la boîte*** *bwatt*
discount **la réduction** *raidewks-yon*
discrimination **la discrimination** *deeskree-mee-nass-yon*
to discuss **discuter** *deeskewtai*
disgusting **dégoûtant(e)** *daigooton f: daigootont,* or **dégueulasse**** *dai-guh-lass*
dish **le plat** *pla*
disk (computer) **la disquette** *deeskett*
distance **la distance** *deestonss;* in the/from a distance **au/de loin** *o/duh lwan*
to dive **plonger** *plonjai*
diving **la plongée** *plonjai;* scuba diving **la plongée sous-marine** *plonjai soo-mareenn* (see also picture below); diving board **le plongeoir** *plonjwar*

les palmes [f] *palmm*
la ceinture de plomb *santewr duh plom*
la bouteille d'oxygène *bootaiy dokseejenn*
le gilet stabilisateur *jeelai stabeeleezatuhr*
la plongeuse *plonjuhz*
le masque *mask*
le détendeur *daitonduhr*
la combinaison *kombee-naizon*
le tuba *tewba*
la console *konsol*

71

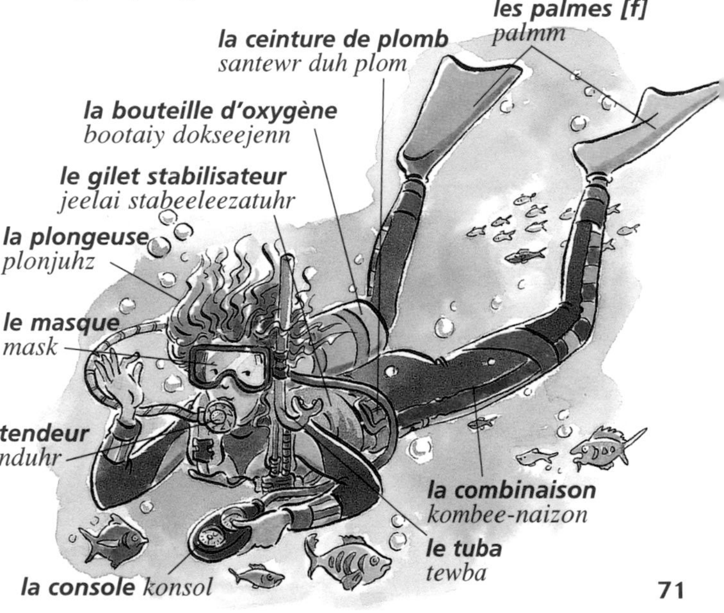

divorced **divorcé(e)** *deevorsai*

dizzy: to be/feel dizzy **avoir la tête qui tourne** *avwar la tet kee toornn*

to do **faire** *fair* (see Useful irregular verbs p. 59); to do up (fasten) **attacher** *atashai*

doctor **le médecin** *med-san*, or **le docteur** *doktuhr*

dodgy (dubious) **louche** *loosh*, or (risky) **risqué(e)** *reeskai*

dog **le chien** *shee-an*

dole: on the dole **au chômage** *o shomaj*

door **la porte** *port*

double **double** *doobl*, or (for two people) **pour deux personnes** *poor duh pairsonn*

down: to go/walk down **descendre** *daissondr*; to be/feel down **être déprimé(e)** *etr depreemai*, or **avoir le cafard*** *avwar luh kafar*

draw (same score) **le match nul** *match newl*

to draw (a picture) **dessiner** *daissee-nai*

dream **le rêve** *rev*

dress **la robe** *rob*

to dress (get dressed) **s'habiller** *sabee-yai*

drink **la boisson** *bwasson*; let's go for a drink **on va prendre un verre/un pot*** *on va prondr un vair/un po*

to drink **boire** *bwar*

to drive **conduire** *kondweer*, or (to go by car) **aller en voiture** *allai on vwatewr*; to drive along/around **rouler** *roolai*

driver **le chauffeur** *sho-fuhr*

to drop (let fall) **laisser tomber** *laissai tombai*, or (let go of) **lâcher** *lashai*; to drop in **passer** *passai*; to drop off (as in "drop me off at the corner") **déposer** *daipozai*; to drop out (of college/a competition) **abandonner** *abondonnai*

drug **la drogue** *drog*; drug addict **le/la drogué(e)** *drogai*; to take drugs **se droguer** *suh drogai*

drunk **soûl(e)** *soo f: sool*; to get drunk **se soûler** *suh soolai*

dry **sec** *sek* **f: sèche** *sesh*

to dry **sécher** *saishai*

dubbed **doublé(e)** *dooblai*

dump (for rubbish) **la décharge** *daisharj*, or (dull, awful place) **le trou*** *troo*; to be down in the dumps **broyer du noir** *brwa-yai dew nwar*

dungarees **la salopette** *salopett*

during **pendant** *pondon*

duty-free **hors taxe** *or taks*

dying: to be dying to (do something) **mourir d'envie de** *mooreer donvee duh*; to be dying of hunger/thirst **mourir de faim/soif** *mooreer duh fam/swaf*

each **chaque** *shak*, or (each one) **chacun(e)** *shakun f: shakewnn*

ear **l'oreille [f]** *oraiy* (see also 'to ache' picture)

early **tôt** *toe*, or (ahead of time) **en avance** *onnavonss*

earphones **les écouteurs [m]** *aikootuhr*

east **l'est [m]** *est*

Easter **Pâques** *pak*

easy **facile** *fasseel*

easy-going **décontracté(e)** *daikontraktai*

to eat **manger** *monjai*, or **bouffer**** *boofai*

EC (or EU) **la CEE** *sai uh uh*

ecology **l'écologie [f]** *aikolojee*

education **l'éducation [f]** *aidewkass-yon*; higher education **les études supérieures [f]** *aitewd sewpair-yuhr*

egg **l'oeuf [m]** *urf pl: uh*

egg *l'oeuf*

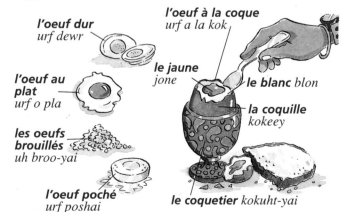

l'oeuf dur *urf dewr*

l'oeuf au plat *urf o pla*

les oeufs brouillés *uh broo-yai*

l'oeuf poché *urf poshai*

l'oeuf à la coque *urf a la kok*

le jaune *jone*

le blanc *blon*

la coquille *kokeey*

le coquetier *kokuht-yai*

elbow **le coude** *kood*
election **l'élection [f]**
aileks-yon
electric **électrique** *ailek-treek*
electricity **l'électricité [f]**
ailek-treesseetai
elevator **l'ascenseur [m]**
assonsuhr
e-mail **le courrier**
électronique *kuhr-yai*
ailek-troneek or **un e-mail**
ee-mail
embarrassing **gênant(e)**
jennon f: jennont; how
embarrassing! **quelle**
honte! *kel-luh ont*
embassy **l'ambassade [f]**
ombassad
emergency **l'urgence [f]**
ewrjonss; emergency exit
la sortie de secours *sortee*
duh suhkoor
empty **vide** *veed*
end (of story) **la fin** *fan*, or
(of road, finger) **le bout** *boo*
engine **le moteur** *motuhr*
England **l'Angleterre [f]**
ongluhtair
English **anglais(e)** *onglai*
f: onglaiz; in English **en**
anglais
to enjoy yourself **s'amuser**
samewzai
enough **assez** *assai;* I've
had enough **j'en ai assez**
jonnai assai
entertainment guide
le guide des spectacles
geed dai spektakl
envelope **l'enveloppe [f]**
onvlop
environment **l'environ-**
nement [m] *onveeronn-mon*
epileptic **épileptique**
aipeelepteek; epileptic fit
la crise d'épilepsie *kreez*
daipeelepsee

equal **égal(e)** *aigal*
erotic **érotique** *airoteek*
escalator **l'escalator [m]**
eskalator
essential **indispensable**
andeesponssabl
EU (European Union)
l'Union Européenne
loon-yon uhropai-enn
Eurocheque **l'Eurochèque**
[m] *uhroshek*
Europe **l'Europe [f]** *uhrop;*
eastern Europe **l'Europe de**
l'est [m] *... duh lest*
western Europe **l'Europe**
occidentale *... okseedontall*
European **européen(ne)**
uhropai-an f: uhropai-enn
evening **le soir** *swar*
everybody **tout le monde**
too luh mond
everything **tout** *too;*
everything else **tout le**
reste *too luh rest*
everywhere **partout** *partoo*
to exaggerate **exagérer**
aigzajairai
exam **l'examen [m]**
aigzaman, or **l'exam***
example **l'exemple [m]**
aigzompl; for example
par exemple
excellent **excellent(e)**
aiksailon f: aiksailont
except **sauf** *sof*
excess: excess baggage
l'excédent de bagages
[m] *aiksaidon duh bagaj;*
excess fare **le supplément**
sewp-laimon
exchange (money) **le**
change *shonj*, or (holiday)
l'échange [m] *aishonj;*
foreign exchange office
le bureau de change
bewro duh shonj; exchange
rate **le taux de change** *toe*
duh shonj

excited **excité(e)** *aikseetai;*
to get excited **s'exciter**
saikseetai
exciting **passionnant(e)**
passyonnon f: passyonnont
excuse **l'excuse [f]** *aiks-kewz;* excuse me **excusez-**
moi *aiks-kewzai-mwa*
exercise **l'exercice [m]**
aigzairseess
exhausted **épuisé(e)**
aipweezai, or **crevé(e)****
kruhvai
exhibition **l'exposition [f]**
aikspozeess-yon
exit **la sortie** *sortee*
exotic **exotique** *aigzoteek*
expensive **cher f: chère**
shair
experience **l'expérience [f]**
aikspair-yonss
to explain **expliquer**
aiks-pleekai
to explore **explorer**
aiks-plorai
extra **supplémentaire**
sewp-laimontair
eye **l'oeil [m]** *uh-yuh*
pl: les yeux *yuh*
fabulous **sensationnel(le)**
sonsass-yonnel, or **sensass***
face **le visage** *veezaj*
to fail (exam) **rater** *rat-ai*
to faint **s'évanouir**
saivannoo-eer, or **tomber**
dans les pommes* *tombai*
don lai pomm
fair (just) **juste** *jewst*
faithful **fidèle** *fee-dell*
to fall **tomber** *tombai;*
to fall for (a person) **tomber**
amoureux de *tombai amoo-ruh duh* **f: ... amoureuse ...**
... amooruhz ..., or (a trick)
se faire avoir** *suh fair*
avwar; to fall out with (a
person) **se fâcher avec**
suh fashai avek

family *la famille* *fameey*
famous (a star) *célèbre* *sailebr*, or (well-known) **(bien) connu(e)** *(bee-an) konnew*
fan (admirer) *le/la fan** *fann*, or (enthusiast) *le/la mordu(e)* *mordew*, or *le/la passionné(e)* *pass-yonnai*
to fancy (in French you say that "someone appeals to you") **plaire à** *plair a*, e.g. Luke fancies her **elle plaît à Luc**; do you fancy (doing something)? **ça te dit de ...?*** *sa tuh dee duh ...*
fantastic **fantastique** *fontasteek*
far **loin** *lwan*
fare *le tarif* *tareef*; full fare *le plein tarif* *plan tareef*; reduced fare *le tarif réduit* *tareef raidwee*
fashion *la mode* *mod*
fashionable **à la mode** *a la mod*
fast (quick) *rapide* *rapeed*, or (quickly) **vite** *veet*
fat (on meat) *le gras* *gra*, or (large) *gros(se)* *gro f: gross*; to get fat *grossir* *grosseer*
father *le père* *pair*
favourite *préféré(e)* *praifairai*
February *février* *faivree-ai*
fed: to be fed up **en avoir marre*** *on-navwar mar*
to feel (as in "to feel happy/good" etc.) *se sentir* *suh sonteer*, or (as in "to feel hot/hungry" etc.) *avoir* *avwar*; to feel like (doing something) *avoir envie de* *avwar onvee duh*
feminist *le/la féministe* *fai-mee-neest*
ferry *le ferry* *fairee*
fever *la fièvre* *fee-aivr*

few **peu de** *puh duh*; a few (as in "I'd like a few") **quelques-un(e)s** *kelkuh-zun f: ...zewnn*, or (as in "a few cakes") **quelques** *kelkuh*
fig *la figue* *feeg*
fight *la bagarre** *bagar*, or (organized) *le combat* *komba*
to fight *se battre* *suh batr*
figure: to have a good figure *être bien fait(e)* *etr bee-an fai f: ... fait*
to fill *remplir* *rompleer*; to fill up (with fuel) *faire le plein* *fair luh plan*
film (at cinema) *le film* *feelm*, or (in camera) *la pellicule* *paileekewl*
to find *trouver* *troovai*; to find out (get information) *se renseigner* *suh ronsenn-yai*, or (discover) *découvrir* *daikoovreer*
fine (penalty) *l'amende [f]* *ammond*, or (OK) **bien** *bee-an* (see also 'weather')
finger *le doigt* *dwa*
to finish *finir* *feeneer*
fire *le feu* *fuh*; fire brigade *les (sapeurs) pompiers [m]* *(sapuhr) pomp-yai*; fire exit *la sortie de secours* *sortee duh suhkoor*

fireworks *le feu d'artifice* *fuh darteefeess*
first (the first) *le premier* *pruhm-yai* f: *la première* *pruhm-yair*, or (at first) *d'abord* *dabor*
first aid *les premiers secours [m]* *pruhm-yai suhkoor*; first aid kit *la trousse à pharmacie* *trooss a farmassee* (see also picture below)
fish *le poisson* *pwasson*
fishing *la pêche* *pesh*; to go fishing *aller à la pêche* *allai a la pesh*
fit (tantrum) *la crise* *kreez*, or (physically fit) *en (pleine) forme* *on (plenn) form*; he's really fit (good-looking) *c'est un beau mec** *sait un bo mek*; to be in fits (of laughter) *avoir le fou rire* *avwar luh foo reer*
to fit *aller* *allai* (see Useful irregular verbs p. 59), e.g. does it fit? *ça te va?*, it fits me well *ça me va bien*
to fix (mend) *réparer* *raiparai*, or (arrange a time/date) *fixer* *feeksai*
fizzy (drink) *gazeux* *gazuh* f: *gazeuse* *gazuhz*

first aid kit *la trousse à pharmacie*

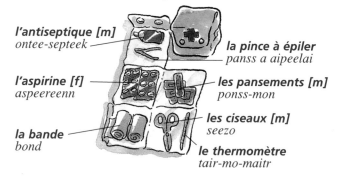

l'antiseptique [m] *ontee-septeek*
la pince à épiler *panss a aipeelai*
l'aspirine [f] *aspeereenn*
les pansements [m] *ponss-mon*
la bande *bond*
les ciseaux [m] *seezo*
le thermomètre *tair-mo-maitr*

flat (apartment) **l'apparte-ment [m]** *apart-mon*, or **l'appart*** *apart*, or (not round) **plat(e)** *pla f: plat*, or (tyre) **dégonflé(e)** *daigonflai*
flavour **le goût** *goo*, or (of ice cream) **le parfum** *parfam*
flea market **le marché aux puces** *marshai o pewss*
flight **le vol** *vol*; flight attendant **l'hôtesse de l'air (f)** *o-tess duh lair*, or (male) **le steward** *stewar*

food **la nourriture** *nooree-tewr*, or **la bouffe**** *boof*; food-poisoning **l'intoxication alimentaire [f]** *antok-seekass-yon alee-montair*
foot **le pied** *pee-ai*; on foot **à pied;** to put your foot in it **faire une gaffe*** *fair ewnn gaff*
football **le football** *foot-bol*, or **le foot*;** American football **le football américain** *foot-bol ammaireekan*

to freak out (lose your cool) **craquer*** *krakai*, or **flipper**** *fleepai*
free **libre** *leebr*, or (no charge) **gratuit(e)** *gratwee f: gratweet*
to freeze **geler** *juhlai*; it's freezing **ça caille**** *sa ka-yuh*
French **français(e)** *fronssai f: fronssaiz*; in French **en français;** French fries **les frites [f]** *freet*

football (soccer) le football   football (American) le football américain

le gardien de but *gardee-an duh bewt*
le supporter *sewp-ortuhr*
l'épaulière [f] *aipol-yair*
le casque *kask*
la meneuse *muh-nurz*
la grille *greey*
le but *bewt*
le ballon *ba-lon*
le footballeur *footballuhr*
l'arbitre [m] *arbeetr*
le crampon *krompon*
le maillot *my-yo*

flirt **le dragueur**** *draguhr f: la dragueuse**** *draguhz*
to flirt **draguer**** *dragai*, or **brancher**** *bronshai*
floor (level) **l'étage [m]** *aitaj*
flop (failure) **le fiasco** *fee-asko*, or **le bide**** *beed*
flower **la fleur** *fluhr*
flu **la grippe** *greep*
fluently **couramment** *koora-mon*
fly **la mouche** *moosh*
to fly **voler** *volai*, or (go by plane) **aller en avion** *allai onnav-yon*
to follow **suivre** *sweevr*

for **pour** *poor*
forbidden **interdit(e)** *antairdee f: antairdeet*
foreigner **l'étranger** *aitronjai f: l'étrangère* *aitronjair*
forest **la forêt** *forai*
to forget **oublier** *ooblee-ai*
to forgive **pardonner** *pardonnai*
fork **la fourchette** *foorshett*
fountain **la fontaine** *fontenn*
frame (picture, bike) **le cadre** *kadr*, or (glasses) **la monture** *montewr*
France **la France** *fronss*

fresh **frais** *frai f: fraîche fraish*
Friday **vendredi [m]** *vondruh-dee*
fridge **le frigo** *freego*
friend **l'ami(e) [m/f]** *amee*, or **le copain*** *kopan f: la copine*** *kopeenn*
friendly **sympathique** *sampateek*, or **sympa***
frightened: to be frightened **avoir peur** *avwar puhr*
from **de** *duh* (see p. 56)
front (of car, train) **l'avant [m]** *avon*, or (of dress, building) **le devant** *duhvon*; in front of **devant**

fruit **le fruit** *frwee*

full **plein(e)** *plan f: plenn,*
or (hotel etc.) **complet**
komplai **f: complète**
komplett; I'm full **j'ai assez**
mangé *jai assai monjai*

fun **amusant(e)**
ammewzon f: ammewzont,
or **marrant(e)*** *maron*
f: maront; to have fun
s'amuser *sammewzai,* or
se marrer** *suh marrai;*
(just) for fun **pour rire**
poor reer; to make fun of
se moquer de *suh mokai*
duh

funfair **la fête foraine** *fett*
forenn

funny (ha! ha!) **drôle** *drol,*
or (peculiar) **bizarre**
beezar

fuss: to make a fuss **faire**
tout un plat* *fair too-tun*
pla

gallery **la galerie** *galree*

game **le jeu** *juh,* or
(football, hockey) **le match,**
or (tennis, cards) **la partie**
partee

garage **le garage** *garaj*

garden **le jardin** *jardan*

garlic **l'ail [m]** *eye*

gas **le gaz** *gaz*

gate (in airport) **la porte**
port

gear (car, bike) **la vitesse**
veetess

general **général** *jai-nairal;*
in general **en général**

generous **généreux**
jai-nairuh **f: généreuse**
jai-nairuhz

geography **la géographie**
jai-o-grafee

German **allemand(e)** *al-*
mon f: al-mond

Germany **l'Allemagne [f]**
al-mann-yuh

to get (buy) **acheter** *ashtai,*
or (fetch) **aller chercher**
allai shairshai, or (obtain)
avoir *avwar,* or (take a
train/taxi) **prendre** *prondr,*
or (understand) **saisir**
saizeer, or **piger**** *peejai;*
to get away (escape)
s'échapper *saishappai;*
to get off (bus, train)
descendre *daissondr;* to
get on (bus, train) **monter**
montai; to get along/on
with (like) **s'entendre avec**
sontondr avek; to get up
se lever *suh luh-vai*

girl **la fille** *feey,* or
(derogatory) **la nana**** *na-na*

girlfriend **la petite amie**
puhteet-amee

to give **donner** *donnai,* or
(as a gift, treat) **offrir** *ofreer,*
or (to pass) **passer** *passai;*
to give back **rendre** *rondr;*
to give up **abandonner**
abondonnai; to give way
(yield) **céder** *saidai*

glass **le verre** *vair*

glasses (spectacles) **les**
lunettes [f] *lew-nett*

glove **le gant** *gon*

go (turn) **le tour** *toor;*
your go **à toi** *a twa;*
whose go is it? **c'est à qui**
le tour? *sai-ta kee luh*
toor; go-kart **le kart** *karrt*

to go **aller** *allai* (see Useful
irregular verbs p. 59), or
(leave) **partir** *parteer;* go
ahead! **vas-y!** *va-zee;* to go
away **s'en aller** *sonn-allai;*
to go back **retourner**
ruhtoor-nai; to go in
entrer *ontrai;* to go out
sortir *sorteer*

goal **le but** *bewt*

goalkeeper **le gardien de**
but *gardee-an duh bewt*

god **le dieu** *dee-uh*

good **bon(ne)** *bon f: bonn,*
or (well-behaved) **sage** *saj,*
or (weather) **beau** *bo* (see
p. 54); good-looking
beau† *bo* **f: belle** *bell;*
good morning/afternoon
bonjour *bonjoor;* good
evening **bonsoir** *bonswar;*
good night **bonne nuit**
bonn nwee

goodbye **au revoir** *o*
ruhvwar, or **salut*** *sa-lew*

gooseberry to be a
gooseberry **tenir la**
chandelle *tuh-neer la*
shondell

gossip **les commérages**
[m] *kommairaj,* or (person)
la commère *kommair*

to gossip **bavarder**
bavardai, or (maliciously)
faire des commérages *fair*
dai kommairaj

government **le**
gouvernement *goovair-*
nuh-mon

graffiti **les graffiti [m]**
grafeetee, or **les tags* [m]**
tag

gram **le gramme** *gram*

grandfather **le grand-père**
gron pair

grandmother **la**
grand-mère *gron mair*

grant **la bourse** *boorss*

grapefruit **le/la**
pamplemousse *pompl-*
mooss

grapes **le raisin** *raizan;*
bunch of grapes **la grappe**
de raisin *grap duh raizan;*
grape harvest **les**
vendanges [f] *vondonj*

grass **l'herbe [f]** *airb*

grateful **reconnaissant(e)**
ruhkonnaisson
f: ruhkonnaissont

†**beau** changes to **bel** *bell* in front of a [m] word beginning with a vowel, or sometimes an "h", e.g. **un bel homme**.

great (terrific)
sensationnel(le) *sonsass-yonnel*, or **génial(e)*** *jainn-yal*
green **vert(e)** *vair f: vairt*
grey **gris(e)** *gree f: greez*
grilled **grillé(e)** *gree-yai*
gross (horrible)
dégueulasse** *dai-guh-lass*
grotty (not very nice)
moche* *mosh*, or (really awful) **minable*** *meennabl*;
to feel grotty **se sentir mal** *suh sonteer mal*
ground **la terre** *tair*;
on the ground **par terre;**
ground floor **le rez-de-chaussée** *rai-duh-shossai*
group **le groupe** *groop*
to grow (person, thing) **grandir** *grondeer*, or (plant) **pousser** *poossai*
to guess **deviner** *duhvee-nai*
guest **l'invité(e) [m/f]** *anveetai*
guide (person, or book) **le guide** *geed*
guilty **coupable** *koopabl*
guitar **la guitare** *geetar*
guy **le gars*** *ga*, or **le type*** *teep*
gym (gymnastics) **la gym** *jeem*, or (gymnasium) **le gymnase** *jeem-naz*
gypsy **le/la gitan(e)** *jeetan f: jeetann*
habit **l'habitude [f]** *abeetewd*
to haggle **marchander** *marshondai*
hair (on head) **les cheveux [m]** *shuh-vuh*, or (on body) **les poils [m]** *pwal*; hairstyle **la coiffure** *kwafewr* (see also picture right)
hairdresser **le coiffeur** *kwafuhr* **f: la coiffeuse** *kwafurz*

half **la moitié** *mwat-yai*, or (with numbers) **demi(e)** *duh-mee*; half a kilo **un demi-kilo** *un duh-mee keelo*; half an hour **une demi-heure** *ewnn duh-mee uhr* (see also 'time' picture); a half bottle **une demi-bouteille** *ewnn duh-mee bootaiy*; half asleep/dressed **à moitié endormi(e) /habillé(e)** *a mwat-yai ondormee/abee-yai*; half-time **la mi-temps** *mee-ton*
ham **le jambon** *jombon*
hamburger **le hamburger** *amboorguhr*
hand **la main** *man*; by hand **à la main;** handmade **fait(e) à la main** *fai a la man f: fait ...*; helping hand **le coup de main** *koo duh ma*

hair **les cheveux**

to hang (something up) **accrocher** *akroshai*; to hang around/out **traîner*** *trainnai*; to hang up (phone) **raccrocher** *rakroshai*
hang-gliding **le deltaplane** *del-taplann*
hangover **la gueule de bois*** *gurl duh bwa*
to happen **se passer** *suh passai*, or **arriver** *areevai*
happy **heureux** *uhruh* **f: heureuse** *uhruhz*
hard **dur(e)** *dewr*
hat **le chapeau** *sha-po*
to hate **détester** *daitestai*, or (a lot) **avoir horreur de** *avwar oruhr duh*
to have **avoir** *avwar*, or (a meal, a drink) **prendre** *prondr*; to have to **devoir** *duhvwar*
hayfever **le rhume des foins** *rewm dai fwan*

bouclés *booklai*
raides *red*
frisés *freezai*
mi-longs *mee-lon*
le sèche-cheveux *sesh shuvuh*
courts *koor*
la mousse *mooss*
la laque *lak*
longs *lon*
roux *roo*
le gel *jel*
bruns *brun*
la brosse *bross*
noirs *nwar*
le peigne *penn-yuh*
la barrette *barett*
blonds *blon*

he *il eel*

head *la tête tett* (see also 'to ache' picture)

health *la santé sontai;* health foods *les produits diététiques prodwee dee-aitai-teek*

healthy (food) *sain(e) san f: senn,* or (person) *en bonne santé on bonn sontai*

to hear *entendre ontondr;* to hear about *entendre parler de ontondr parlai duh*

heart *le coeur kuhr;* to be heart-broken *avoir le coeur brisé avwar luh kuhr breezai*

heating *le chauffage sho-faj*

heavy *lourd(e) loor f: loord*

helicopter *l'hélicoptère [m] aileekoptair*

hell *l'enfer [m] onfair*

hello *bonjour bonjoor,* or *salut* sa-lew*

helmet *le casque kask*

help *l'aide [f] ed;* help! *au secours! o suhkoor*

to help *aider aidai;* to help yourself *se servir suh sairveer*

her (as in "her bag") *son son f: sa sa pl: ses sai,* or (as in "it's her" and after "of", "to", "with", etc.) *elle el,* or (as in "I see her") *la la*

here *ici ee-see;* here is/are *voici vwa-see*

hi *salut* sa-lew*

hiccups *le hoquet o-kai*

to hide (something) *cacher kashai,* or (yourself) *se cacher suh kashai*

hi-fi (system) *la chaîne (hi-fi) shenn (ee-fee)*

high *haut(e) o f:ote*

hiking: to go hiking *faire une randonnée fair ewnn rondonnai*

hill *la colline koleenn*

him (as in "it's him" and after "of", "than", "to", "with", etc.) *lui lwee,* or (as in "I see/know him") *le luh*

Hindu *hindou(e) andoo*

hippie *le/la hippie eepee,* or *le/la bab* bab*

his (as in "his bike") *son son f: sa sa pl: ses sai*

history *l'histoire [f] eestwar*

hit (success) *le succès sewk-sai,* or (song) *le tube* tewb*

to hit (strike) *frapper frappai,* or (knock into) *heurter uhrtai*

to hitch (a ride) *faire du stop* fair dew stop*

hitch-hiker *l'auto-stoppeur oto-stopuhr f: l'auto-stoppeuse oto-stopuhz*

HIV positive *séropositif sairo-pozeeteef f: séropositive sairo-pozeeteev*

hobby *le hobby o-bee*

to hold *tenir tuhneer*

hole *le trou troo*

holiday *les vacances [f] vakonss,* or (bank holiday) *le jour férié joor fair-yai;* holiday camp *le camp de vacances kom duh vakonss*

home *la maison maizon;* home game *le match à domicile match a domeesseel;* at (my/your etc.) home *chez moi/toi shai mwa/twa*

homeless (people) *les sans-abri [m/f] son-zabree,* or *le/la SDF ess dai eff*

homework *les devoirs [m] duhvwar*

homosexual *homosexuel(le) omosseksewell,* or *homo**

honest (law-abiding) *honnête o-net,* or (truthful) *sincère sansair*

honey *le miel mee-ell*

to hope *espérer aispairai*

horn (of car) *le klaxon klakson*

horoscope *l'horoscope [m] oroskop*

horrible *horrible oreebl*

horoscope
l'horoscope

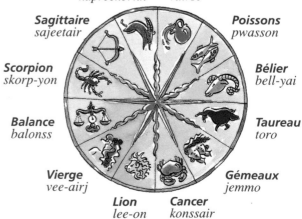

Capricorne *kapreekornn*

Verseau *vairso*

Sagittaire *sajeetair*

Poissons *pwasson*

Scorpion *skorp-yon*

Bélier *bell-yai*

Balance *balonss*

Taureau *toro*

Vierge *vee-airj*

Gémeaux *jemmo*

Lion *lee-on*

Cancer *konssair*

horror film **le film d'horreur** *feelm doruhr*
horse **le cheval** *shuhval*
hospital **l'hôpital [m]** *opeetal*
host **l'hôte [m]** *ote*
hostess **l'hôtesse [f]** *otess*
hot **chaud(e)** *sho f: shode,* or (spicy) **épicé(e)** *ai-peessai;* to be hot (person) **avoir chaud** *avwar sho,* or (weather) it is hot **il fait chaud** *eel fai sho*
hotel **l'hôtel [m]** *otel*
hour **l'heure [f]** *uhr* (see also 'time' picture)
house **la maison** *maizon*
hovercraft **l'aéroglisseur [m]** *a-airogleessuhr*
how **comment** *kommon;* how are you? **comment vas-tu?/allez-vous?** *kommon-va-tew/talai-voo;* how many/much? **combien?** *kombee-an*
to hug (someone) **serrer (quelqu'un) dans ses bras** *sairai (kelkun) don sai bra*
human **humain(e)** *ew-man f: ew-menn;* human rights **les droits de l'homme [m]** *drwa duh lomm*
humour **l'humour [m]** *ew-moor*
hungry: to be hungry **avoir faim** *avwar fan*
hurry: in a hurry **pressé(e)** *praissai*
to hurry **se dépêcher** *suh daipaishai*
to hurt **faire mal** *fair mal* (see also 'to ache')
hypocrite **l'hypocrite [m/f]** *eepokreet*
hysterics (nervous fit) **la crise de nerfs** *kreez duh nair,* or (laughter) **le fou rire** *foo reer*

I **je** *juh*
ice **la glace** *gla-ss;* ice cream **la glace;** ice cube **le glaçon** *gla-sson;* ice rink **la patinoire** *patee-nwar*
idea **l'idée [f]** *eedai*
idiot **l'idiot(e) [m/f]** *eed-yo f: eed-yott*
if **si** *see*
ill **malade** *malad*
illegal **illégal(e)** *ee-laigal*
to imagine **imaginer** *ee-majee-nai*
immigrant **l'immigré(e) [m/f]** *ee-meegrai*
important **important(e)** *amporton f: amportont*
in **dans** *don,* or (with months, years and [f] names of countries) **en** *on,* e.g. in June **en juin,** in France **en France,** or (with town names and [m] and [pl] names of countries) **à** *a,* e.g. in Paris **à Paris,** in the US **aux États-Unis** (see Au à la, à l', aux p. 57); to be in (at home) **être là** *etr la;* the in thing **le must***, or **le top***
inclusive **(tout) compris** *(too) kompree*
independent **indépendant(e)** *andaipondon f: andaipondont*
India **l'Inde [f]** *and*
infection **l'infection [f]** *anfekss-yon*
information **les renseignements [m]** *ronsainn-yuhmon*
injection **la piqûre** *peekewr*
injury **la blessure** *blaissewr;* injury time (in sports) **les arrêts de jeu [m]** *arrai duh juh*
innocent **innocent(e)** *ee-nosson f: ee-nossont*

insect **l'insecte [m]** *ansekt;* insect bite **la piqûre d'insecte** *peekewr dansekt;* insect repellent **le produit anti-insectes** *prodwee ontee ansekt*
inside **à l'intérieur** *a lantair-yuhr;* inside out **à l'envers** *a lonvair*
to insist **insister** *ansseestai*
instead of **au lieu de** *o lee-uh duh*
instructor **le professeur** *professuhr,* or (ski, driving) **le moniteur** *monneetuhr f: **la monitrice** *monneetreess*
instrument **l'instrument [m]** *anstrew-mon* (see also picture below)
insult **l'insulte [f]** *assewlt*

instruments *les instruments* (see also band picture)

le violoncelle *vee-olonsell*
le violon *vee-olon*
le cor *kor*
le piano *pee-anno*
la clarinette *klaree-nett*
le hautbois *o-bwa*
la trompette *trompett*
la flûte *flewt*
le trombone *trombonn*

insurance **l'assurance [f]** assewronss

intercom **l'interphone [m]** antairfonn

interested: to be interested in **s'intéresser à** santairaissai a

interesting **intéressant(e)** antairaisson f: antairaissont

international **international(e)** antair-nass-yonnal

Internet **Internet** internet or **le Net** net

interval (theatre) **l'entracte [m]** ontrakt

interview (for job) **l'entretien [m]** ontr-tee-an, or (with reporter) **l'interview [f]** antairvew

to introduce (to person) **présenter** praizontai

invitation **l'invitation [f]** anveetass-yon

to invite **inviter** anveetai

Ireland **l'Irlande [f]** eerlond

Irish **irlandais(e)** eerlondai f: eerlon-daiz

island **l'île [f]** eel

it (referring to a [m] thing) **il** eel, or (referring to a [f] thing) **elle** el, or (when unclear what "it" refers to) **ça** sa; it is **c'est** sai

Italy **l'Italie [f]** eetalee

jacket **la veste** vest, or (short, bomber-style) **le blouson** bloozon (see picture below)

jam **la confiture** konfeetewr

January **janvier** jonvee-ai

jazz **le jazz** jazz

jealous **jaloux** jaloo **f: jalouse** jalooz

jeans **le (blue-)jean** (bloo-)djeen

jellyfish **la méduse** maidewz

jewellery **les bijoux [m]** beejoo (see picture below)

Jewish **juif** jweef **f: juive** jweev

job **le travail** trav-eye, or **le boulot*** boolo, or **le job*** djob, or (weekend, vacation) **le petit boulot*** puhtee boolo

to join (club, party) **s'inscrire à** sanskreer a

joke **la plaisanterie** plaizontree, or **la blague** blag

to joke **plaisanter** plaizontai, **or blaguer*** blagai

judo **le judo** jewdo

to juggle **jongler** jonglai

juice **le jus** jew

jukebox **le juke-box** jewk-boks

July **juillet** jwee-yai

to jump **sauter** so-tai

June **juin** jwan

junk **le bric-à-brac** bree-ka-brak; junk shop **le brocanteur** brokontuhr

just: to have just done (something) **venir de faire** vuhneer duh fair

to keep **garder** gardai, or (not to stop) **ne pas arrêter de** nuh pa-zaraitai duh; to keep an eye on **surveiller** sewrvai-yai

key **la clé** klai

keyboard **le clavier** klavyai

kick **le coup de pied** koo duh pee-ai

kid **le/la gamin(e)** ga-man f: ga-meenn, or **le/la gosse*** goss

to kill **tuer** tewai; to kill yourself (laughing) **être mort(e) de rire*** etr mor duh reer f: ... mort ...

kilo **le kilo** keelo

jacket **la veste**   jewellery **les bijoux**

le blouson bloozon

la boucle d'oreille bookl doraiy

la chaîne shenn

le collier kolee-ai

la broche brosh

le pin's peenz

la bague bag

la boucle bookl

la gourmette goormet

le bracelet brasslai

le col kol

la veste vest

la manche monsh

le bouton booton

la poche posh

kite *le cerf-volant*

la poignée
pwann-yai

la ficelle
feessell

la queue
kuh

kilometre **le kilomètre**
keelomaitr
kind (nice) **gentil(le)** *jontee*
f: jonteey
kiss **le baiser** *baizai*, or
la bise *beez*, or **le bisou**
beezoo
to kiss **embrasser**
ombrassai, or (one another)
s'embrasser *sombrassai*
kit (equipment) **le matériel**
matair-yell
kitchen **la cuisine**
kweezeenn
kite **le cerf-volant** *sair
volon* (see also picture above)
knee **le genou** *juh-noo*
knickers **le slip** *sleep*
knife **le couteau** *kooto*
to know (facts) **savoir**
savwar, or (person, place)
connaître *konnaitr*
kosher **kascher** *kashair*
lager **la bière (blonde)**
bee-air (blond)
laid-back **décontracté(e)**
daikontraktai
lake **le lac** *lak*
lamb **l'agneau [m]** *ann-yo*
land **la terre** *tair*
language **la langue** *long*
laptop **un ordinateur
portable** *ordee-natuhr
portabl*
laser **le laser** *lazair*
last **le dernier** *dairnn-yai*
f: la dernière *dairnn-yair*;
at last **enfin** *onfan*

late (not early) **tard**
tar, or (not on time)
en retard *on ruhtar*
to laugh **rire** *reer*,
or **rigoler*** *reegolai*;
to have a laugh **se marrer***
suh marai; to laugh at (a
person, thing) **se moquer de**
suh mokai duh; to burst out
laughing **éclater de rire**
aiklatai duh reer
launderette **la laverie**
lavree
lazy **paresseux** *paraissuh*
f: paresseuse *paraissuhz*
leaf **la feuille** *fuh-yuh*
to learn **apprendre** *aprondr*
leather **le cuir** *kweer*
to leave **laisser** *laissai*, or
(go away) **partir** *parteer*; to
leave alone **laisser tranquille**
laissai tronkeel
left **la gauche** *goshe*;
on the left **à gauche**; left-
handed **gaucher** *go-shai*
f: gauchère *go-shair*
leg **la jambe** *jomb*
lemon **le citron** *seetron*
to lend **prêter** *praitai*
leotard **le collant** *kollon*
less **moins** *mwan*
lesson **le cours** *koor*
letter **la lettre** *letr*
lettuce **la salade verte**
sa-lad vairt
liar **le menteur** *montuhr*
f: la menteuse *montuhz*
library **la bibliothèque**
beeblee-otek
licence **le permis** *pairmee*;
driving licence **le permis de
conduire** *pairmee duh
kondweer*

lie (fib) **le mensonge**
monsonj
to lie (fib) **mentir** *monteer*
life **la vie** *vee*
lifeguard **le/la
surveillant(e) de baignade**
sewrvai-yon duh bainn-yad
f: sewrvai-yont ...
lifejacket **le gilet de
sauvetage** *jeelai duh sovtaj*
lifestyle **le mode de vie**
mode duh vee
lift (elevator) **l'ascenseur [m]**
assonsuhr
light (electric or not
darkness) **la lumière**
lew-mee-air, or (not dark)
clair(e) *klair*, or (not heavy)
léger *laijai* **f: légère** *laijair*
lighter **le briquet** *breekai*
like **comme** *komm*; what's
he/she like? **il/elle est
comment?** *eel/el ai kommon*
to like **aimer** *aimmai*; I like
him/her **je l'aime bien**
juh laimm bee-an; I'd like
je voudrais *juh voodrai*, or
j'aimerais *jaimm-rai*
likely **probable** *probabl*;
not likely! **pas question!**
pa kesst-yon
lilo **le matelas
pneumatique** *matela
pnuh-mateek*
line **la ligne** *leenn-yuh*
lip **la lèvre** *laivr*
to listen **écouter** *aikootai*
litre **le litre** *leetr*
little (small) **petit** *puhtee*
f: petite *puhteet*; a little (of)
un peu (de) *un puh duh*
live (broadcast) **en direct**
on deerekt

to live **vivre** *veevr*, or (dwell) **habiter** *abeetai;* to live it up **mener la grande vie** *muhnnai la grond vee*

liver **le foie** *fwa*

living room **le salon** *salon*

loaded (with money) **bourré(e) de fric**** *boorai duh freek*

loads of **des tas de** *dai ta duh*

to loathe **haïr** *a-eer*

local (regional) **de la région** *duh la raij-yon*, or (in/from this part of town) **du quartier** *dew kartee-ai,* or **du coin*** *dew kwan*

to lock **fermer à clé** *fairmai a klai*

London **Londres** *londr*

lonely **seul(e)** *surl*

long **long(ue)** *lon f: long,* or (a long time) **longtemps** *lonton;* how long? (time) **combien de temps?** *kombee-an duh ton*

loo (see 'toilet')

to look **regarder** *ruhgardai;* to look after (care for) **soigner** *swannyai* or (take charge of) **s'occuper de** *sokekpai duh;* to look for **chercher** *shairshai;* to look forward to **attendre avec impatience** *atondr avek ampass-yonss;* to look like **ressembler à** *ruhssomblai a*

to lose **perdre** *pairdr*

lost **perdu(e)** *pairdew;* to get lost **se perdre** *suh pairdr;* get lost! (clear off!) **fiche le camp*** *feesh luh kon* or **fous le camp**** *foo luh kon;* lost property **les objets trouvés [m]** *objai troovai*

lots (a lot) **beaucoup** *bo-koo,* or **plein*** *plan*

loud **fort(e)** *for f: fort*

lousy **nul(le)** *newl*

love **l'amour [m]** *a-moor;* in love **amoureux** *a-mooruh f: amoureuse* *a-mooruhz;* love-life **les amours** *a-moor;* to make love **faire l'amour** *fair la-moor*

to love **aimer** *aimai*, or (adore) **adorer** *adorai*

lovely (pretty) **joli(e)** *jo-lee,* or (nice, sweet) **mignon(ne)** *meenn-yon f: meenn-yonn*

low **bas(se)** *ba f: bass;* low-cut **décolleté(e)** *daikoltai*

low-down: to get the low-down (on something) **se faire tuyauter*** *suh fair twee-yotai*

luck **la chance** *shonss;* bad luck **pas de chance** *pa duh shonss;* good luck! **bonne chance!** *bonn shonss*

luckily **heureusement** *uhruhz-mon*

luggage **les bagages [m]** *bagaj;* hand-luggage **les bagages à main** *bagaj a man*

lunch **le déjeuner** *daijuh-nai;* to have lunch **déjeuner** *daijuh-nai*

lyrics **les paroles [f]** *parol*

machine **la machine** *masheenn*

macho **macho*** *matcho*

mad **fou** *foo f:* **folle** *fol* (see also 'crazy')

madam **madame** *ma-damm*

magazine **le magazine** *magazeenn*

mail (letters) **le courrier** *koor-yai* (see also 'e-mail')

to make **faire** *fair* (see Useful irregular verbs p. 59), or (earn) **gagner** *gann-yai,* or (as in "it makes me ill/jealous/happy") **rendre** *rondr;* to make up (invent) **inventer** *anvontai,* or (be friends again) **se réconcilier** *suh raikonseel-yai*

make-up **le maquillage** *ma-kee-yaj* (see also picture on right)

man **l'homme [m]** *omm*

to manage (cope) **se débrouiller** *suh daibroo-yai;* to manage to (succeed) **arriver à** *areevai a*

many **beaucoup de** *bo-koo duh;* not many **pas beaucoup de** *pa bo-koo duh*

map **la carte** *kart,* or (of town) **le plan** *plon*

March **mars** *marss*

margarine **la margarine** *margareenn*

mark (stain) **la tache** *tash,* or (at school) **la note** *not*

market **le marché** *marshai*

match (for a candle) **l'allumette [f]** *alewmett,* or (sport) **le match** *match*

material (cloth) **le tissu** *teessew*

maths **les maths [f]** *matt*

matter: it doesn't matter **ça ne fait rien** *sa nuh fai ree-an;* what's the matter? **qu'est-ce qui se passe?** *kess-kee-suh pass*

mature **mûr(e)** *mewr*

May **mai** *mai*

mayonnaise **la mayonnaise** *my-o-naiz*

me (as in "it's me" and after "of", "than", "to", "with", etc.) **moi** *mwa,* or (as in "he sees/knows me") **me** *muh*

meal **le repas** *ruh-pa*

make-up le maquillage

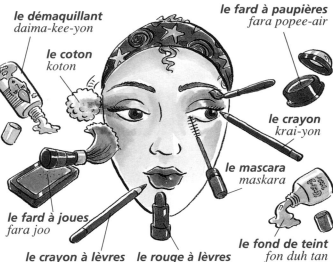

le démaquillant *daima-kee-yon*

le coton *koton*

le fard à paupières *fara popee-air*

le crayon *krai-yon*

le mascara *maskara*

le fard à joues *fara joo*

le fond de teint *fon duh tan*

le crayon à lèvres *krai-yon a laivr*

le rouge à lèvres *rooj a laivr*

to mean **vouloir dire** *voolwar deer;* to mean to **avoir l'intention de** *avwar lantonss-yon duh*
meat **la viande** *vee-ond*
media (TV, radio, papers) **les médias [m]** *maid-ya*
medicine (medication) **le médicament** *maideekamon,* or (science) **la médecine** *maidseenn*
Mediterranean (sea) **la Méditerranée** *maideetairannai*
medium (size) **moyen(ne)** *mwa-yan f: mwa-yenn,* or (cooking) **à point** *a pwan*
to meet (by chance) **rencontrer** *ronkontrai,* or (by arrangement) **retrouver** *ruhtroovai*
melon **le melon** *muhlon;* watermelon **la pastèque** *pastek*
menu **la carte** *kart,* or (set menu) **le menu** *muh-new*

mess **le désordre** *daizordr,* or **la pagaille*** *pag-eye*
message **le message** *messaj*
method **la méthode** *mai-tod*
metre **le mètre** *maitr*
microwave **le micro-ondes** *meekro-ond*
middle **le milieu** *meel-yuh;* in the middle (of) **au milieu (de)**
midnight **minuit** *meenn-wee*
milk **le lait** *lai;* milk shake **le milk-shake** *meelk shaik*
mind: do you mind? (does it bother you?) **ça te/vous dérange?** *sa tuh/voo daironj;* I don't mind (it doesn't bother me) **ça ne me dérange pas** *sa nuh muh daironj pa,* or (it's all the same to me) **ça m'est égal** *sa mai-tai-gal*
minute (time) **la minute** *mee-newt*
mirror **le miroir** *meerwar*

Miss **mademoiselle** *mad-mwazel*
to miss (as in "I missed the train") **rater** *ratai,* or (to long for: in French you say "something is missing to you") **manquer** *monkai,* e.g. I miss you **tu me manques,** he misses Paris **Paris lui manque**
mistake **l'erreur [f]** *eruhr;* to make a mistake **se tromper** *suh trompai*
to mix (or to mix up) **mélanger** *mailonjai,* or (muddle) **s'embrouiller** *sombroo-yai*
mixed up (in your mind) **perturbé(e)** *pairtewrbai*
to moan (complain) **râler*** *ralai*
mobile (phone) **le (téléphone) portable** *(tai-lai-fonn) portabl*
model (fashion) **le mannequin** *mann-kan*
modern **moderne** *modairnn*
moment: in a moment **dans un instant** *donzun nanston;* at the moment **en ce moment** *on suh mommon*
Monday **lundi [m]** *lundee*
money **l'argent [m]** *arjon,* or **le fric*** *freek;* money belt **la ceinture porte-billets** *santewr port bee-yai*
month **le mois** *mwa*
monument **le monument** *monnew-mon*
mood: in a good/bad mood **de bonne/mauvaise humeur** *duh bonn/movaiz ew-muhr*
moody (temperament) **lunatique** *lewnnateek*
moon **la lune** *lewnn*
moped **la mobylette** *mobeelett*

more (as in "more handsome" and "more slowly") **plus** *plew*, or (as in "I want more" and "I like it more") **plus** *plewss*, or (as in "[some] more?") **encore** *onkor*

morning **le matin** *matan*

mosque **la mosquée** *moskai*

mosquito **le moustique** *moosteek*; mosquito bite **la piqûre de moustique** *peekewr duh moosteek*; mosquito repellent **l'anti-moustique [m]** *ontee-moosteek*

most (as in "most handsome") **le/la/les plus** *luh/la/lai plew*, or (as in "I want the most" and "I like it the most") **le plus** *luh plewss*, or (as in "most of the time/people") **la plupart de** *la plewpar duh*; to make the most of **profiter de** *profeetai duh*

mother **la mère** *mair*

motor **le moteur** *motuhr*

motorbike **la moto*** *moto*, or **la bécane*** *baikann*

motorway **l'autoroute [f]** *otoroot*

mountain **la montagne** *montann-yuh*

mouse (animal/computer) **la souris** *soo-ree*

mouth **la bouche** *boosh*

to move **bouger** *boojai*, or (change address) **déménager** *daimai-najai*; move over! **pousse-toi!** *pooss twa*

movie **le film** *feelmm*

movies **le cinéma** *see-naima*, or **le ciné*,** or **le cinoche*** *see-nosh*

Mr **monsieur** *muhss-yuh*

Mrs **madame** *madamm*

much **beaucoup** *bo-koo*

mugged: to get mugged **se faire agresser** *suh fair agraissai*

murder **le meurtre** *murtr*

muscle **le muscle** *mewsskl*

museum **le musée** *mewzai*

mushroom **le champignon** *shompeenn-yon*

music **la musique** *mewzeek*

musician **le/la musicien(ne)** *mewzeess-yan* f: *mewzeess-yenn*

Muslim **musulman(e)** *mewzewlmon* f: *mewzewlmann*

must (to have to) **devoir** *duhvwar*; I must **je dois** *juh dwa*

mustard **la moutarde** *mootard*

my **mon** *mon* f: **ma** *ma* pl: **mes** *mai*

naïve **naïf** *na-eef* f: **naïve** *na-eev*

naked **nu(e)** *new*

name **le nom** *nom*; first name **le prénom** *prai-nom*; last name **le nom de famille** *nom duh fameey*; what's your name? **comment tu t'appelles/ vous vous appelez?** *komon tew ta-pell/voo voo-za-puhlai*

napkin **la serviette** *sairvee-ett*

narrow **étroit(e)** *aitrwa* f: *aitrwatt*

nasty **désagréable** *daizagrai-abl*, or (person, animal) **méchant(e)** *maishon* f: *maishont*

national **national(e)** *nass-yonnal*

nationality **la nationalité** *nass-yonnaleetai*

natural **naturel(le)** *natewrel*

nature **la nature** *natewr*

naughty **vilain(e)** *veelan* f: *veelenn*

near **près de** *prai duh*

nearest **le/la plus proche** *plew prosh*

nearly **presque** *presk*

necessary **nécessaire** *naissaissair*

neck **le cou** *koo*

to need **avoir besoin de** *avwar buhzwan duh*

needle **l'aiguille [f]** *aigweey*

neighbour **le/la voisin(e)** *vwazan* f: *vwazeenn*

neighbourhood **le quartier** *kart-yai*

nerve **le nerf** *nair*; nerve-racking **angoissant(e)** *ong-wasson* f: *ong-wassont*; to get on (someone's) nerves **taper sur les nerfs* (de quelqu'un)** *ta-pai sewr lai nairf (duh kelkun)*; what a nerve! **quel culot!*** *kel kewlo*

nervous: to be/feel nervous **être tendu(e)** *etr tondew*, or (have butterflies) **avoir le trac*** *avwar luh trak*

never **jamais** *jammai*; never mind! (it doesn't matter) **ça ne fait rien!** *sa nuh fai ree-an*, or (too bad) **tant pis!** *ton pee*

new **nouveau**[†] *noo-vo* f: **nouvelle** *noo-vel*; New Year **le nouvel an** *noo-vel on*; New Zealand **la Nouvelle-Zélande** *noo-vel zailond*

news **les nouvelles [f]** *noo-vel*, or (TV, radio, press) **les informations [f]** *anformass-yon*, or **les infos*** *anfo*; news stand **le kiosque** *kee-osk*

---

84 [†]**nouveu** changes to **nouvel** *noovell* in front of a [m] word beginning with a vowel or sometimes an "h".

newsagent's (for papers) **le marchand de journaux** *marshon duh joorno*, or (for cigarettes) **le tabac** *taba*
newspaper **le journal** *joornal*
next **prochain(e)** *proshan* f: *proshenn*; next to **à côté de** *a kotai duh*
nice (likeable) **sympa*** *sampa*; nice and ... (as in "nice and cold") **bien** *bee-an*
nickname **le surnom** *sewr-nom*, or (shortened name) **le diminutif** *dee-mee-newteef*
night **la nuit** *nwee*; last night **hier soir** *ee-air swar*
nightmare **le cauchemar** *koshmar*
no **non** *non*; no entry/smoking **défense d'entrer/de fumer** *daifonss dontrai/duh fewmai*; no way! **pas question!** *pa kesst-yon*
nobody **personne** *pairsonn*; nobody else **personne d'autre** *pairsonn dotr*
noise **le bruit** *brwee*
normal **normal(e)** *nor-mal*

north **le nord** *nor*; north of **au nord de** *o nor duh*
nose **le nez** *nai*
nosy **curieux** *kewr-yuh* f: **curieuse** *kewr-yuhz*; to be nosy **fourrer son nez partout*** *foorai son nai partoo*
not (with a verb, as in "it's not working") **ne ... pas** *nuh ... pa*, or (without a verb, as in "not me") **pas** *pa* (see Negatives p. 60)
note (money) **le billet** *bee-yai*
notebook **le carnet** *karnai*
nothing **rien** *ree-an*; nothing else **rien d'autre** *ree-an dotr*
novel **le roman** *rommon*
November **novembre** *novombr*
now **maintenant** *mant-non*
nowhere **nulle part** *newl par*
nuclear **nucléaire** *newklai-air*
number **le numéro** *new-mairo*

nurse **l'infirmier** *anfeerm-yai* f: **l'infirmière** *anfeerm-yair*
nuts **les noix [f]** *nwa* (see picture below)
nutter (crazy person) **le fou** *foo* f: **la folle** *fol*, or **le/la cinglé(e)**** *sanglai*
obnoxious **odieux** *od-yuh* f: **odieuse** *od-yuhz*
obscene **obscène** *obsenn*
obsession **l'obsession [f]** *obsaiss-yon*
obvious **évident(e)** *aiveedon* f: *aiveedont*
o'clock (see picture for 'time')
October **octobre** *oktobr*
odd (strange) **bizarre** *beezar*; the odd one out **l'exception [f]** *eksepss-yon*
of **de** *duh* (see p. 56)
off (switched off) **éteint(e)** *aitan* f: *aitant*; (see also to get, to put, to take, to turn, etc.)
offended **vexé(e)** *veksai*
to offer **offrir** *offreer*
office **le bureau** *bewro*
official **officiel(le)** *ofeess-yell*

nuts *les noix*

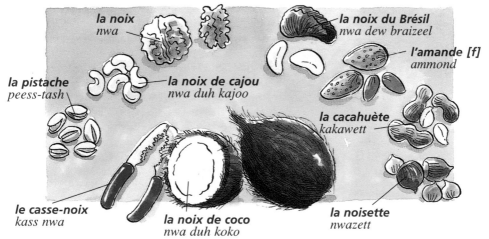

la noix *nwa*
la noix du Brésil *nwa dew braizeel*
l'amande [f] *ammond*
la pistache *peess-tash*
la noix de cajou *nwa duh kajoo*
la cacahuète *kakawett*
le casse-noix *kass nwa*
la noix de coco *nwa duh koko*
la noisette *nwazett*

often **souvent** *soovon;*
how often? **combien de
fois?** *kombee-an duh fwa*
oil **l'huile [f]** *weel*
OK **d'accord** *da-kor,* or **OK***,
or (I'm/it's OK) **ça va** *sa va*
old **vieux**[†] *vee-uh* **f: vieille**
vee-aiy; how old are you?
quel âge as-tu? *kel aj a tew;*
old-fashioned **démodé(e)**
dai-modai, or **ringard(e)***
rangar **f: rangard**
olive **l'olive [f]** *oleev*
omelette **l'omelette [f]**
omm-lett
on **sur** *sewr,* or (switched
on) **allumé(e)** *alew-mai;* on
Sundays **le dimanche** *luh
dee-monsh;* to be on (as in
"where's the film on?")
passer *passai*
one-way **à sens unique**
a sonss ew-neek
onion **l'oignon [m]** *onn-yon*
only **seulement** *surlmon;*
only daughter/son **la fille/le
fils unique** *feey/feess
ew-neek*
open **ouvert(e)** *oovair
f: oovairt;* in the open air
en plein air *on plenn-air*
to open **ouvrir** *oovreer*
opera **l'opéra [m]** *opaira*
opinion **l'avis [m]** *avee*
opportunity **l'occasion [f]**
okaz-yon
opposite (facing) **en face**
on fass, or (not the same)
le contraire *kontrair*
optician's **chez
l'opticien(ne) [m/f]** *shai
lopteess-yan* **f: ... lopteess-
yen**
optimistic **optimiste**
optee-meest
or **ou** *oo*
orange (fruit) **l'orange [f]**
oronj, or (colour) **orange**

orchestra **l'orchestre [m]**
orkestr
order **l'ordre [m]** *ordr,* or
(for food, drink) **la
commande** *kommond*
to order (food, drink)
commander *kommondai*
ordinary **ordinaire**
ordee-nair
to organize **organiser**
organneezai
original **original(e)**
oreejeennal
other **autre** *otr;*
the other one **l'autre [m/f]**
otherwise **sinon** *see-non*
our **notre** *notr* **pl: nos** *no*
out: to be out (not at home)
être sorti(e) *etr sortee;*
out of order (not working)
en panne *on pann* (see also
to find, to go, etc.)
outdoor **de plein air** *duh
plenn-air;* to sleep outdoors
dormir à la belle étoile
dormeer a la bel aitwal
outrageous **monstrueux**
monss-trew-uh
f: monstrueuse
monss-trew-uhz
outside **à l'extérieur** *a lex-
tair-yuhr,* or **dehors** *duh-or*
oven **le four** *foor*
over (not under) **par-dessus**
par duhssew, or (finished)
fini(e) *fee-nee;* over here
par ici *par ee-see;* over
there **là-bas** *la-ba;* over the
top **exagéré(e)** *egzajairai*
overdraft **le découvert**
daikoovair
overrated **surestimé(e)**
sewr-esstee-mai
to overtake **doubler**
dooblai
to owe **devoir** *duhvwar*
own: on your own **tout(e)
seul(e)** *too surl* **f: toot surl**

owner **le/la propriétaire**
propree-aitair
to pack (bags) **faire les
valises** *fair lai valeez*
package tour **le voyage
organisé** *vwa-yaj
organneezai*
padlock **le cadenas**
kad-na, or (on bike)
l'antivol [m] *onteevol*
page **la page** *paj*
pain: to be a pain (nuisance)
être embêtant(e) *etr
ombaiton* **f: ombaitont**
to paint **peindre** *pandr*
palace **le palais** *palai*
pan (saucepan) **la casserole**
kass-rol, or (frying) **la poêle**
pwal
panic **la panique** *panneek*
paper **le papier** *pap-yai*
paperback (book) **le livre
de poche** *leevr duh posh*
parachute **le parachute**
parashewt
parcel **le colis** *kolee*
parents **les parents [m]**
pa-ron
park **le jardin public**
jardan pewbleek, or
(large) **le parc** *park*
to park **se garer** *suh ga-rai*
parking space **le parking**
parkeeng
part (not all) **la partie**
partee, or (for bike etc.) **la
pièce** *pee-ess;* to take part
participer *parteesseepai*
party **la fête** *fett,* or
(political) **le parti** *partee*
to party **faire la fête** *fair
la fett*
pass (for travel) **la carte
(d'abonnement)** *kart
(dabonn-mon);* ski pass
le forfait *forfai*
to pass **passer** *passai,* or
(exam) **réussir** *rai-ewsseer*

---

86 [†]*vieux* changes to *vieil (vee-ai)* in front of a [m] word beginning with a vowel and sometimes "h", e.g. *un vieil homme*

passenger *le passager*
passajai f: la passagère
passajair
passport *le passeport*
passpor
pasta *les pâtes [f] patt*
path *le chemin shuh-man*
patient *patient(e) pass-*
yon f: pass-yont
pattern *le motif moteef*
pavement *le trottoir*
trotwar
to pay *payer pai-yai;*
to pay back *rembourser*
romboorsai
peace *la paix pai*
peaceful *tranquille*
tronkeel
peach *la pêche pesh*
peanut *la cacahuète*
kakawett
pear *la poire pwar*
peas *les petits pois [m]*
puhtee pwa
pedestrian *le piéton pee-*
aiton; pedestrian crossing
le passage (pour) piétons
passaj (poor) pee-aiton
pen *le stylo steelo;* pen pal
le/la correspondant(e)
ko-respondon
f: ko-respondont
pencil *le crayon krai-yon*
people *les gens [m/f] jon*
pepper (spice) *le poivre*
pwavr, or (vegetable)
le poivron pwavron
perfect *parfait(e) parfai*
f: parfett
performance *la*
représentation ruhprai-
zontass-yon, or (cinema)
la séance sai-onss
perhaps *peut-être puh-tetr*
period (menstruation)
les règles [f] raigl
person *la personne*
pairsonn

phone booth *la cabine téléphonique*

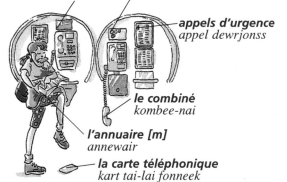

le téléphone à carte
tai-lai-fonn a kart
le téléphone à pièces
tai-lai-fonn a pee-ess
appels d'urgence
appel dewrjonss
le combiné
kombee-nai
l'annuaire [m]
annewair
la carte téléphonique
kart tai-lai fonneek

petrol *l'essence [f] essonss;*
lead-free petrol *le sans*
plomb son plom; petrol
station *la station-service*
stass-yon sairveess
pharmacy *la pharmacie*
farmassee
philosophy *la philosophie*
feelo-zofee
phobia *la phobie fobee*
phone *le téléphone tai-*
lai-fonn; phone booth
la cabine téléphonique
ka-beenn tai-lai-fonneek;
phone call *le coup de fil*
koo duh feel (see also
picture above)
to phone *téléphoner*
tai-lai-fonnai, or *passer un*
coup de fil* passai un koo
duh feel; to phone back
rappeler rap-lai
photo *la photo foto*
photographer
le/la photographe fotograf
to pick (choose) *choisir*
shwazeer, or (gather)
cueillir kuh-yeer; to pick up
(from floor/table, etc.)
ramasser rammassai

picnic *le pique-nique peek*
neek (see also picture p. 88)
picture (drawing) *le dessin*
daissan, or (painting)
le tableau tablo
pie (meat/vegetable)
la tourte toort, or (sweet)
la tarte tart
piece *le morceau morso*
pig *le cochon koshon*
pigeon *le pigeon peejon*
pill *la pilule peelewl;* to be
on the pill *prendre la pilule*
prondr la peelewl
PIN (personal identification
number) *le code*
confidentiel kod
konfeedonsee-ell
pinball *le flipper fleepuhr*
pineapple *l'ananas [m]*
annannass
pink *rose roz*
pity: it's a pity! *c'est*
dommage! sai dommaj
pizza *la pizza peedza*
place *l'endroit [m] ondrwa,*
or (seat, position) *la place*
plass; (at/to) my/your place
chez moi/toi shai mwa/twa
plan *le plan plon*

picnic *le pique-nique*

le banc bon

le frisbee *freez-bee*

la poubelle *poobell*

le fromage *fromaj*

l'eau [f] o

le pain pan

la pastèque *pastek*

le raisin raizan

la glacière *glass-yair*

le thermos tairmoss

le saucisson sosseesson

le tire-bouchon teer booshon

l'essuie-tout [m] esswee-too

le panier pann-yai

le canif kaneef

plane (aircraft) *l'avion [m]* av-yon

plant *la plante* plont

plaster (for cut or blister) *le pansement* ponss-mon, or (cast) *le plâtre* platr

plastic *le plastique* plasteek

plate *l'assiette [f]* ass-yett

play (in theatre) *la pièce* pee-yess

to play *jouer* joo-ai

player *le joueur* joo-uhr f: *la joueuse* joo-uhz

please *s'il vous plaît* seel voo plai, or (to a friend) *s'il te plaît* seel tuh plai

plug (for water) *la bonde* bond, or (for electrics) *la prise* preez

plum *la prune* prewn

pocket *la poche* posh; pocket-money *l'argent de poche [m]* arjon duh posh

poem *le poème* po-emm

to point *indiquer* andeekai, or (with a finger) *montrer du doigt* montrai dew dwa

police *la police* poleess; police officer *l'agent de police [m]* ajon duh poleess, or *le gendarme* jondarm, or *le flic** fleek; police station *le commissariat de police* komeess-areea duh poleess

polite *poli(e)* polee

politics *la politique* poleeteek

pollution *la pollution* polewss-yon

poor *pauvre* povr

popular *populaire* popewlair

pork *le porc* por

posh (elegant) *chic* sheek

positive (not negative) *positif* pozeeteef f: *positive* pozeeteev, or (sure) *sûr(e)* sewr

possible *possible* posseebl

post (letters) *le courrier* kooree-ai; post-box *la boîte aux lettres* bwat o letr; post office *la poste* post

postcard *la carte postale* kart postal

poster *le poster* postair

potato *la pomme de terre* pomm duh tair; mashed potato *la purée (de pomme de terre)* pewrai (duh pomm duh tair)

pound (UK money) *la livre (sterling)* leevr (stairleeng)

practical *pratique* prateek

to practise (sport) *s'entraîner* sontrainnai, or (piano, violin) *travailler* trav-eye-ai

prawn *la crevette* kruhvett

to prefer *préférer* praifairai

pregnant *enceinte* onsant

to prepare *préparer* praiparai

present (gift) *le cadeau* kado

to pretend *faire semblant* fair somblon

pretty *joli(e)* jolee

price *le prix* pree

printer (machine) *l'imprimante [f]* ampree-mont

prison *la prison* preezon

private *privé(e)* preevai

prize *le prix* pree

problem *le problème* problemm

programme *le programme* programm, or (TV, radio) *l'émission [f]* ai-meess-yon

progress *le progrès* prograi

promise *la promesse* pro-mess

proof *la preuve* prurv

prostitute *le/la prostitué(e)* prostee-tewai

Protestant ***protestant(e)***
proteston f: protestont
proud ***fier f: fière*** *fee-air*
psychological
psychologique *pseekolojeek*
public ***public f: publique***
pewbleek
to pull ***tirer*** *teerai;*
to pull someone's leg
faire marcher quelqu'un*
fair marshai kelkun
to punch ***donner un coup***
de poing *donnai un koo*
duh pwan
puncture: to have a puncture
(tyre) ***avoir (le pneu) crevé***
avwar (luh pnuh) kruhvai
pure ***pur(e)*** *pewr*
purpose: on purpose
exprès *aiksprai*
purse ***le porte-monnaie***
port monnai
to push ***pousser*** *poossai*
to put ***mettre*** *metr;* to put
away ***ranger*** *ronjai;* to put
off (postpone) ***remettre à***
plus tard *ruh-metr a plew*
tar, or (discourage)
dissuader *deess-ew-adai,*
or (disgust) ***dégoûter***
daigootai; to put on
(clothes) ***mettre*** *metr;* to
put (someone) up ***loger***
lojai; to put up with
supporter *sewportai*
puzzle ***le puzzle*** *pewzl*
quality ***la qualité*** *ka-leetai*
quantity ***la quantité***
konteetai
to quarrel ***se disputer***
suh deespewtai
quarter ***le quart*** *kar*
(see also time)
question ***la question***
kest-yon
queue ***la queue*** *kuh*
to queue ***faire la queue***
fair la kuh

quick ***rapide*** *rapeed*
quickly ***vite*** *veet*
quiet (calm) ***tranquille***
tronkeel, or (not loud) ***bas***
ba f: basse bass; to be/keep
quiet ***se taire*** *suh tair*
quite (as in "quite pretty")
assez *assai,* or (as in "I quite
agree") ***tout à fait*** *too-ta-fai*
quiz ***le jeu*** *juh,* or
le concours *konkoor*
race ***la course*** *koorss*
racist ***raciste*** *rasseest*
racket (tennis etc.)
la raquette *rakett*
radiator ***le radiateur***
rad-yatuhr
radio ***la radio*** *rad-yo;*
radio cassette player
la radiocassette
rad-yo ka-sett
raft ***le radeau*** *ra-do*
railway ***le chemin de fer***
shuh-man duh fair;
French railways ***la SNCF***
ess enn sai eff
rain ***la pluie*** *plwee;*
it's raining ***il pleut***
eel pluh
rape ***le viol*** *vee-ol*
rare (unusual) ***rare*** *rar,*
or (barely cooked)
saignant(e) *senn-yon*
f:senn-yont
rash ***l'irritation [f]***
eereetass-yon
raspberry ***la***
framboise *frombwaz*
raw ***cru(e)*** *krew*
razor ***le rasoir*** *razwar;*
razor blade ***la lame de***
rasoir *lamm duh razwar*
reaction ***la réaction***
rai-aks-yon
to read ***lire*** *leer*
ready ***prêt(e)*** *prai f:*
prait
real ***vrai(e)*** *vrai*

to realize ***se rendre***
compte *suh rondr komt*
really (truly, extremely)
vraiment *vrai-mon,* or
(extremely) ***vachement****
vash-mon
reason ***la raison*** *raizon*
recent ***récent(e)*** *raisson*
f: raissont
reception ***la réception***
rai-seps-yon
recipe ***la recette*** *ruhsett*
to recognize ***reconnaître***
ruhkonnaitr
to recommend
recommander
ruhkommondai
record (sport) ***le record***
ruhkor
to record ***enregistrer***
onruh-jeestrai
red ***rouge*** *rooj;* to blush
rougir *roojeer* (see also 'hair')

rain ***la pluie***

l'arc-en-ciel [m]
ar-konss-yell

le parapluie
paraplwee

la flaque d'eau
flak doh

l'imper* [m]
ampair

la goutte de pluie
goot duh plwee

la botte de caoutchouc
bott duh ka-ootchoo

reduced (in sales) **soldé(e)**
soldai
refund **le remboursement**
romboorss-mon
to refuse **refuser** *ruhfewzai*
region **la région** *raij-yon*
registered (post, letter)
recommandé(e)
ruhkommondai, or (luggage)
enregistré(e) *onruhjeestrai*
regular **régulier** *raigewl-yai*
f: **régulière** *raigewl-yair*
rehearsal **la répétition**
raipaiteess-yon
to relax **se détendre** *suh*
daitondr
relaxed **décontracté(e)**
daikontraktai
relief **le soulagement**
soolaj-mon
religion **la religion**
ruhleej-yon
to remember **se souvenir**
de *suh soov-neer duh*
remote **isolé(e)** *eezolai*;
remote control **la télé-**
commande *tailai-kommond*
to rent **louer** *loo-ai*;
for rent **à louer**

to repair **réparer**
raiparai
to repeat **répéter**
raipaitai
to reply **répondre**
raipondr
rescue **les secours [m]**
suhkoor
to rescue **sauver** *sovai*
research **la recherche**
ruh-shairsh
reservation **la réservation**
raizairvass-yon
reserved **réservé(e)**
raizairvai
responsible **responsable**
raisponsabl
rest (break) **le repos** *ruhpo*,
or (remainder) **le reste** *rest*
to rest **se reposer** *suh*
ruhpozai
restaurant **le restaurant**
restoron, or **le resto***
result **le résultat** *raizewlta*
return **le retour** *ruhtoor*, or
(ticket) **l'aller-retour [m]**
allai ruhtoor
revenge: to get your revenge
se venger *suh vonjai*

to reverse **faire marche**
arrière *fair marsh ar-yair*;
to reverse the charges (phone)
appeler en PCV *appuhlai*
on pai sai vai
rice **le riz** *ree*
rich **riche** *reesh*
rid: to get rid of
se débarrasser de
suh daibarrassai duh
ride: to go for a ride (bike/
car) **faire un tour** *fair un*
toor; to take someone for a
ride (trick) **faire marcher**
quelqu'un *fair marshai*
kelkun
rider (horse) **le cavalier**
kaval-yai; **la cavalière**
kaval-yair
riding **l'équitation [f]**
aikeetass-yon
(see also picture below)
right (correct) **exact** *egzakt*,
or (fair) **juste** *jewst*, or (not
left) **la droite** *drwat*; you
are right **tu as/vous avez**
raison *tew a/voo-zavai*
raizon; on the right **à**
droite; right away **tout de**
suite *tood sweet*;
right-of-way **la**
priorité, *pree-oreetai*
to ring **sonner** *sonnai*
(see also 'phone')
riot **l'émeute [f]**
emmurt; to have a riot
(wild time) **s'éclater****
saiklatai
to rip **déchirer**
daisheerai
ripe **mûr(e)** *mewr*
rip-off: it's a rip-off
c'est de l'arnaque**
sai duh lar-nak
risk **le risque** *reesk*
river **la rivière** *reev-*
yair, or (large)
le fleuve *flurv*

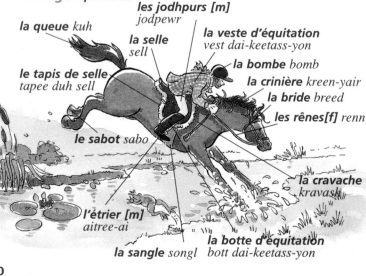

riding **l'équitation**

les jodhpurs [m]
jodpewr

la queue *kuh*

la selle
sell

le tapis de selle
tapee duh sell

la veste d'équitation
vest dai-keetass-yon

la bombe *bomb*

la crinière *kreen-yair*

la bride *breed*

les rênes[f] *renn*

le sabot *sabo*

la cravache
kravash

l'étrier [m]
aitree-ai

la botte d'équitation
bott dai-keetass-yon

la sangle *songl*

road *la route* root, or (in town) *la rue* rew;
road map *la carte routière* kart root-yair
rock (boulder, rock-face) *le rocher* roshai, or (music) *le rock* rok
roll (bread) *le petit pain* puhtee pan
roller blades *les rollers (m)* roluhr
romance (love affair/story) *l'histoire d'amour [f]* eestwar da-moor
romantic *romantique* ro-monteek
roof *le toit* twa; roof rack *la galerie* galree
room *la pièce* pee-ess, or (hotel/bedroom) *la chambre* shombr; single/double room *la chambre simple/double* shombr sampl/doobl; twin room *la chambre à deux lits* shombr a duh lee
rope *la corde* kord
rotten (off) *pourri(e)* pooree, or (mean, unfair) *moche** mosh
round (of drinks) *la tournée* toor-nai, or (shape) *rond(e)* ron f: rond
roundabout *le rond-point* ron-pwan
route *l'itinéraire [m]* eetee-nairair
to row (a boat) *ramer* ramai
to rub *frotter* frotai; to rub it in *remuer le couteau dans la plaie* ruhmewai luh kooto don la plai; to rub out *effacer* aifassai
rubber band *l'élastique [m]* ailasteek
rubbish *les ordures [f]* ord-ewr; rubbish bin *la poubelle* poobel; to talk rubbish *dire des bêtises* deer dai baiteez

sailing boat *le voilier* or *le dériveur*

le spinnaker, or le spi* spee(nakhur)
le mât ma
le voilier vwall-yai
la grand-voile gron vwal
le dériveur daireevuhr
la bôme bomm
l'ancre [f] onkr
la cabine ka-been
le canot kanno
le pare-battage par battaj
la rame ramm
le gilet de sauvetage jeelai duh sov-taj
le foc fok
la bouée boo-ai
le gouvernail goovairnn-eye
la barre bar
l'écoute de grand-voile [f] aikoot duh gron vwal

rude *impoli(e)* ampolee, or (crude) *grossier* gross-yai; f: *grossière* gross-yair
rugby *le rugby* rewgbee
ruins *les ruines [f]* rween
rule *la règle* raigl
rumour *la rumeur* rewmuhr
to run *courir* kooreer; to run away *s'enfuir* sonfweer; to run out (expire) *expirer* ekspeerai
rush hour *l'heure de pointe [f]* uhr duh pwant
sad *triste* treest
safe *en sécurité* on saikew-reetai, or (for valuables) *le coffre-fort* kofr for
safety *la sécurité* saikewreetai; safety belt *la ceinture de sécurité* santewr duh saikewreetai; safety pin *épingle de sûreté* aipangl duh sewr-tai

sailing: sailing boat (yacht) *le voilier* vwall-yai, or (dinghy) *le dériveur* daireevuhr; to go sailing *faire de la voile* fair duh la vwal (see also picture above)
salad *la salade* salad; fruit salad *la salade de fruits* salad duh frwee; green salad *la salade verte* salad vairt; mixed salad *la salade composée* salad kompozai; salad dressing (French dressing) *la vinaigrette* vee-naigrett
salami *le saucisson* sosseesson
sale: for sale *à vendre* a vondr
sales (reduced prices) *les soldes [f]* solld
salmon *le saumon* so-mon

91

salt **le sel** *sell*
same **le/la même** *memm*
sand **le sable** *sabl*
sandal **la sandale** *sondal*
sandwich **le sandwich**
sondweesh
sanitary towel **la serviette**
hygiénique *sairv-yett*
eejai-neek
sarcastic **sarcastique**
sarkasteek
Saturday **samedi [m]**
sammdee
sauce **la sauce** *sosse*
sausage **la saucisse** *sosseess*
to save (rescue) **sauver**
sovai, or (money)
économiser *aiko-no-meezai*
savoury (not sweet) **salé(e)**
sa-lai
to say **dire** *deer*
scared: to be scared **avoir**
peur *avwar puhr*, or
avoir la trouille** *avwar*
la troo-yuh; scared stiff
mort(e) de peur *mor duh*
puhr f: mort ...
scarf (long) **l'écharpe [f]**
aisharp, or (square)
le foulard *foolar*
scary **effrayant(e)**
efrai-yon f: efrai-yont
scenery **le paysage**
pai-ee-zaj
school (primary) **l'école [f]**
aikol, or (high/secondary)
le lycée *lee-sai*, or
le collège *kolej*
science **la science** *see-onss*
scissors **les ciseaux [m]**
seezo
score **le score** *skor*
to score (a goal, point)
marquer un but/un point
markai un bewt/un pwan
Scotland **l'Écosse [f]** *aikoss*
Scottish **écossais(e)**
aikossai f: aikossaiz

to scratch (yourself)
se gratter *suh gratai*
to scream **crier** *kree-ai*
screen **l'écran [m]** *aikron*
scruffy **crade**** *krad*
sculpture **la sculpture**
skewl-tewr
sea **la mer** *mair*
seafood **les fruits de mer**
[m] *frwee duh mair*
seasick: to be seasick
avoir le mal de mer
avwar luh mal duh mair
season **la saison** *saizon;*
season ticket **la carte**
d'abonnement *kart*
dabonn-mon
seat (place) **la place** *plass,*
or (chair) **le siège** *see-aij*
second (measurement of
time) **la seconde** *suhgond;*
second-hand **d'occasion**
dokaz-yon
secret **le secret** *suhkrai*
secretary **le/la secrétaire**
suhkraitair
to see **voir** *vwar;*
to see again **revoir** *ruhvwar;*
see you soon **à bientôt**
a bee-anto
to seem **sembler** *somblai*
selfish **égoïste** *aigo-eest*
self-service (restaurant)
le self(-service)*
self(-sairveess)
to sell **vendre** *vondr*
to send **envoyer**
onvwa-yai
sense **le sens** *sonss;*
it doesn't make sense
ça n'a pas de sens
sa na pa duh sonss
sensible **raisonnable**
raizonnabl
sensitive **sensible**
sonsseebl
September **septembre**
septombr

serious **sérieux** *sair-yuh*
f: sérieuse *sair-yuhz*
service **le service** *sairveess*
sewing **la couture**
kootuhr
sex (gender) **le sexe** *seks,*
or (intercourse) **les rapports**
(sexuels) [m] *rappor*
(seksewell)
sexist **sexiste** *sekseest*
sexy **sexy** *seksy*
shade **l'ombre [f]** *ombr;*
in the shade **à l'ombre**
shame **la honte** *ont;* what
a shame! **(quel) dommage!**
kel dommaj
shampoo **le shampooing**
shompwan
shape **la forme** *form*
to share **partager** *partajai*
shattered (tired) **nase****
naz, or **crevé(e)**** *kruhvai*
to shave **se raser**
suh ra-zai
shaving cream **la crème à**
raser *kremm a ra-zai*
she **elle** *el*
sheet **le drap** *dra*
shirt **la chemise** *shuh-meez*
shock **le choc** *shok*
shoe **la chaussure**
sho-sewr, or **la pompe****
pomp, or **la godasse****
godass; athletics shoes
les baskets [f] *baskett,* or
les tennis [f] *tai-neess*
shop **le magasin** *magazan,*
or **la boutique** *booteek*
shopping: to go shopping
(for groceries etc.) **faire des**
courses *fair dai koorss,* or
(for clothes etc.) **faire les**
magasins *fair lai magazan;*
shopping centre **le centre**
commercial *sontr*
kommairsee-al; window
shopping **le lèche-vitrines**
lesh-veetreenn

short **court(e)** *koor f: koort;*
short cut **le raccourci**
ra-koorsee; short-sighted
myope *mee-op*
shorts **le short** *short*
shoulder **l'épaule [f]** *aipole*
to shout **crier** *kree-ai,* or
hurler *ewrlai*
show (performance) **le**
spectacle *spek-takl*
to show **montrer** *montrai;*
to show off **frimer**** *freemai*
shower **la douche** *doosh*
shut **fermé(e)** *fair-mai;*
shut up! **tais-toi!** *tai-twa,*
or **taisez-vous** *taizai-voo*
shy **timide** *tee-meed*
sick (ill) **malade** *malad;*
to be sick (vomit) **vomir**
vo-meer; to feel sick (queasy)
avoir mal au coeur *avwar*
mal o kuhr
side **le côté** *kotai*
sightseeing **le tourisme**
tooreezm
sign (with hand etc.) **le**
signe *seenn-yuh,* or (on
road etc.) **le panneau** *panno*
signature **la signature**
seenn-yatewr
Sikh **sikh** *seek*
silence **le silence**
seelonss
silly **bête** *bet*
simple **simple**
sampl
since **depuis**
duhpwee
to sing **chanter**
shontai
singer **le chanteur**
shontuhr f: la
chanteuse *shontuhz*
single (ticket) **l'aller**
simple [m] *allai*
sampl, or (unmarried)
célibataire
saileebatair

Sir **Monsieur** *muhss-yuh*
sister **la soeur** *suhr,* or
la frangine* *fronjeenn*
to sit down **s'asseoir**
sass-war
sitting down **assis(e)**
assee f: asseez
size **la taille** *tie*
skate **le patin** *patan*
skate board **la planche**
à roulettes *plonsh a*
roolett, or **le skate***
skate
skating: ice-skating
le patin (à glace) *patan*
(a gla-ss); roller skating
les rollers (m) *roluhr*
to ski **skier** *skee-ai*
skiing **le ski** *skee;* water-
skiing **le ski nautique**
skee noteek; to go skiing
faire du ski *fair dew*
skee; ski resort **la station**
de ski *stass-yon duh skee*
(see also picture)
skin **la peau** *po*
skirt **la jupe** *jewp*
skiver **le/la tire-au-flanc***
teer-o-flon
sky **le ciel** *see-ell*
slang **l'argot [m]** *argo*

to sleep **dormir** *dor-meer;*
to sleep in **faire la grasse**
matinée *fair la grass matee-*
nai; to sleep with someone
coucher avec quelqu'un
kooshai avek kelkun

to ski *skier*

la **télécabine** *tailai-ka-beenn*

le **télésiège** *tailai-see-aij*

la **luge** *lewj*

le **surf** *suhrf*

la **piste**
peest

le **monoski**
monno-ski

hors-piste
or *peest*

le **bandeau**
bon-do

les **lunettes [f]**
lew-nett

le **téléski** *tailai-skee*

le **gant** *gon*

la **combinaison**
kombee-naizon

le **forfait**
for-fai

le **bâton**
ba-ton

la **banane**
ba-nann

la **doudoune**
doodoonn

le **fuseau**
fewzo

le **ski** *skee*

la **chaussure de ski**
sho-sewr duh skee

sleeper (on train)
la couchette kooshett
sleeping bag *le sac de couchage* sak duh kooshaj
slice *la tranche* tronsh
to slip *glisser* gleessai
slob *le/la plouc*** plook
slow *lent(e)* lon f: lont
slowly *lentement* lont-mon
sly *rusé(e)* rewzai
small *petit(e)* puhtee f: puhteet
smart (cunning) *malin* malan f: *maligne* maleenn, or (elegant) *chic* sheek
smell *l'odeur [f]* oduhr
to smell *sentir* sonteer, or (stink) *puer* pewai
smile *le sourire* sooreer
to smile *sourire* sooreer
to smoke *fumer* few-mai
smoking (sign) *fumeurs* few-muhr; non-smoking *non fumeurs* non-few-muhr
snack *le casse-croûte* kass-kroot
snail *l'escargot* eskargo
snake *le serpent* sairpon
sneaky (cunning) *rusé(e)* rewzai
to sneeze *éternuer* aitair-new-ai
sniff *renifler* ruhneeflai
snobbish *snob* snob
snore *ronfler* ronflai
snow *la neige* nej; snowball *la boule de neige* bool duh nej (see also 'weather')
so (as in "it's so easy") *tellement* tell-mon, or *si* see, or (as in "so, be quick") *alors* alor; so-so (not great) *pas génial(e)*** pa jainn-yal
soaking (wet) *trempé(e)* trompai

soap *le savon* sa-von; soap opera *le feuilleton* fuh-yuh-ton
sob *sangloter* songlotai
soccer (football) *le football* footbol, or *le foot*** (see also football)
society *la société* soss-yaitai
sock *la chaussette* sho-sett
socket (electrical) *la prise* preez
soft *doux* doo f: *douce* dooss, or (not firm) *mou* moo f: *molle* mol; soft drink *la boisson non alcoolisée* bwasson nonnal-koleezai
software *le logiciel* lojeess-yel
soldier *le soldat* solda
solid *solide* soleed
some *du* dew f: *de la* duh la *pl: des* dai, or (as in "some [of them]" and "some people") *certain(e)s* sairtan f: sairtenn
somebody *quelqu'un* kelkun; somebody else *quelqu'un d'autre* kelkun dotr
something *quelque chose* kelkuh-shoze; something else *quelque chose d'autre* kelkuh-shoze dotr
sometimes *quelquefois* kelkuh-fwa
somewhere *quelque part* kelkuh-par; somewhere else *ailleurs* eye-uhr
song *la chanson* shonsson
soon *bientôt* bee-anto
sorry (excuse me/forgive me) *pardon* par-don, or (as in "I'm really sorry") *désolé(e)* daizolai
sort *le genre* jonr
sound *le son* son

soup *la soupe* soop, or *le potage* potaj
south *le sud* sewd; south of *au sud de* o sewd duh
souvenir *le souvenir* soov-neer
space *l'espace [m]* esspass, or (room) *la place* plass
Spain *l'Espagne [f]* esspann-yuh
spare (extra) *en trop* on tro; spare part *la pièce de rechange* pee-ess duh ruh-shonj; spare time *le temps libre* ton leebr, or *les loisirs [m]* lwazeer
to speak *parler* parlai
speaker (loudspeaker) *le haut-parleur* o-par-luhr
special *spécial(e)* spess-yal
speciality *la spécialité* spess-yal-eetai
speed *la vitesse* veetess; at full speed *à toute vitesse* a toot veetess
to spend (money) *dépenser* daiponsai, or (time) *passer* passai
spice *l'épice [f]* aipeess
spicy *épicé(e)* aipeessai
spider *l'araignée [f]* arainn-yai
spinach *les épinards [m]* aipee-nar
to spit *cracher* krashai
to split (divide) *partager* partajai, or (leave) *filer*** feelai; to split up (relationship) *se séparer* suh saiparai
to spoil (ruin) *gâcher* gashai, or (to damage) *abîmer* abeemmai
spoiled (child) *gâté(e)* ga-tai
spontaneous *spontané(e)* sponta-nai
spoon *la cuillère* kwee-yair

sport *le sport* *spor;* sports centre *le centre sportif* *sontr sporteef*

sporty (athletic) *sportif* *sporteef f: sportive* *sporteev*

spot (pimple) *le bouton* *booton,* or (place) *l'endroit [m]* *ondrwa*

sprain *l'entorse [f]* *ontorss*

spring (season) *le printemps* *pranton,* or (water) *la source* *soorss*

spy *l'espion(ne) [m/f]* *esp-yon f: esp-yonn*

square (in town) *la place* *plass,* or (not trendy) *ringard(e)* rangar f: rangard*

squash (game) *le squash* *skwash*

stadium *le stade* *stad*

stairs *l'escalier [m]* *eskall-yai*

stamp *le timbre* *tambr;* book of stamps *le carnet de timbres* *kar-nai duh tambr*

to stand (bear) *supporter* *sewportai* e.g. I can't stand ... *je ne supporte pas ... ,* or (not sit) *être debout* *etr duhboo;* to stand up *se lever* *suh luhvai;* to stand up for *défendre* *daifondr*

stand-by (ticket, passenger) *le stand-by*

star (in sky) *l'étoile [f]* *aitwal,* or (of film) *la vedette* *vuhdett,* or *la star*

start *le début* *daibew,* or (of race) *le départ* *daipar*

starter (first course) *le hors-d'oeuvre [m]* or *duhvr,* or *l'entrée [f]* *ontrai*

station (train) *la gare* *gar,* or (underground, radio) *la station* *stass-yon* (see also bus)

statue *la statue* *sta-tew*

to stay *rester* *restai*

steak *le steak,* or *l'entrecôte [f]* *ontr-kote*

to steal *voler* *volai*

steep *raide* *red*

step (footstep) *le pas* *pa,* or (stair) *la marche* *marsh;* stepbrother *le demi-frère* *duh-mee frair;* stepfather *le beau-père* *bo pair;* stepmother *la belle-mère* *bel mair;* stepsister *la demi-soeur* *duh-mee suhr*

stereo: personal stereo *le baladeur* *baladuhr*

stereotype *le stéréotype* *stairai-oteep*

to stick (glue) *coller* *kolai*

stiff *raide* *red;* to be/feel stiff *avoir des courbatures* *avwar dai koorbatewr*

still (even now) *toujours* *toojoor,* or (not moving) *immobile* *ee-mobeel*

to sting *piquer* *peekai*

stingy (not generous) *radin(e)* radan f: radeenn*

to stink *puer* *pewai*

to stir *remuer* *ruhmewai,* or (cause trouble) *provoquer* *provokai*

stomach *l'estomac [m]* *esto-ma,* or (tummy) *le ventre* *vontr;* upset stomach *l'indigestion [f]* *andeejest-yon* (see also 'ache' picture)

stone *la pierre* *pee-air*

to stop *arrêter* *araitai,* or (to prevent) *empêcher* *ompeshai*

stopover (on journey) *l'escale [f]* *esskal,* or *l'étape [f]* *aitap*

storm *la tempête* *tompet,* or (with thunder) *l'orage [m]* *oraj*

story *l'histoire [f]* *eestwar,* or (plot) *le scénario* *sai-naree-o,* or (in newspaper) *l'article [m]* *arteekl*

straight (not curved) *droit(e)* *drwa f: drwat,* or (directly) *directement* *deerekt-mon,* or (old-fashioned) *pas cool** *pa kool,* or *coincé(e)** *kwansai,* or (not gay) *hétérosexuel(le)* *aitairo-seksewel,* or *hétéro*;* straight ahead *tout droit* *too drwa*

strange *étrange* *aitronj*

strawberry *la fraise* *fraiz*

street *la rue* *rew;* high/main street *la rue principale* *rew pransseepal*

stress *le stress*

strict *strict(e)* *streekt*

strike *la grève* *graiv*

string *la ficelle* *feessel*

striped *rayé(e)* *rai-yai*

strong *fort(e)* *for f: fort*

stubborn *têtu(e)* *taitew*

stuck (unable to move) *coincé(e)* *kwansai;* stuck-up *prétentieux* *praitonss-yuh f: prétentieuse* *praitonss-yuhz*

student *l'étudiant(e) [m/f]* *aitewd-yon f: aitewd-yont*

to study *étudier* *aitewd-yai*

stuff (things) *les trucs* [m]* *trewk,* or *le barda*** *barda*

stuffy (no air) *mal aéré(e)* *mal a-airai*

stunning (amazing) *stupéfiant(e)* *stewpaif-yon f: stewpaif-yont,* or (lovely) *sensationnel(le)* *sonsass-yonnell;* she's stunning *elle est canon** *el ai kannon*

stupid *stupide* *stewpeed,* or *bête* *bet;* to act stupid *faire l'idiot(e)* *fair leed-yo f: ... leed-yot;* a stupid thing *une bêtise* *baiteez*

style **le style** *steel*
subconsciously
inconsciemment
ankonsee-ammon
subject **le sujet** *sewjai*
subtitle **le sous-titre** *soo-teetr*
subtle **subtil(e)** *sewb-teel*
suburbs **la banlieue** *bonl-yuh*
to succeed **réussir** *rai-ewseer*
success **le succès** *sewksai*
such **tellement** *tell-mon*, or **si** *see*
suddenly **tout à coup** *too ta koo*
suede **le daim** *dam*
to suffer **souffrir** *soofreer*
sugar **le sucre** *sewkr*
to suggest **proposer** *propozai*
suit (man's) **le costume** *kostewm*, or (woman's) **le tailleur** *tie-yuhr*
to suit (look good) **aller bien** *allai bee-an*; it suits you **ça te/vous va bien** *sa tuh/voo va bee-an*
suitcase **la valise** *va-leez*

summer **l'été [m]** *aitai*;
summer camp **le camp de vacances** *kom duh vakonss*
sun **le soleil** *solaiy*; sun block **l'écran total [m]** *aikron to-tal*; sun cream **la crème solaire** *kremm solair*
to sunbathe **se faire bronzer** *suh fair bronzai* (see also picture below)
sunburned: to be/get sunburned **prendre un coup de soleil** *prondr un koo duh solaiy*
Sunday **dimanche [m]** *dee-monsh*
sunglasses **les lunettes de soleil [f]** *lew-nett duh solaiy*
sunny **ensoleillé(e)** *onssolai-yai*
sunset **le coucher du soleil** *kooshai dew solaiy*
sunstroke **l'insolation [f]** *anssolass-yon*
superficial **superficiel(le)** *sewpairfeess-yel*
supermarket **le supermarché** *sewpair-marshai*

superstitious **superstitieux** *sewpair-steess-yuh*
f: superstitieuse *sewpair-steess-yuhz*
supper **le dîner** *dee-nai*
supplement **le supplément** *sewplai-mon*
to suppose **supposer** *sewpozai*
supposed to **censé(e)** *sonssai*
sure **sûr(e)** *sewr*
to surf (sport/Internet) **surfer** *suhrfai* (see also picture below)
surprise **la surprise** *sewrpreez*
suspense **le suspense** *sewsponss*
to swallow **avaler** *avalai*
to swap **échanger** *aishonjai*
to swear (promise) **jurer** *jewrai*
swearword **le gros mot** *gro mo*
sweat **la sueur** *sewuhr*
to sweat **transpirer** *tronspeerai*
sweater **le pull-over** *pewlovair*, or **le pull**

to sunbathe **se faire bronzer**   to surf **surfer**

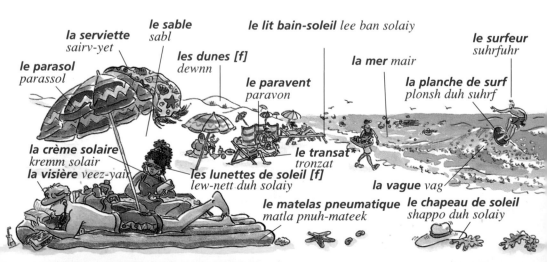

la serviette *sairv-yet*
le sable *sabl*
le lit bain-soleil *lee ban solaiy*
le surfeur *suhrfuhr*
le parasol *parassol*
les dunes [f] *dewnn*
la mer *mair*
le paravent *paravon*
la planche de surf *plonsh duh suhrf*
la crème solaire *kremm solair*
la visière *veez-yair*
le transat* *tronzat*
les lunettes de soleil [f] *lew-nett duh solaiy*
la vague *vag*
le matelas pneumatique *matla pnuh-mateek*
le chapeau de soleil *shappo duh solaiy*

sweatshirt **le sweat-shirt**
sweet **le bonbon** *bonbon*,
or (sugary) **sucré(e)**
sewkrai, or (cute)
mignon(ne) *meenn-yon*
f: meenn-yonn
to swim **nager** *najai*, or
(to go swimming, to go for
a dip) **se baigner** *suh benn-yai* (see also picture below)
swimming **la natation**
natass-yon; swimming pool
la piscine *peesseenn*;
swimming costume/trunks
le maillot de bain
my-o duh ban
swing **la balançoire**
balonswar
Switzerland **la Suisse**
sweess
swollen **enflé(e)** *enflai*
synagogue **la synagogue**
see-nagog
table **la table** *tabl*; table
football **le baby-foot**
baibee foot; table tennis
le tennis de table *tai-neess*
duh tabl
tacky (unstylish) **moche***
mosh

to take **prendre** *prondr*, or
(to lead) **emmener**
omm-nai; to take away
emporter *omportai*; to
take off **enlever** *onluhvai*,
or (plane) **décoller**
daikolai; to take part
participer *parteesseepai*
take-away (food) **(les plats)**
à emporter [m] *(pla) a*
omportai, or (café) **l'endroit**
vente à emporter [m]
ondrwa vont a omportai
to talk **parler** *parlai*
talkative **bavard(e)** *bavar*
f: bavard
tall **grand(e)** *gron f: grond*
tampon **le tampon** *tompon*
tan **le bronzage** *bronzaj*
tanned **bronzé(e)** *bronzai*
tap **le robinet** *robee-nai*
tape (cassette) **la cassette**
kassett
tart **la tarte** *tart*, or (small)
la tartelette *tartuh-lett*
taste **le goût** *goo*
to taste (as in "taste it")
goûter *gootai*, or (as in
"it tastes sweet") **avoir un**
goût *avwar un goo*

taxi **le taxi** *taksee;* taxi
stand **la station de taxis**
stass-yon duh taksee
tea (drink) **le thé** *tai*, or
(afternoon snack) **le goûter**
gootai, or (evening meal)
le dîner *dee-nai*
to teach (in school/university)
enseigner *onssain-yai*, or
(as in "that'll teach him")
apprendre *approndr*
teacher **le professeur**
professuhr
team **l'équipe [f]** *aikeep;*
to be part of a team **faire**
partie d'une équipe *fair*
partee dewnn aikeep
tear: in tears **en larmes;**
to burst into tears **fondre**
en larmes *fondr on larm*
to tease **taquiner**
ta-kee-nai, or (to be joking)
plaisanter *plaizontai*
teenager **l'adolescent(e)**
[m/f] *adolesson*
f: adolessont, or **l'ado***
telephone (see phone)
television **la télévision**
tailaiveez-yon, or **la télé***;
on television **à la télé***;
cable TV **le câble** *kabl;*
to have cable TV **être**
câblé(e) *etr kablai*;
digital TV **la télé* numérique**
tailai newmaireek
to tell (say) **dire** *deer*, or
(recount) **raconter** *rakontai*;
to tell off **gronder** *grondai*,
or **engueuler**** *onguhlai*
temperature
la température
tompairatewr; to have a
temperature **avoir de la**
fièvre *avwar duh la*
fee-aivr
temporary **temporaire**
tomporair
tennis **le tennis** *tai-neess*

to swim *nager*

le bonnet de bain
bonnai duh ban

le brassard (de
natation) *brassar*
(duh natass-yon)

le slip (de bain)
sleep (duh ban)

le dos crawlé
do krolai

le crawl
krol

la bouée
boo-ai

la brasse
brass

le (maillot) deux pièces
(my-oh) duh pee-ess

le maillot une pièce
my-oh ewnn pee-ess

le bermuda *bair-mewda*

97

tent **la tente** *tont*
(see also campsite)
term (school, university)
le trimestre *tree-mestr;*
beginning of term
la rentrée *rontrai*
terrible **terrible** *tai-reebl*
terrific **formidable** *for-meedabl,* or **extra*** *ekstra*

what time is it?
quelle heure est-il?

neuf heures et quart *nurf uhr ai kar*

trois heures *trwa-zuhr*

huit heures moins dix *wee-tuhr mwan deess*

onze heures vingt *onz-uhr van*

une heure moins le quart *ewn uhr mwan luh kar*

dix heures et demi *deez uhr ai duh-mee*

midi/minuit *meedee/meenn-wee*

terrorism **le terrorisme** *terroreesm*
test (at school)
l'interrogation [f] *antair-ogass-yon*
textbook **le manuel** *manewel*
Thames (river) **la Tamise** *tameez*
than **que** *kuh,* or (with numbers) **de** *duh*
to thank **remercier** *ruh-mairss-yai*
thankful (for) **reconnaissant(e) de** *ruhkonnaisson duh* **f:** *ruhkonaissont duh*
thank you **merci** *mairsee*
that **ce**[†] *suh* **f: cette** *set;*
that one **celui-là** *suhlwee-la* **f: celle-là** *sell-la*
thaw (ice) **fondre** *fondr,* or (food) **décongeler** *dai-konjuhlai*
the **le** *luh* **f: la** *la,* or (in front of a vowel, or sometimes "h") **l' pl: les** *lai* (see also Nouns p. 56)
theatre **le théâtre** *tai-atr*
their **leur** *luhr*
them (as in "I see/know them") **les** *lai,* or (as in "it's them" and after "of", "than", "to", "with", etc.)
eux *uh* **f: elles** *el*
theme **le thème** *tem;*
theme park **le parc (d'attraction) à thème** *park (datraksyon) a tem*
then **alors** *alor*
therapy **la thérapie** *tairapee*
there **là** *la;* there is/are **il y a** *eel-ee-a*
these **ces** *sai;* these ones **ceux-ci** *suh-see* **f: celles-ci** *sel-see*
they **ils** *eel* **f: elles** *el*

thick **épais(se)** *aipai* **f: aipaiss,** or (stupid) **bête** *bet,* or **lourd(e)*** *loor* **f: loord*
thief **le voleur** *voluhr* **f: la voleuse** *voluhz*
thin **mince** *manss*
thing **la chose** *shoze,* or **le truc*** *trewk,* or **le machin*** *mash-an*
things (belongings)
les affaires [f] *afair*
to think **penser** *ponsai*
thirsty: to be thirsty
avoir soif *avwar swaf*
this **ce**[†] *suh* **f: cette** *set;*
this one **celui-ci** *suh-lwee-see* **f: celle-ci** *sel-see*
those **ces** *sai;* those ones **ceux-là** *suh-la* **f: celles-là** *sel-la*
thread **le fil** *feel*
threat **la menace** *muh-nass*
thrill **le frisson** *freesson*
thriller **le film à suspense** *feelm a sewsponss,* or **le thriller*** *treeluhr*
throat **la gorge** *gorj;* sore throat **l'angine [f]** *onjeenn*
through **à travers** *a travair;* to go through **traverser** *travairsai*
to throw **lancer** *lonsai;* to throw away/out **jeter** *juhtai;* to throw up (be sick) **vomir** *vo-meer*
thug **le voyou** *vwa-yoo*
Thursday **jeudi [m]** *juhdee*
ticket **le billet** *bee-yai,* or **le ticket** *teekai;* ticket machine **le distributeur de billets** *dee-stree-bew-tuhr duh bee-yai;* ticket office **le guichet** *geeshai;* ticket collector **le contrôleur** *kontroluhr* **f: la contrôleuse** *kontroluhz;* ticket stamping machine **le composteur** *kompostuhr*

†**ce** changes to **cet** (*set*) in front of a [m] word beginning with a vowel or sometimes an "h", e.g. **cet homme**.

to tickle **chatouiller**
shatoo-yai
tide **la marée** *marai*
to tidy up **ranger** *ronjai*
to tie **attacher** *atashai*, or
(knot) **nouer** *noo-ai*
tights **les collants [m]** *kolon*
time (hour) **l'heure [f]** *uhr*,
or (occasion) **la fois** *fwa*; on
time **à l'heure**; to have time
avoir le temps *avwar luh
ton*; what time is it? **quelle
heure est-il?** *kel uhr ai-
teel* (see also picture on left)
timetable (train/bus)
l'horaire [m] *orair*, or
(school) **l'emploi du temps
[m]** *omplwa dew ton*
tint (for hair) **le
shampooing colorant**
shompwan koloron
tinted (hair) **teint(e)** *tan*
f: tant, or (glass) **teinté(e)**
tantai
tiny **minuscule** *meenew-
skewl*
tip (end) **le bout** *boo*, or
(money) **le pourboire**
poorbwar
tissue (hanky) **le mouchoir
(en papier)** *mooshwar (on
pap-yai)*
to **à** *a* (see also p. 57), or
(with [f] country names)
en *on*
toast **le pain grillé** *pan
gree-yai*, or **le toast** *tost*
today **aujourd'hui**
o-joor-dwee
together **ensemble**
onsombl
toilet **les toilettes [f]**
twalett, or **les WC [m]**
vai sai; women's/men's
dames/messieurs
damm/mess-yuh; toilet
paper **le papier hygiénique**
pap-yai eejaineek

toll **le péage** *pai-aj*
tomato **la tomate** *to-mat*;
tomato sauce **la sauce
tomate** *sosse to-mat*
tomorrow **demain** *duh-man*
the day after tomorrow
après-demain *aprai-duh-
man*
tongue **la langue** *long*
tonight **ce soir** *suh swar*
too (too much) **trop** *tro*, or
(also) **aussi** *o-see*
tool **l'outil [m]** *ootee*

tools **les outils**

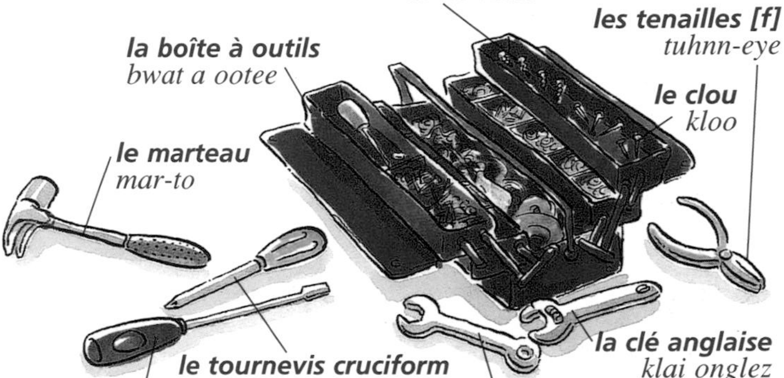

la vis *veess*
les tenailles [f] *tuhnn-eye*
la boîte à outils *bwat a ootee*
le clou *kloo*
le marteau *mar-to*
la clé anglaise *klai onglez*
le tournevis cruciform *toorn-veess krewseeform*
la clé *klai*
le tournevis *toorn-veess*

to touch **toucher** *tooshai*;
to touch wood **toucher du
bois** *tooshai dew bwa*
tour (day trip) **l'excursion
[f]** *ekskewrss-yon*, or
(concerts) **la tournée**
toor-nai; package tour
le voyage organisé
vwa-yaj organneezai
tourist **le/la touriste**
tooreest; tourist office
l'office du tourisme [m]
ofeess dew tooreesm

tooth **la dent** *don*
(see also 'ache' picture)
toothbrush **la brosse à
dents** *bross a don*
toothpaste **le dentifrice**
donteefreess
top (bottle) **le bouchon**
booshon, or (not bottom,
item of clothing) **le haut** *o*
topless **seins nus** *san new*;
to sunbathe topless **faire du
monokini*** *fair dew
monnokee-nee*
torch (pocket) **la lampe de
poche** *lomp duh posh*, or
(flaming) **la torche** *torsh*

touristy **touristique**
tooreesteek
towel **la serviette** *sairv-yet*
town **la ville** *veel*; town
centre **le centre-ville** *sontr-
veel*; old town **la vieille
ville** *vee-aiy veel*; town hall
l'hôtel de ville [m] *otel
duh veel*
toy **le jouet** *jooai*
traffic **la circulation**
seerkewlass-yon; traffic jam
l'embouteillage [m]
ombootai-yaj; traffic lights
les feux [m] *fuh*, or **le feu
rouge** *fuh rooj*

99

train **le train**

le tableau des départs
tablo dai daipar
le tableau des arrivées
tablo dai-zareevai

Arrivées   Départs

le guichet *geeshai*

la locomotive *lokomoteev*

le bar *bar*   **le wagon** *vagon*

non-fumeurs *non few-muhr*

le wagon restaurant *vagon restoron*

la couchette *kooshett*

le chariot
sharee-o

le chef de gare
shef duh gar

train **le train** *tran* (see also
picture above)
to train (for sport)
s'entraîner *sontrainnai*, or
(for a job) **former** *for-mai*
trainers **les baskets [f]**
baskett, or **les tennis [f]**
tai-neess
tramp **le clochard** *kloshar*,
or **le clodo**** *klodo*

to translate **traduire**
tradweer
to travel **voyager** *vwa-
yajai*
travel agency **l'agence
de voyages [f]** *ajonss
duh vwa-yaj*
traveller **le voyageur**
vwa-yajuhr **f: la
voyageuse** *vwa-yajuhz;*
traveller's cheque
le traveller's chèque
trav-luhrz shek
tree **l'arbre [m]** *arbr*
trendy **branché(e)****
bronshai
trip (long) **le voyage**
vwa-yaj, or (short)
l'excursion [f]
ekskewrss-yon
trolley (for baggage/
shopping) **le chariot**
sharee-o
trouble **les ennuis [m]**
onnwee
trousers **le pantalon**
pontalon
true **vrai(e)** *vrai*
to trust **avoir confiance**
avwar konf-yonss
truth **la vérité** *vaireetai*
to try **essayer** *essai-yai*
T-shirt **le tee-shirt**
Tuesday **mardi [m]**
mardee
tuna **le thon** *ton*
tunnel **le tunnel** *tewnell*
to turn **tourner** *toor-
nai*; to turn around/back
faire demi-tour *fair duh-
mee toor*; to turn down
(music/heat) **baisser** *baissai;*
to turn off (light/TV) **éteindre**
aitandr; to turn on (light/TV)
allumer *alew-mai*; to turn
up (music/heat) **monter**
montai, or (arrive) **arriver**
areevai

twin (brother/sister)
le jumeau *jew-mo*
f: la jumelle *jew-mell*
typical **typique** *teepeek*
tyre **le pneu** *pnuh;* tyre
pressure **la pression (de
gonflage)** *press-yon (duh
gonflaj)*
ugly **laid(e)** *lai f: laid*
umbrella **le parapluie**
paraplwee
unbelievable **incroyable**
ankrwayabl
under **sous** *soo*
underground (trains)
le métro *maitro*
to understand **comprendre**
komprondr
underwear **les sous-
vêtements [m]**
soo-vet-mon
unemployed (person)
le chômeur *shommuhr*
f: la chômeuse *shommuhz,*
or (out of work) **au chômage**
o shommaj
unemployment **le chômage**
shommaj
unfortunately
malheureusement
maluh-ruhz-mon
United States
les États-Unis [m]
aita-zewnnee
university **l'université [f]**
ewnnee-vairsee-tai
unusual (rare) **rare** *rar*, or
(different) **original(e)**
oreejeennal
up: to go/walk up **monter**
montai
uptight **coincé(e)****
kwansai
urgent **urgent(e)** *ewrjon
f: ewrjont*
us **nous** *noo*
to use **se servir de**
suh sairveer duh

used: to be used to
avoir l'habitude de
avwar labeetewd duh
useful utile *ewteel*
useless (of no use) **inutile**
eennewteel, or (no good)
nul(le)* *newl*
usual (customary)
habituel(le) *abeetew-el;*
as usual **comme d'habitude**
komm dabeetewd
usually d'habitude
dabeetewd
vacation les vacances [f]
vakonss
vaccination la vaccination
vakseennass-yon
valid valable *valabl*
valuables les objets de
valeur [m] *objai duh*
valuhr
vanilla la vanille *vanneey*
vegetable le légume
laigewmm
vegetarian végétarien(ne)
vaijaitar-yan
f: vaijaitar-yenn
vending machine le
distributeur automatique
dee-stree-bew-tuhr
otommateek

very très *trai*, or
vachement* *vash-mon;*
very much **beaucoup** *bo-koo*
video la vidéo *veedai-o;*
video recorder
le magnétoscope
mann-yaito-skop
view la vue *vew*, or
(opinion) **l'avis [m]** *avee*
village le village *veelaj*
vine la vigne *veenn-yuh*
vineyard le vignoble
veenn-yobl
visit la visite *veezeet*
to visit (a place) **visiter**
veezeetai, or (a person)
rendre visite à *rondr*
veezeet a
vital indispensable
andeess-ponsabl
volleyball le volley(-ball)
volai(-bal)
vote le vote *vote*
wacky farfelu(e)
farfuh-lew, or **dingue***
dang, or **original(e)**
oreejeennal
to waffle **parler pour ne**
rien dire *parlai poor nuh*
ree-an deer, or **radoter***
ra-dotai

wage la paye *paiy*
waist la taille *tie-y*
waistcoat le gilet *jeelai*
to wait **attendre** *a-tondr*
waiter le serveur *sairvuhr*
waiting room la salle
d'attente *sal da-tont*
waitress la serveuse
sairvuhz
to wake up **se réveiller**
suh raivai-yai
Wales le pays de Galles
pai-ee duh gal
wall le mur *mewr*
walk la promenade
promm-nad, or **la balade***
balad, or **la randonnée**
rondonnai
to walk **marcher** *marshai*,
or (to go on foot) **aller à**
pied *allai a pee-ai;* to walk
around/about **se promener**
suh promm-nai
wallet le portefeuille
portuh-fuh-y
to want **vouloir** *voolwar*
(see Useful irregular verbs
p. 59)
war la guerre *gair*
wardrobe l'armoire [f]
armwar

water l'eau   **wine le vin**

l'eau minérale
plate [f]
o mee-nairal
platt

la cascade
kaskad

le glaçon
glasson

le rouge
rooj

le blanc
blon

la demi-bouteille
duh-mee bootaiy

le rosé
rozai

le pichet
peeshai

l'eau minérale
gazeuse [f]
o mee-nairal
gazuhz

la carafe
karaf

un verre d'eau
un vair doh

le tire-bouchon
teer booshon

le bouchon
booshon

un verre de vin
un vair duh van

warm **(assez) chaud(e)**
(assai) sho f: ... shode
to warm up **réchauffer**
raishofai, or (for a sport)
s'échauffer *saishofai*
warning **l'avertissement**
[m] *avairteess-mon*
wart **la verrue** *verew*
to wash **laver** *lavai*, or
(yourself) **se laver;**
to wash up **faire la vaisselle**
fair la vaissell
washing: washing machine
le lave-linge *lav-lanj;*
washing powder **la lessive**
laisseev; washing-up
la vaisselle *vaissell;*
washing-up liquid **le liquide**
vaisselle *leekeed vaissell*
wasp **la guêpe** *gaip*
waste (of food/money etc.)
le gaspillage *gaspee-yaj;*
waste of time **la perte de**
temps *pairt duh ton*
to waste (food/money)
gaspiller *gaspee-yai*, or
(time/opportunity) **perdre**
pairdr
watch **la montre** *montr*
to watch (look at) **regarder**
ruhgardai, or (keep an eye
on) **surveiller** *sewrvai-yai;*
watch out! **attention!**
attonss-yon, or (to a friend)
fais gaffe!* *fai gaf*
water **l'eau [f]** *o*
(see also picture p. 101)

waterproof **imperméable**
ampair-mai-abl
way (direction) **la direction**
deereks-yon, or (route)
le chemin *shuh-man*, or
(manner) **la façon** *fasson;*
to be/get in the way **gêner**
jennai; to get your own
way **arriver à ses fins**
areevai a sai fan; no way!
pas question! *pa kest-yon*
we **nous** *noo*, or **on** *on*
weak **faible** *faibl*, or
(coffee, tea) **léger** *laijai*
f: **légère** *laijair*
to wear **porter** *portai;*
to wear out (exhaust)
épuiser *aipweezai*, or
(overuse) **user** *ewzai*
weather **le temps** *ton;*
what's the weather like?
quel temps fait-il? *kel ton*
fai-teel; weather forecast
la météo *maitai-o*
(see also picture below)
Web site **le site Web**
seet web
Wednesday **mercredi [m]**
mairkruh-dee
week **la semaine** *suh-*
menn
weekend **le week-end**
weight **le poids** *pwa;*
to lose weight **maigrir**
maigreer; to put on weight
grossir *grosseer*
weird **bizarre** *beezar*

welcome **bienvenu(e)**
bee-an-vuh-new;
you're welcome! **de rien!**
duh ree-an
well **bien** *bee-an;*
well-behaved **sage** *saj;*
well-cooked **bien cuit(e)**
bee-an kwee f: ... kweet;
well-known **très connu(e)**
trai konnew; to be well
aller bien *allai bee-an*
Welsh **gallois(e)** *galwa*
f: *galwaz*
west **l'ouest [m]** *oo-est*
wet **mouillé(e)** *moo-yai*
what (as in "what?") **quoi**
kwa, or (as in "what do you
want?") **qu'est-ce que**
kess-kuh; what is this/it?
qu'est-ce que c'est? *kess-*
kuh sai; about/in/with what?
de/dans/avec quoi?
duh/don/avek kwa;
what a ...! (as in "what a
great hat!") **quel(le) ...!** *kel*
wheel **la roue** *roo;* steering
wheel **le volant** *volon*
wheelchair **le fauteuil**
roulant *fotuh-y roolon*
when **quand** *kon*
where **où** *oo*
which (as in "which [one]?")
lequel *luhkel* f: **laquelle**
lakell, or (as in "which
bike/cake etc?") **quel(le)** *kel*
while (during) **pendant que**
pondon kuh

weather
le temps

il pleut
eel pluh

c'est couvert
sai koovair

il fait beau
eel fai bo

il neige
eel naij

white **blanc** *blon* **f: blanche**
blonsh
who **qui** *kee;* whose **à qui**
a kee
whole **entier** *ont-yai*
f: entière *ont-yair*
why **pourquoi** *poorkwa*
wide **large** *larj*
widow **la veuve** *verv*
widower **le veuf** *verf*
wild (not tame) **sauvage**
sovaj; to be/go wild (about)
être/devenir fou (de)
etr/duh-vuh-neer foo (duh)
f: ... folle *... fol*
to win **gagner** *gann-yai*
wind **le vent** *von*
(see also picture below)
windmill **le moulin à vent**
moolan a von
window **la fenêtre**
fuh-netr, or (shop) **la vitrine**
veetreenn
windscreen **le pare-brise**
par-breez; windscreen
wiper **l'essuie-glace [m]**
esswee-gla-ss
windsurfer (board)
la planche à voile
plonsh a vwal, or (person)
le/la planchiste *plonsheest*
wine **le vin** *van*
(see also picture p. 101);
wine-tasting **la dégustation**
daigewstass-yon
winner **le/la gagnant(e)**
gann-yon **f:** *gann-yont*

winter **l'hiver [m]** *eevair*
wish **le voeu** *vuh;* best
wishes (in a letter) **amitiés**
ammeet-yai, or (Christmas,
birthday) **meilleurs voeux**
mai-yuhr vuh
to wish (hope) **souhaiter**
soo-aitai
with **avec** *avek*
without **sans** *son*
woman **la femme** *famm,*
or (lady) **la dame** *damm*
wonderful **formidable**
for-meedabl
wood **le bois** *bwa*
wool **la laine** *lenn*
word **le mot** *mo;* words (of
song) **les paroles [f]** *parol*
work **le travail** *trav-eye,* or
le boulot** *boolo*
to work **travailler**
trav-eye-ai, or **bosser****
bossai, or (function)
marcher *marshai*
world **le monde** *mond;*
World Wide Web **le World
Wide Web;** out of this
world **extraordinaire**
ekstra-ordee-nair, or **extra***
worried **inquiet** *ank-yai*
f: inquiète *ank-yet*
to worry **s'inquiéter**
sank-yaitai
worse **pire** *peer*
worth: to be worth **valoir**
valwar
wrist **le poignet** *pwanyai*

to write **écrire** *aikreer*
writer **l'écrivain [m]**
aikreevan
wrong (incorrect) **faux** *fo*
f: fausse *fosse,* or (unfair)
injuste *anjewst;* to be
wrong (not right) **avoir tort**
avwar tor, or (mistaken)
se tromper *suh trompai;*
what's wrong? **qu'est-ce
qui ne va pas?** *kess kee
nuh va pa*
to yawn **bâiller** *buy-ai*
year **l'année [f]** *annai*
yellow **jaune** *jone*
yes **oui** *wee,* or (after
negative question) **si** *see*
yesterday **hier** *ee-yair*
yogurt **le yaourt** *ya-oort*
you (as in "you like him")
tu *tew,* or **vous** *voo,* or
(as in "it's you" and after
"and", "for", "than", etc.)
toi *twa,* or **vous** *voo,* or (as
in "he knows you") **te** *tuh,*
or **vous** *voo* (see p. 58 for
when to use 'tu' or 'vous')
young **jeune** *juhnn*
your (to friend) **ton** *ton*
f: ta *ta* **pl: tes** *tai,* or (polite
form) **votre** *votr* **pl: vos** *vo*
youth hostel **l'auberge de
jeunesse [f]** *o-bairj duh
juhnness*
zero **zéro** *zairo*
zip **la fermeture éclair**
fair-muh-tewr aiklair

il y a un orage
eel ee a unnoraj

il fait froid
eel fai frwa

il fait chaud
eel fai sho

il fait du vent
eel fai dew von

à *at,* or *to,* or *in* (see also p. 57)

abîmer *to damage,* or *to spoil*

l'abricot [m] *apricot*

l'accent [m] *accent*

accepter *to accept*

l'accident [m] *accident*

accrocher *to hang (up)*

l'accueil [m] *reception,* or *welcome*

accueillir *to welcome*

acheter *to buy*

l'acteur [m] *actor*

l'actrice [f] *actress*

l'addition [f] *sum,* or *bill*

l'adolescent(e) or **l'ado* [m/f]** *teenager*

adorer *to love,* or *to adore*

l'adresse [f] *address*

l'adulte [m/f] *adult*

l'adversaire [m/f] *opponent*

l'aérobic [m] *aerobics*

l'aéroglisseur [m] *hovercraft*

l'aéroport [m] *airport*

les affaires [f] *things,* or *business;* **une bonne affaire** *a bargain*

l'affiche [f] *poster,* or *notice*

affreux (f: affreuse) *awful*

l'Afrique [f] *Africa*

agacer *to annoy*

l'âge [m] *age*

l'agence de voyages [f] *travel agency*

l'agenda [m] *diary*

l'agent (de police) [m] *(police) officer*

l'agneau [m] *lamb*

agresser *to attack;* **se faire agresser** *to get mugged*

l'aide [f] *help,* or *aid*

aider *to help*

l'aiguille [f] *needle*

l'ail [m] *garlic*

ailleurs *somewhere else*

aimer *to like,* or *to love;* **aimer bien** *to like*

l'air [m] *air;* **en plein air** *in the open air;* **air conditionné** *air-conditioned*

aise: à l'aise *comfortable*

ajouter *to add*

l'album [m] *album*

l'alcool [m] *alcohol*

alcoolisé(e) *alcoholic*

l'Algérie [f] *Algeria*

l'Allemagne [f] *Germany*

aller (see p. 59) *to go,* or *to fit,* or *to suit;* **s'en aller** *to leave*

l'aller [m] *the journey out;* **l'aller-retour** *return (journey/ticket);* **l'aller simple** *single*

l'allergie [f] *allergy*

s'allonger *to lie down*

allumer *to light,* or *to switch on*

l'allumette [f] *match*

alors *then,* or *so*

l'alpinisme [m] *mountaineering*

l'amande [f] *almond*

l'ambassade [f] *embassy*

l'ambulance [f] *ambulance*

l'amende [f] *fine*

amener *to bring*

amer (f: amère) *bitter*

américain(e) *American*

l'Amérique [f] *America*

l'ami(e) [m/f] *friend;* **le/la petit(e) ami(e)** *boy/girlfriend*

l'amitié [f] *friendship;* **amitiés** *best wishes*

l'amour [m] *love;* **les amours [f]** *love-life;* **faire l'amour** *to make love*

amoureux (f: amoureuse) *in love*

l'ampoule [f] *lightbulb,* or *blister*

amusant(e) *fun,* or *funny*

s'amuser *to have fun*

l'an [m] *year*

l'ananas [m] *pineapple*

l'ancre [f] *anchor*

l'andouillette [f] *spicy sausage made from tripe*

l'angine [f] *sore throat*

anglais(e) *English*

l'Angleterre [f] *England*

angoissant(e) *nerve-racking*

animé(e) *lively*

l'année [f] *year*

l'anniversaire [m] *birthday,* or *anniversary*

l'annonce [f] *advertisement;* **les petites annonces** *classified ads*

l'annuaire [m] *phone directory*

annuler *to cancel*

l'antibiotique [m] *antibiotic*

antiseptique *antiseptic*

l'antivol [m] *lock* (for bikes/cars)

août *August*

l'appareil-photo [m] *camera*

l'appartement or **l'appart* [m]** *flat*

l'appel [m] *call*

appeler *to call*

s'appeler *to be called*

l'appétit [m] *appetite;* **bon appétit** *enjoy your meal*

apporter *to bring*

apprendre *to learn,* or *to teach*

s'approcher *to get/come near*

appuyer *to press*

après *after*

l'après-midi [m/f] *afternoon*

arabe *Arab*

l'araignée [f] *spider*

l'arbitre [m] *umpire*

l'arbre [m] *tree*

l'arc-en-ciel [m] *rainbow*

l'arête [f] *fish bone,* or *ridge*

l'argent [m] *money;* **l'argent liquide [m]** *cash*

l'argot [m] *slang*

l'arnaque**: c'est de l'arnaque** *it's a rip-off*
l'arrêt [m] *stop;* **l'arrêt de bus** *bus stop;* **les arrêts de jeu** *injury time*
arrêter *to arrest, or to stop*
les arrhes [f] *deposit*
l'arrière [m] *back (not front)*
arriver *to arrive, or to happen;* **arriver à (faire quelque chose)** *to manage to (do something)*
l'art [m] *art*
l'article [m] *article*
l'artisanat [m] *crafts*
l'artiste [m/f] *artist*
l'ascenseur [m] *lift*
l'Asie [f] *Asia*
l'aspirine [f] *aspirin*
s'asseoir *to sit down*
assez *enough, or quite*
l'assiette [f] *plate;* **l'assiette anglaise** *plate of cold meats*
assis(e) *sitting down*
l'assurance [f] *insurance*
l'asthme [m] *asthma*
l'atelier [m] *workshop*
attacher *to fasten*
attendre *to wait*
l'attention [f] *attention, or care;* **faire attention** *to be careful;* **attention!** *watch out!*
attraper *to catch*
l'auberge [f] *inn;* **l'auberge de jeunesse [f]** *youth hostel*
augmenter *to increase*
aujourd'hui *today*
au revoir *goodbye*
aussi *also, or too;* **aussi ... que** *as ... as*
l'Australie [f] *Australia*
australien(ne) *Australian*
l'auteur [m/f] *author*
authentique *genuine*
l'autocollant [m] *sticker*
automatique *automatic*
l'automne [m] *autumn*
l'autoroute [f] *motorway*

l'auto-stoppeur (f: l'auto-stoppeuse) *hitch-hiker*
autour *around*
autre *other*
l'autre [m/f] *the other one*
avaler *to swallow*
avance: en avance *early*
avancer *to go/move forwards*
avant *before;* **avant-hier** *the day before yesterday*
l'avant [m] *front*
l'avantage [m] *advantage*
avec *with*
aventureux (f: aventureuse) *adventurous*
avertir *to warn*
l'avertissement [m] *warning*
aveugle *blind*
l'avion [m] *plane*
l'avis [m] *opinion*
l'avocat [m] *avocado, or* **(f: l'avocate)** *lawyer*
avoir (see p. 59) *to have;* **se faire avoir*** *to be had/tricked*
avril *April*

le baby-foot* *table football*
les bagages [m] *luggage*
la bagarre* *fight*
la bagnole* *car*
la bague *ring*
la baguette *French bread*
se baigner *to go for a swim*
bâiller *to yawn*
le bain *bath;* **prendre un bain de soleil** *to sunbathe*
le baiser *kiss*
baisser *to lower*
le bal *dance;* **le bal populaire** *village dance*
la balade *walk, or outing*
le baladeur *personal stereo*
Balance *(star sign) Libra*
le balcon *balcony*
balèze** *terrific, or strong*
la balle *ball*

les balles** *slang for francs*
le ballet *ballet*
le ballon *ball, or balloon*
la banane *banana, or bum bag*
le banc *bench*
la bande *band, or bandage, or gang;* **la bande dessinée** *comic book/strip*
le bandeau *headband*
la banlieue *suburbs*
la banque *bank*
le bar *bar*
baratiner** *to chat up, or to natter*
la barbe *beard*
le barda** *things, or stuff*
la barque *boat*
la barre *bar, or (sailing) tiller*
la barrette *hair-slide*
bas(se) *low;* **en bas** *down below, or downstairs*
le basket *basketball*
les baskets [f] *basketball shoes, or trainers*
le bateau *boat*
le bâtiment *building*
le bâton *stick, or pole*
la batte *bat*
la batterie *battery, or drums*
le batteur *drummer*
se battre *to fight*
le baudrier *(climbing) harness*
bavarder *to chat, or to gossip*
la bavette *(food) type of steak*
BCBG (bon chic, bon genre) *French equivalent of yuppie, or sloane*
la BD (la bande dessinée) *comic book/strip*
beau (f: belle) *beautiful, or good-looking;* **il fait beau** *it's fine weather;* **le beau-père** *stepfather, or father-in-law*

beaucoup *many,* or *a lot*
le beauf* *short for* **le beau-frère** *brother-in-law,* (but used as derogatory term for a narrow-minded man who lacks taste)
la bécane** *motorbike*
le beignet *doughnut*
belge *Belgian*
la Belgique *Belgium*
Bélier (star sign) *Aries*
belle (see 'beau');
la belle-mère *stepmother,* or *mother-in-law*
bénévole *voluntary,* or *unpaid*
le bermuda *bermuda shorts,* or *long swimming trunks*
le besoin *need;* **avoir besoin de** *to need*
la bestiole* *bug (insect)*
bête *silly,* or *stupid*
la bêtise *stupid thing;* **dire des bêtises** *to talk nonsense*
le beurre *butter*
la bibliothèque *library*
le bide** *belly;* **être/faire un bide**** *to be a flop*
bien *well,* or *good;*
bien cuit(e) *well-cooked;*
bien frais *nice and cold;*
aller bien *to be well*
bientôt *soon;* **à bientôt** *see you soon*
bienvenu(e) *welcome*
la bière *beer;*
la bière blonde *lager;*
la bière brune *bitter*
le bifteck *steak*
les bijoux [m] *jewellery*
le billet *ticket;* **le billet de 10 francs** *10 franc note;*
le billet doux *love letter*
le biscuit *biscuit*
la bise *kiss*
le bisou *kiss*
bizarre *odd,* or *weird*
la blague *joke*

blaguer* *to joke*
blanc(he) *white*
la blessure *injury*
bleu(e) *blue*
le bleu *bruise*
blond(e) *blond*
le/la blond(e) *the blond guy/girl*
le blouson *short, bomber-style jacket*
le boeuf *beef*
boire *to drink*
le bois *wood*
la boisson *drink*
la boîte *box,* or *can,* or **(slang)** *office,* or *night-club;*
la boîte à outils *tool box;*
aller en boîte* *to go clubbing*
le bol *bowl;* **pas de bol!*** *no luck!* (see also 'ras le bol'*)
la bombe *bomb,* or *riding hat*
la bôme (sailing) *boom*
bon(ne) *good*
le bonbon *sweet*
bonjour *hello*
le bonnet *hat;* **le bonnet de bain** *swimming cap*
bonsoir *good evening*
la bosse *bump,* or *lump,* or (skiing) *mogle*
bosser** *to work*
la botte *boot;* **la botte de caoutchouc** *welly;* **la botte d'équitation** *riding boot*
la bouche *mouth*
la boucherie *butcher's s*
le bouchon de l'objectif *lens cap*
bouclé(e) *curly*
la boucle *buckle,* or *curl;*
la boucle d'oreille *earring*
le boudin *black pudding*
la bouée *buoy,* or *rubber ring*
la bouffe** *grub* (food)
bouffer** *to scoff* (eat)
bouger *to move*

la bougie *candle*
bouilli(e) *boiled*
le bouillon *broth,* or *thin soup*
la boulangerie *bakery*
boules *bowling game played with heavy metal balls*
le boulot* *job,* or *work;* **le petit boulot*** *weekend/ holiday job*
le bouquin* *book*
bourré(e)* *jam-packed,* or (slang) *drunk;* **bourré(e) de fric**** *loaded* (with money)
la bourse *purse,* or *grant,* or **(la Bourse)** *Stock Exchange*
bousiller** *to wreck*
la boussole *compass*
le bout *end,* or *tip*
la bouteille *bottle;*
la bouteille d'oxygène *oxygen bottle*
la boutique *shop*
le bouton *button,* or *spot*
le bowling *ten pin bowling*
le bracelet *bracelet*
branché(e)** *trendy*
brancher *to plug in,* or (slang) *to flirt,* or *to chat up;* **ça (ne) me branche pas**** *it doesn't appeal to me*
le bras *arm*
le brassard (de natation) *armband* (for swimming)
la brasse *breast-stroke*
la brasserie *large restaurant with a bar and café*
le bric-à-brac *junk*
la bride (riding) *bridle*
la brioche *soft, slightly sweet bun or loaf*
le briquet *lighter*
la brocante *second-hand furniture/things*
le brocanteur *junk/ second-hand dealer*
la broche *brooch*
la brochette *kebab*

le bronzage *tan*
bronzé(e) *tanned*
se bronzer (or **se faire bronzer**) *to sunbathe*
la brosse *brush;* **la brosse à cheveux** *hairbrush*
le brouillard *fog*
le bruit *noise;* **le bruit qui court** *rumour*
brûler *to burn*
brun(e) *brown*
le bureau *office,* or *desk*
le bus *bus*
le but *goal*

ça *this,* or *that;* **ça va** *OK,* or *all right,* or (question) *how are you?*
la cabine *cabin;* **la cabine téléphonique** *phone booth*
la cacahuète *peanut*
cacher *to hide*
le cadeau *present*
le cadenas *padlock*
le cafard *cockroach;* **avoir le cafard*** *to be/feel down*
le café *café,* or (black) *coffee;* **le café-crème** *coffee with cream/milk*
cailler** *to be freezing cold*
la caisse *check-out* (cash till), or *crate* (box)
la calculette *calculator*
le caleçon *boxer shorts, underpants,* or *leggings*
calme *calm*
calmer *to calm down*
la calorie *calorie;* **à basses calories** *low-calorie*
le cambriolage *burglary*
le caméscope *camcorder*
le camion *lorry*
la campagne *countryside*
camper *to camp*
le camping *campsite;* **le camping-car** *camper van;* **le camping-gaz** *camping stove,* or *camping gas*

le Canada *Canada*
le canal *canal*
le canard *duck*
Cancer (star sign) *Cancer*
le canif *penknife*
le canoë *canoe*
le canon *canon;* **elle est canon*** *she's stunning*
le canot *small boat*
la capitale *capital* (city)
la capote** *condom*
Capricorne (star sign) *Capricorn*
le car *coach*
la carafe *jug*
la caravane *caravan*
le carnaval *carnival*
le carnet *notebook*
la carotte *carrot*
le carrefour *crossroads*
la carrière *career*
la carte *card,* or *map,* or *menu;* **la carte d'abonnement** *season ticket;* **la carte bleue** *visa card;* **la carte de crédit** *credit card;* **la carte orange** *Paris bus and metro pass;* **la carte postale** *postcard;* **la carte routière** *road map;* **la carte téléphonique** *phonecard*
le cas *case;* **au cas où** *in case*
la cascade *waterfall*
le casque *helmet*
la casquette *cap*
le casse-croûte *snack*
le casse-noix *nutcracker*
casser *to break;* **casse-bonbons*/casse-pieds*** *dead boring,* or *really annoying*
se casser *to get broken,* or (slang) *to leave,* or *to go;* **casse-toi!**** *get lost!*
la casserole *saucepan*
la cassette *cassette,* or *tape;* **le lecteur de cassettes** *cassette player*

le cassis *blackcurrant*
le cassoulet *meat and bean casserole*
la catastrophe *disaster*
la cathédrale *cathedral*
catholique *catholic*
le cauchemar *nightmare*
la cause *cause;* **à cause de** *because of*
la caution *deposit*
le cavalier (f: **la cavalière**) *rider,* or *dance partner*
la cave *cellar*
la caverne *cave*
le CD *CD;* **le lecteur de CD** *CD player*
ce (f: **cette**) *this,* or *that*
céder *to give in,* or *to give way*
la CE *EC (European Community)*
la ceinture *belt;* **la ceinture de plomb** *weight belt;* **la ceinture porte-billets** *money belt*
célèbre *famous*
célibataire *single* (unmarried)
celle (see 'celui')
celui (f: **celle**) *the one;* **celui-ci** *this one;* **celui-là** *that one*
le cendrier *ashtray*
censé(e): être censé(e) (faire quelque chose) *to be supposed to (do something)*
le centime (100 centimes equals one French franc)
le centre *centre;* **le centre commercial** *shopping centre;* **le centre sportif** *sports centre;* **le centre-ville** *town centre*
les céréales [f] *cereal*
le cerf-volant *kite*
la cerise *cherry*
la cervelle *brain*
ces *these,* or *those*
c'est *it is*
cette (see 'ce')

chacun(e) *each one*
la chaîne *chain,* or *TV channel;* **la chaîne hi-fi** *hi-fi system*
la chaise *chair;* **la chaise longue** *deck-chair*
la chambre *room,* or *bedroom;* **la chambre d'hôte** *bed and breakfast (guest house)*
le champignon *mushroom*
la chance *luck*
le change *exchange;* **le bureau de change** *foreign exchange office;* **le taux de change** *exchange rate*
changer *to change*
la chanson *song*
chanter *to sing*
le chanteur (f: la chanteuse) *singer*
la Chantilly (or **la crème Chantilly**) *whipped cream*
le chapeau *hat;* **le chapeau de soleil** *sunhat*
chaque *each*
la charcuterie *meat products such as ham, salami, pâté, etc.* or *shop selling these*
le chariot *trolley* (for shopping/luggage)
le chat *cat*
le château *castle*
chaud(e) *hot*
le chauffage *heating*
le chauffeur *driver*
la chaussette *sock*
le chausson *slipper,* or *pump;* **le chausson d'escalade** *climbing shoe;* **le chausson aux pommes** *apple turnover*
la chaussure *shoe,* or *(walking/ski) boot*
le chef *chef,* or *boss;* **le chef de gare** *station master*
le chemin *path,* or *route,* or *way;* **le chemin de fer** *railway*
la chemise *shirt*

le chèque *cheque*
le chéquier *cheque-book*
cher (f: chère) *dear,* or *expensive*
chercher *to look for*
le cheval *horse;* **le hamburger/steak à cheval** *hamburger/steak with an egg on top*
les cheveux [m] *hair*
la cheville *ankle*
la chèvre *goat*
chez (at) *the home/place of;* **chez moi** (at) *my place*
chic *posh,* or *elegant,* or *nice*
le chien *dog*
les chips [f] *crisps*
le choc *shock*
le chocolat *chocolate*
le choeur *choir*
choisir *to choose*
le choix *choice*
le chômage *unemployment;* **au chômage** *unemployed,* or *on the dole*
le chômeur (f: la chômeuse) *unemployed person*
la chose *thing*
la choucroute *sauerkraut*
chouette* *nice,* or *great*
le chou-fleur *cauliflower*
chrétien(ne) *Christian*
chuchoter *to whisper*
le cidre *cider*
le ciel *sky*
la cigarette *cigarette*
le cimetière *cemetery*
le cinéma or **le ciné*** *cinema*
cinglé(e)* *crazy*
la circulation *traffic*
circuler *to move* (along)
les ciseaux [m] *scissors*
le citron *lemon;* **le citron pressé** *drink of freshly squeezed lemon juice with sugar and water*

clair(e) *clear,* or *light*
la clarinette *clarinet*
classique *classical*
la clé *key,* or *spanner;* **la clé anglaise** *adjustable spanner*
le/la client(e) *customer*
le clignotant *indicator*
climatisé(e) *air-conditioned*
le/la clochard(e) *tramp*
le/la clodo** *tramp*
la clope** *cigarette*
le clou *nail*
le cochon *pig*
le coeur *heart;* **avoir le coeur brisé** *to be heart-broken;* **avoir mal au coeur** *to feel sick/queasy*
le coffre (car) *boot;* **le coffre-fort** *safe* (box for valuables)
se cogner (contre) *to bump into,* or *to hit*
le coiffeur (f: la coiffeuse) *hairdresser*
la coiffure *hairstyle*
le coin *corner;* **du coin*** *local*
coincé(e) *stuck,* or *(slang) uptight*
le col *collar,* or *(mountain) pass*
la colère *anger;* **en colère** *angry*
le colis *parcel*
le collant *leotard,* or *tights*
collectionner *to collect*
le collège *secondary/high school*
le collier *necklace*
la colline *hill*
la colonie de vacances *children's summer camp*
le combat *fight*
combien? *how many/much?*
la combinaison *overalls,* or *wetsuit,* or *ski suit*
le combiné (phone) *receiver*
la comédie *comedy;* **jouer la comédie** *to put on an act*

la commande *order,* or *controls*
commander *to order*
comme *like,* or *as*
comment *how*
les commérages [m] *gossip*
la commère *gossip* (a person)
la compagnie *company;* **la compagnie aérienne** *airline*
le compas *compass*
complet (f: complète) *full,* or *booked up*
composter *to stamp,* or *to punch* (a hole)
le composteur *man/machine that punches hole in ticket*
comprendre *to understand*
le comprimé *pill,* or *tablet*
compris(e) *understood,* or *included*
le comptoir *counter*
le concert *concert*
le concombre *cucumber*
le concours *contest,* or *exam*
conduire *to drive*
la confiance *trust*
la confiserie *confectionery, confectioner's* (shop)
la confiture *jam*
confondre *to mix up,* or *to confuse*
confortable *comfortable*
connaître *to know*
connu(e) *known,* or *well-known*
le conseil *advice*
la consigne (de bagages) *left-luggage office*
la console *console*
constipé(e) *constipated*
le consulat *consulate*
contagieux (f: contagieuse) *contagious*
content(e) *happy,* or *pleased*
le contraceptif *contraceptive*

le/la contractuel(le) *traffic warden*
le contraire *opposite*
contrarié(e) *upset,* or *annoyed*
contre *against*
le contrôle *test,* or *inspection*
contrôler *to control,* or *to inspect*
le contrôleur (f: la contrôleuse) *ticket inspector*
cool* *cool,* or *fab*
le copain* (f: la copine*) *friend*
copier *to copy*
le coquetier *eggcup*
les coquillages [m] *shellfish*
la coquille *shell*
le cor *horn*
la corde *rope*
le corps *body*
correct(e) *correct*
la correspondance (trains, planes) *connection*
le/la correspondant(e) *pen pal*
la Corse *Corsica*
cosmopolite *cosmopolitan*
le costume *suit,* or *costume*
la côte *coast*
le côté *side;* **à côté de** *next to*
la côtelette (food) *chop*
le coton *cotton,* or *cotton wool*
le cou *neck*
coucher *to sleep,* or *to spend the night*
se coucher *to go to bed*
le coucher du soleil *sunset*
la couchette *sleeper,* or *berth*
le coude *elbow*
la couette *duvet*
la couleur *colour*
le coup *blow,* or *shock;*
le coup d'envoi *kick-off;*
le coup de fil *phone call;*

le coup de main (helping) *hand;* **le coup de pied** *kick;*
le coup de poing *punch;*
le coup de soleil *sunburn*
coupable *guilty*
la coupe *cut,* or (ice cream) *dish;* **la Coupe du monde** *World Cup*
couper *to cut*
le courage *courage;* **courage!** *cheer up!*
courageux (f: courageuse) *brave,* or *courageous*
couramment *fluently,* or *commonly*
courant(e) *common;* **être au courant de** *to know about*
la courbature *ache;* **avoir des courbatures** *to be stiff*
courir *to run*
le courrier *post,* or *mail*
le cours *course,* or *lesson*
la course *race,* or *errand*
les courses [f] *shopping*
court(e) *short*
le/la cousin(e) *cousin*
le couteau *knife*
coûter *to cost*
la coutume *custom*
couvert(e) *covered;* **c'est couvert** (weather) *it's overcast*
la couverture *blanket,* or *cover*
crado** *scruffy*
le crampon (on boot) *stud*
craquer *to crackle,* or (slang) *to crack up,* or *to lose it*
la cravache (riding) *whip*
la cravate *tie*
le crawl (swimming) *crawl*
le crayon *pencil*
la crème *cream;* **le (grand) crème** (large) *coffee with milk/cream;* **la crème anglaise** *custard;* **la crème patissière** *confectioner's custard;*
la crème solaire *sun cream*
la crêpe *pancake*

crevé(e)** exhausted, or shattered
crever to burst, or to puncture
la crevette prawn
crier to scream, or to shout
la crinière mane
la crise fit, or crisis
critiquer to criticize
croire to believe
la croix cross
le croque-madame ham and cheese toasted sandwich with an egg on top
le croque-monsieur ham and cheese toasted sandwich
le crottin small goat's cheese
cru(e) raw
les crudités [f] dish of salad and/or raw vegetables
la cuillère spoon
le cuir leather
la cuisine kitchen
le cuisinier cook
la cuisinière cook, or stove
le culot* cheek, or nerve
le culte cult
culturel(le) cultural
curieux (f: curieuse) curious, or odd, or nosy

d'abord first
d'accord OK, or all right; **être d'accord** to agree
la dame lady
dangereux (f: dangereuse) dangerous
dans in
danser to dance
le danseur (f: la danseuse) dancer
la date (calendar) date
de from, or of (see also p. 56)
le dé dice, or thimble
se débarrasser de to get rid of
débile** stupid, or feeble-minded

debout standing
se débrouiller to cope
le début start, or beginning
le/la débutant(e) beginner
le déca* a decaff. coffee
décaféiné(e) decaffeinated
la décapotable open top car
le décapsuleur bottle opener
décembre December
les déchets [m] rubbish
déchirer to rip
décider to decide
décoller (plane) to take off
décolleté(e) low-cut
décontracté(e) casual, or relaxed, or laid-back
le découvert overdraft
découvrir to discover
décrire to describe
déçu(e) disappointed
défendu(e) forbidden
la défense defence; **défense d'entrer/de fumer** no entry/smoking; **la défense de l'environnement** environmental conservation
déglinguer** to bust, or to fall to pieces
dégonflé(e) (tyre) flat, or (slang) chicken (cowardly)
dégoûtant(e) disgusting
dégoûter to disgust
le degré degree
dégueulasse** revolting, or gross
la dégustation tasting
déjà already
déjeuner to have lunch
le déjeuner lunch; **le petit déjeuner** or **le petit déj*** breakfast
délicieux (f: délicieuse) delicious
délirer to be delirious; **tu délires*!** you must be out of your mind!

demain tomorrow; **après-demain** the day after tomorrow
demander to ask
se demander to wonder
le démaquillant make-up remover
déménager to move house
dément(e)* fab, or cool
demi(e) half; **il est dix heures et demie** it's half past ten; **le demi-frère** stepbrother, or half-brother; **la demi-soeur** stepsister, or half-sister; **le demi-tarif** half-price
le demi-tour U-turn; **la demi-bouteille** half-bottle
la démocratie democracy
démodé(e) old-fashioned
démolir to demolish, or to wreck
la dent tooth
le dentifrice toothpaste
le/la dentiste dentist
le déodorant deodorant
le départ departure
dépasser to exceed, or to overtake
se dépêcher to hurry
dépendre to depend
dépenser to spend
déposer to drop off
déprimant(e) depressing
déprimé(e) depressed
depuis since, or for
déranger to disturb; **ça te/vous dérange?** do you mind?
le dériveur sailing dinghy
le dernier (f: la dernière) last, or latest
derrière behind
le derrière bottom
des some, or of the, or any
désagréable unpleasant
descendre to go/walk down, or to get off
se déshabiller to undress

désolé(e) sorry, or desolate
le désordre mess
le dessert dessert
le dessin picture, or drawing; **le dessin animé** cartoon
dessiner to draw
dessus above, or on top
le détail detail
le détendeur (diving) regulator
se détendre to relax
détester to hate
le détour detour
devant in front of
devenir to become
deviner to guess
devoir to have to, or to owe
les devoirs [m] homework
diabétique diabetic
le dialecte dialect
la diarrhée diarrhoea
le dictionnaire or **le dico*** dictionary
le dieu god
différent(e) different
difficile difficult
dimanche Sunday
le diminutif shortened name
la dinde turkey
le dîner supper
dingue* crazy
diplomatique diplomatic, or tactful
dire to say, or to tell; **ça te dit de ...?** would you like to ...?
direct(e) direct; **en direct** live
la direction direction
discuter to discuss, or to argue
la dispute argument
se disputer to quarrel
le disquaire music store
le disque disk, or record
la disquette floppy disk

le distributeur distributor;
le distributeur (automatique) vending machine; **le distributeur (automatique) de billets** cash dispenser, or ticket machine
divorcé(e) divorced
le docteur doctor
le doigt finger
le dollar dollar
le dommage harm, or damage; **quel dommage!** what a shame!
donner to give
dormir to sleep; **dormir à la belle étoile** to sleep out under the stars
le dortoir dormitory
le dos back; **le dos crawlé** (swimming) backstroke, or back crawl
la douane customs
double double
doubler to double, or to dub, or to overtake
douce (see 'doux')
la douche shower
la doudoune* puffa jacket
doué(e) talented
doux (f: douce) soft, or sweet
draguer** to flirt, or to chat/pick up
le dragueur** (f: la dragueuse**) flirt
le drap sheet
la drogue drug
le/la drogué(e) drug addict
droit(e) straight; **tout droit** straight ahead
le droit law, or right; **avoir le droit** to be allowed; **les droits de l'homme [m]** human rights
la droite right
drôle funny
du some, or of the, or any

les dunes [f] dunes
dur(e) hard, or difficult

l'eau [f] water; **l'eau (minérale) plate/gazeuse** still/sparkling (mineral) water
l'échange [m] exchange
échanger to exchange, or to swap
s'échapper to escape
l'écharpe [f] scarf
s'échauffer to warm up
les échecs [m] chess
échouer to fail
éclater to explode; **éclater de rire** to burst out laughing
l'école [f] school; **l'école des beaux-arts** art school
l'écologie [f] ecology
écossais(e) Scottish
l'Écosse [f] Scotland
l'écoute [f] (sailing) sheet
écouter to listen
les écouteurs [m] earphones
l'écran [m] screen; **l'écran total [m]** sun block
écrire to write
l'écrivain [m] writer
l'éducation [f] education
effacer to rub out
effrayant(e) scary
égal(e) equal; **ça m'est égal!** I don't care!
l'église [f] church
égoïste selfish
l'élastique [m] elastic, or rubber band
l'élection [f] election
électrique electric
elle she, or her
l'embarquement [m] boarding; **la salle d'embarquement** departure lounge
embêtant(e) annoying
l'embouteillage [m] traffic jam

embrasser *to kiss*
embrouiller *to muddle,* or *to confuse*
l'émission [f] *programme* (on TV/radio)
emmener *to take*
empêcher *to prevent*
emporter *to take,* or *to take away;* **les plats à emporter [m]** *take-away dishes*
emprunter *to borrow*
enceinte *pregnant*
encore *again,* or *still;* **encore un peu** *a little more;* **pas encore** *not yet*
l'endroit [m] *place*
énervant(e) *annoying*
énerver *to annoy*
l'enfant [m/f] *child*
l'enfer [m] *hell*
enfin *at last*
enflé(e) *swollen*
s'enfuir *to run away*
engueuler** *to tell off*
s'engueuler** *to have a row*
enlever *to take off*
les ennuis [m] *trouble,* or *problems*
s'ennuyer *to be bored*
ennuyeux (f: ennuyeuse) *boring,* or *annoying,* or *worrying*
enregistré(e) (luggage) *checked in,* or (post) *registered*
l'enregistrement [m] *check-in*
enregistrer *to record,* or (luggage) *to check in*
enrhumé(e): être enrhumé(e) *to have a cold*
enseigner *to teach*
ensemble *together*
ensoleillé(e) *sunny*
entendre *to hear*
s'entendre *to get on/along*

entendu *understood,* or *fine*
entier (f: entière) *whole*
l'entorse [f] *sprain*
l'entracte [m] *interval,* or *intermission*
s'entraîner *to train*
entre *between*
l'entrecôte [f] *type of steak*
l'entrée [f] *entrance,* or *first course,* or *main course;* **entrée libre** *free admission*
entrer *to come/go in*
l'entretien [m] *interview,* or *upkeep*
l'enveloppe [f] *envelope*
l'envers [m] *wrong side;* **à l'envers** *inside out,* or *upside-down*
environ *approximately,* or *about*
l'environnement [m] *environment*
envoyer *to send*
épais(se) *thick*
l'épaule [f] *shoulder*
l'épaulière [f] *shoulder pad*
épicé(e) *hot,* or *spicy*
l'épice [f] *spice*
épileptique *epileptic*
les épinards [m] *spinach*
l'épingle [f] *pin;* **l'épingle de sûreté** *safety pin*
l'éponge [f] *sponge*
épouvantable *dreadful*
épuisé(e) *exhausted*
l'équipe [f] *team*
l'équitation [f] *riding*
érotique *erotic*
l'erreur [f] *mistake*
l'escalade [f] *climbing*
escalader *to climb*
l'escale [f] *stopover*
l'escalier [m] *stairs;* **l'escalier roulant (m)** *escalator*
l'escargot [m] *snail*

l'espace [m] *space*
l'Espagne [f] *Spain*
espérer *to hope*
l'esprit [m] *spirit;* **l'esprit mal tourné** *dirty mind*
l'essai [m] *test,* or *attempt*
essayer *to try*
l'essence [f] *petrol*
essoufflé(e) *out of breath*
l'essuie-glace [m] *windscreen wiper*
l'essuie-tout [m] *kitchen paper*
l'est [m] *east;* **les pays de l'Est [m]** *eastern Europe*
est-ce que ... ? (see Questions p. 60)
l'estomac [m] *stomach*
et *and*
l'étage [m] *floor* (level)
l'étagère [f] *shelf*
les États-Unis [m] *United States*
l'été [m] *summer*
éteindre *to switch off*
éteint(e) (switched) *off*
éternuer *to sneeze*
l'étoile [f] *star*
étrange *strange*
l'étranger (f: l'étrangère) *foreigner;* **à l'étranger** *abroad*
être (see p. 59) *to be*
l'étrier [m] *stirrup*
étroit(e) *narrow*
les études [f] *studies;* **les études supérieures [f]** *higher education*
l'étudiant(e) [m/f] *student*
étudier *to study*
l'Europe [f] *Europe*
européen(ne) *European*
s'évanouir *to faint*
l'événement [m] *event*
évident(e) *obvious*
éviter *to avoid*
exact *right,* or *correct*
exagéré(e) *exaggerated,* or *over the top*

exagérer *to exaggerate*
l'examen [m] *exam(ination)*
l'excédent [m] *surplus;*
l'excédent de bagages [m]
excess baggage
excellent(e) *excellent*
excentrique *eccentric*
l'exception [f] *exception,*
or odd one out
excité(e) *excited*
s'exciter *to get excited*
l'excursion [f] *tour, or trip*
excusez-moi *excuse me*
l'exercice [m] *exercise*
exotique *exotic*
l'expérience [f] *experience,*
or experiment
expirer *to run out, or to*
expire
expliquer *to explain*
l'exposition [f] *exhibition*
exprès *on purpose*
l'express [m] *espresso*
coffee, or fast train
l'extérieur [m] *outside*
extra* *brilliant, or fab*
extraordinaire
extraordinary

fabriquer *to make, or to*
manufacture
face: en face de *opposite*
fâché(e) *cross, or angry*
se fâcher *to get cross/angry,*
or to fall out with
facile *easy*
la façon *manner, or way*
faible *weak*
la faiblesse *weakness*
la faim *hunger;* **avoir faim**
to be hungry
faire (see p. 59) *to make, or*
to do
fait: il fait froid/beau
it's cold/fine (weather)
la falaise *cliff*
la famille *family*
fantastique *fantastic*

farci(e) *stuffed*
le fard *make-up;* **le fard à**
joues *blusher;* **le fard à**
paupières *eye shadow*
fatigué(e) *tired*
fauché(e)** *broke*
la faute *fault, or mistake*
le fauteuil *armchair;* **le**
fauteuil roulant *wheelchair*
faux (f: fausse) *false, or*
wrong
félicitations *congratulations*
le/la féministe *feminist*
la femme *woman, or wife*
la fenêtre *window*
la ferme *farm*
fermé(e) *closed*
fermer *to close;* **fermer à**
clé *to lock*
la fermeture *closure, or*
fastening; **la fermeture**
éclair *zip*
la fête *party;* **faire la fête**
to party; **la fête foraine**
funfair
fêter *to celebrate*
le feu *fire;* **le feu d'artifice**
fireworks; **le feu rouge**
traffic lights
la feuille *leaf, or* (paper)
sheet
le feuilleton *soap opera,*
or serial
les feux [m] *lights;*
les feux de signalisation
traffic lights
février *February*
la ficelle *string*
ficher* *to do, or to put;*
fiche-moi la paix!* *leave me*
alone!; **fiche le camp!*** *get*
lost!
se ficher de* *not to give a*
damn
fidèle *faithful*
fier (f: fière) *proud*
la fièvre *fever*
le fil *thread*

la fille *girl, or daughter*
le film *film*
le fils *son*
la fin *end*
finir *to finish*
la fixation (ski) *binding*
fixer *to fix* (a date/price), *or*
to stare
la flaque d'eau *puddle*
le flash (camera) *flash*
la fléchette *dart*
la fleur *flower*
le fleuve (large) *river*
le flic** *cop*
le flingue** *gun*
le flipper *pinball*
flipper** *to flip* (to become
excited/depressed/scared)
flotter *to float, or* (slang) *to*
rain
la flûte *flute*
le foc (sailing) *jib*
le foie *liver;* **le foie gras**
rich goose or duck liver pâté
la fois *time, or occasion*
folle (see 'fou')
la folle *mad woman*
foncé(e) *dark*
le fond *bottom, or back* (of
throat/room etc); **le fond de**
teint *foundation* (make-up)
fondre *to melt;* **fondre en**
larmes *to burst into tears*
la fondue (savoyarde) *dish*
of hot melted cheese with
bread; **la fondue**
bourguignonne *thin strips*
of meat cooked at table
la fontaine *fountain*
le football *or* **le foot***
football; **le football**
américain *American football*
le footballeur (f: la
footballeuse) *football player*
le footing *jogging*
la forêt *forest*
le forfait *set price, or* (ski)
lift pass

la formation training
la forme shape; **en forme** fit, or well
former to train
formidable wonderful, or terrific
fort(e) loud, or strong
fou (f: folle) mad, or crazy
le fou madman
la foudre lightning
le foulard scarf
la foule crowd
le four oven
la fourchette fork
la fourmi ant
frais (f: fraîche) fresh, or chilled
la fraise strawberry
la framboise raspberry
français(e) French
la France France
le frangin* brother
la frangine* sister
frapper to hit, or to knock
le frein brake
le frère brother
le fric* dosh (money)
le frigo* fridge
frileux (f: frileuse) sensitive to the cold
frimer* to boast, or to show off
les fringues* [f] clothes
le frisbee frisbee
frisé(e) very curly
la frisée type of lettuce with very curly leaves
le frisson shiver, or thrill
frit(e) fried
les frites [f] chips, or French fries
froid(e) cold
le fromage cheese
la frontière border, or frontier
le fruit fruit
les fruits de mer [m] seafood

fumer to smoke
le fumeur (f: la fumeuse) smoker
fumeurs smoking; **non-fumeurs** non-smoking
furax* livid, or furious
le fuseau (de ski) ski pants

gâcher to spoil
la gaffe* blunder; **faire gaffe*** to watch out; **faire une gaffe*** to put your foot in it
gaffer* to blunder, or to put your foot in it
le/la gagnant(e) winner
gagner to win, or to earn
la galère: quelle galère*! what a mess/disaster!
la galerie gallery, or roof rack
gallois(e) Welsh
le gant glove
le garçon boy, or waiter
garder to keep, or to look after
le/la gardien(ne) guard, or caretaker; **le gardien de but** goalkeeper
la gare railway station; **la gare routière** bus station
se garer to park
le gars* guy
le gaspillage waste
gaspiller to waste
gâté(e) spoiled
le gâteau cake
la gauche left
le gaz gas
gazeux (f: gazeuse) fizzy
le gazole diesel
le gel gel, or frost
geler to freeze
Gémeaux (star sign) Gemini
gênant(e) embarrassing, or a nuisance
le gendarme police officer
gêner to bother, or to be/get in the way

génial(e) inspired, or brilliant, or great
le genou knee
le genre type, or gender
les gens [m/f] people
gentil(le) kind, or nice
la géographie geography
le gigot d'agneau leg of lamb
le gilet cardigan, or waistcoat; **le gilet de sauvetage** life jacket; **le gilet stabilisateur** (diving) buoyancy aid
le/la gitan(e) gypsy
le gîte house for rent in the countryside
la glace ice, or ice cream, or mirror
la glacière cool box
le glaçon ice cube
glisser to slip, or to slide
le goal* goalie
la godasse* shoe
gonflé(e) swollen, or (slang) cheeky
la gorge throat
la gourde water bottle, or flask
gourmand(e) greedy
la gourmette chain bracelet
le goût taste, or flavour
goûter to taste
le goûter tea (afternoon snack)
la goutte drop; **la goutte de pluie** raindrop
le gouvernail rudder, or helm
le gouvernement government
le gramme gram
grand(e) big, or tall, or large
la grand-mère grandmother
le grand-père grandfather
la Grande-Bretagne Britain
grandir to grow

le gras fat
gratter to scratch
gratuit(e) free
la Grèce Greece
la grenouille frog
la grève strike
la grille iron gate, or grid, or (American football) facemask
grillé(e) grilled, or toasted
la grimpe* (rock) climbing
grimper to climb
le grimpeur (f: la grimpeuse) (rock) climber
la grippe flu
gris(e) grey
gros(se) large, or fat
grossier (f: grossière) rude, or crude
grossir to get fat, or to put on weight
la grotte cave
le groupe group, or band
la guêpe wasp
la guerre war
la gueule mouth; **la gueule de bois*** hangover
le guichet ticket office, or (bank) counter
le/la guide guide
le guidon handlebars
la guitare guitar
le/la guitariste guitarist
le gymnase gymnasium
la gymnastique or **la gym*** gymnastics, or excercise classes

s'habiller to get dressed
habiter to live
l'habitude [f] habit; **d'habitude** usually; **comme d'habitude** as usual; **avoir l'habitude de** to be used to
habituel(le) usual
haïr to loathe
l'haleine [f] breath
le hamac hammock

handicapé(e) disabled
le haricot bean
le hasard chance
haut(e) high
le haut top; **le haut-parleur** loudspeaker
le hautbois oboe
l'hélicoptère [m] helicopter
l'herbe [f] grass
l'héroïne [f] heroine
le héros hero
hésiter to hesitate
l'heure [f] hour, or time; **à l'heure** on time; **les heures de pointe/d'affluence** rush hour; **quelle heure est-il?** what time is it?; **trois heures** three o'clock
heureusement luckily
heureux (f: heureuse) happy
le hibou owl
hier yesterday
hindou(e) Hindu
l'histoire [f] story, or history
l'hiver [m] winter
l'homme [m] man
homosexuel(le) or **homo*** homosexual
honnête honest
la honte shame; **quelle honte!** how embarrassing!
l'hôpital [m] hospital
le hoquet hiccups
l'horaire [m] timetable
l'horoscope [m] horoscope
l'horreur [f] horror; **avoir horreur de** to hate
horrible horrible
le hors-d'oeuvre [m] first course, or starter
hors de out of; **hors-jeu** offside; **hors-piste** off piste; **hors saison** off season; **hors taxe** duty-free
l'hôte [m] host, or [m/f] guest

l'hôtel [m] hotel; **l'hôtel de ville** town hall
l'hôtesse [f] hostess; **l'hôtesse de l'air** (female) flight attendant
l'huile [f] oil
l'huître [f] oyster
humain(e) human
l'humeur [f] mood; **de bonne/mauvaise humeur** in a good/bad mood
l'humour [m] humour
hurler to yell
hyper* extremely
l'hypocrite [m/f] hypocrite

ici here; **par ici** over here
l'idée [f] idea; **l'idée fixe** obsession
l'idiot(e) [m/f] idiot; **faire l'idiot(e)*** to act stupid
ignoble vile
il he, or it
l'île [f] island; **les îles anglo-normandes** the Channel Islands
il y a there is/are, or ago
l'immigré(e) [m/f] immigrant
immobile still
imperméable waterproof
l'imperméable or **l'imper*** [m] raincoat
impoli(e) rude
important(e) important
importé(e) imported
impossible impossible
impressionnant(e) impressive
l'imprimante [f] printer
l'inconvénient [m] drawback, or disadvantage
incroyable unbelievable
l'Inde [f] India
l'indicatif [m] area code
l'indigestion [f] upset stomach
indiquer to point, or to show

indispensable *essential,* or *vital*

l'infirmier (f: l'infirmière) *nurse*

les informations or **les info*** [f] *news,* or *information*

l'informatique [f] *computing*

l'infusion [f] *herb tea*

injuste *unfair,* or *wrong*

inquiet (f: inquiète) *worried*

s'inquiéter *to worry*

s'inscrire *to join,* or *to sign up for,* or *to register*

l'insolation [f] *sunstroke*

l'instant [m] *moment;* **à l'instant** *now*

l'instrument [m] *instrument*

l'insulte [f] *insult*

insupportable *unbearable*

intelligent(e) *intelligent*

l'intention [f] *intention;* **avoir l'intention de** *to mean to*

interdit(e) *forbidden*

intéressant(e) *interesting*

s'intéresser à *to be interested in*

l'intérieur [m] *inside*

l'interphone [m] *intercom*

introduire *to insert*

inutile *useless*

l'invitation [f] *invitation*

l'invité(e) [m/f] *guest*

inviter *to invite,* or *to ask out*

irlandais(e) *Irish*

l'Irlande [f] *Ireland*

isolé(e) *isolated*

l'Italie [f] *Italy*

l'itinéraire [m] *route*

jaloux (f: jalouse) *jealous*

jamais *never*

la jambe *leg*

le jambon *ham*

janvier *January*

le jardin *garden;* **le jardin public** *park*

jaune *yellow*

le jaune (d'oeuf) *(egg) yolk*

je (or j') *I*

le jean *jeans;* **en jean** *(made of) denim*

jeter *to throw,* or *to throw away/out*

le jeu *game,* or *quiz;* **les jeux vidéos** *video games;* **la salle de jeux vidéos** *(amusement) arcade*

jeudi *Thursday*

jeune *young*

les jodhpurs [m] *jodhpurs*

le jogging *jogging*

joli(e) *pretty*

la joue *cheek*

jouer *to play*

le jouet *toy*

le joueur (f: la joueuse) *player*

le jour *day;* **le jour de congé** *day off;* **le jour férié** *national holiday;* **à jour** *up-to-date*

le journal *newspaper,* or *personal diary*

le/la journaliste *journalist*

la journée *day,* or *daytime*

joyeux (f: joyeuse) *happy,* or *cheerful*

juif (f: juive) *Jewish*

juillet *July*

juin *June*

le jumeau *twin (brother)*

la jumelle *twin (sister)*

les jumelles [f] *binoculars*

la jupe *skirt*

jurer *to swear*

le jus *juice*

jusqu'à *until*

juste *fair,* or *just*

kascher *kosher*

le kayak *canoe,* or *kayak*

le kilo *kilo*

le kilomètre *kilometre*

le kiosque *news stand*

le kir *white wine with blackcurrant;* **le kir royale** *champagne with blackcurrant*

le klaxon *horn*

la (or l') *the,* or *her,* or *it*

là *there;* **là-bas** *over there*

le lac *lake*

le/la lâche *coward*

lâcher *to let go*

laid(e) *ugly*

la laine *wool*

laisser *to leave,* or *to let;* **laisser tomber** *to drop,* or *to let go,* or *(slang) to let down,* or *stand (someone) up;* **laisser tranquille** *to leave alone*

le laissez-passer *(entry) pass*

le lait *milk*

la lame *blade*

la lampe *lamp,* or *light;* **la lampe de poche** *torch*

lancer *to throw*

la langue *language,* or *tongue*

le lapin *rabbit*

les lardons [m] *small pieces of bacon*

la laque *hair-spray*

laquelle *which (one)*

large *wide*

la larme *tear*

la latte *(sailing) batten*

le lavabo *wash basin*

le lave-linge *washing machine*

laver *to wash*

se laver *to wash (yourself)*

la laverie *launderette*

le (or l') *the,* or *him,* or *it*

le lèche-vitrines *window shopping*

léger (f: légère) *light*

le légume *vegetable*

le lendemain the next day
lent(e) slow
la lentille lentil; **la lentille (de contact)** contact lens; **la lentille souple/dure** soft/hard contact lens
lequel which (one)
les the, or them
la lessive washing powder, or laundry
la lettre letter
leur their, or them
se lever to get up
la lèvre lip
la librairie bookshop
libre free
la licence degree
le lieu place; **au lieu de** instead of
la ligne line
le linge washing, or linen (sheets etc.)
Lion (star sign) Leo
lire to read
le lit bed; **le grand lit** double bed; **le lit bain-soleil** sun-lounger
le litre litre
la littérature literature
le livre book; **le livre de poche** paperback book
la livre (sterling) pound
location (de) for hire/rent
la locomotive (train) engine
le logement accommodation
loger (quelqu'un) to put (someone) up
le logiciel software
loin far
les loisirs [m] leisure, or free time
long(ue) long
longtemps a long time
louche dodgy, or dubious
louer to rent, or to hire
lourd(e) heavy
la luge toboggan

lui him, or her, or it
la lumière light
lundi Monday
la lune moon
les lunettes [f] glasses; **les lunettes de soleil** sunglasses; **les lunettes de ski** ski goggles
le lycée secondary/high school

ma my
le machin* thing
la machine machine
macho* macho
madame Mrs, or madam
mademoiselle Miss
le magasin shop; **le grand magasin** department store; **faire les magasins** to go around the shops
la magnésie chalk (for climbing); **le sac à magnésie** chalk bag
le magnétoscope video recorder
mai May
maigrir to get thin, or to lose weight
le maillet mallet
le maillot swimming trunks, or swimsuit, or team shirt/jersey; **le maillot deux-pièces** bikini; **le maillot une pièce** one piece swimsuit
la main hand
maintenant now
la mairie town hall
mais but
la maison house, or home
mal bad, or wrong, or badly; **avoir mal** to hurt; **avoir mal à la tête/aux dents** to have a headache/toothache; **le mal de mer** seasickness; **le mal du pays** homesickness
malade ill, or sick

malheureusement unfortunately
malheureux (f: malheureuse) unhappy, or upset
malin (f: maligne) cunning, or clever (smart)
la manche sleeve; **la Manche** the Channel; **le tunnel sous la Manche** the Channel tunnel
manger to eat
la manifestation or **la manif*** demonstration
le mannequin (fashion) model
manquer to miss
le manteau coat
le maquillage make-up
le marchand stallholder, or salesman; **le marchand de journaux** newsagent; **le marchand de fruits et légumes** greengrocer
marchander to bargain
la marche step, or (sport) walking; **faire marche arrière** to reverse
le marché market; **le marché aux puces** flea market
marcher to walk, or to be in working order; **faire marcher quelqu'un*** to have someone on
mardi Tuesday
la marée tide
la margarine margarine
le mari husband
le mariage wedding
le Maroc Morocco
marquer to mark; **marquer un but/un point** to score a goal/point
marrant(e)* fun, or funny
marre*: en avoir marre* to be fed up
se marrer* to have a laugh

marron brown
le marron chestnut
mars March
le marteau hammer
le mascara mascara
le masque mask
le mât mast
le match match, or game;
le match à domicile home
match/game
le matelas mattress;
le matelas pneumatique air
bed
le matelot sailor
le matériel kit, or equipment
le matin morning
la matinée morning, or
afternoon performance; **faire
la grasse matinée** to sleep in
late
mauvais(e) bad
le mazout (fuel) oil
le mec* guy, bloke
le/la mécanicien(ne)
mechanic or train driver
méchant(e) wicked, or
naughty
le médecin doctor
la médecine medicine (the
science)
les médias [m] media
le médicament medicine
(medication)
la Méditerranée the
Mediterranean
la méduse jellyfish
meilleur(e) better
le/la meilleur(e) best
mélanger to mix
le melon melon
le/la même same
la menace threat
le/la mendiant(e) beggar
le meneur (f: la meneuse)
leader, or cheerleader
le mensonge lie, or fib
le menteur (f: la menteuse)
liar

mentir to lie
le menu set menu
la mer sea
merci thank you
mercredi Wednesday
la mère mother
**merveilleux
(f: merveilleuse)** wonderful
messieurs gentlemen
la météo weather forecast
le mètre metre
le métro underground, or
tube
le metteur en scène
(film/movie) director, or (play)
producer
mettre to put, or to put on
le meurtre murder
le micro microphone
le micro-ondes microwave
le microbe bug
midi midday, or noon
le miel honey
le/la mien(ne) mine
mieux better; **se sentir
mieux** to feel better; **il vaut
mieux ...** it is better to ...
le/la mieux best
mignon(ne) sweet, or cute
le milieu middle, or
environment
le millefeuille cream slice
mi-longs (cheveux)
shoulder length (hair)
minable* pathetic
mince thin; **mince!*** damn!
la minette* babe (girl)
mineur(e) under age
minuit midnight
le miroir mirror
mixte mixed, or (school) co-ed
la mobylette moped
moche* lousy, or ugly
la mode fashion; **à la mode**
fashionable
le mode method; **le mode
de vie** lifestyle; **le mode
d'emploi** user instructions

moi me
moins less; **au moins** at
least; **huit heures moins dix**
ten to eight; **une heure
moins le quart** a quarter to
one
le mois month
la moitié half
molle (see 'mou')
mon my
le monde world
le moniteur/la monitrice
instructor
la monnaie money, or
change
le monokini bikini bottoms;
en monokini topless
le monoski monoski
monsieur Mr, or Sir
**monstrueux (f:
monstrueuse)** outrageous
la montagne mountain
le montant total amount
monter to go/walk up
la montre watch
montrer to show
le monument monument
se moquer de to make fun
of
le moral morale; **remonter
le moral à quelqu'un** to
cheer someone up
le morceau piece
mordre to bite
mordu(e)* de madly in love
with, or mad about
le mors (riding) bit
mort(e) dead
la morue cod
la mosquée mosque
le mot word; **le gros mot**
swearword; **les mots croisés
[m]** crossword
le motard biker, or police
on motorbike
le motif pattern, or motive
la moto motorbike
mou (f: molle) soft

la mouche *fly*
le mouchoir *handkerchief*
mouillé(e) *wet*
la moule *mussel;* **moules marinières** *mussels in white wine*
le moulin à vent *windmill*
mourir *to die*
le mousqueton *karabiner*
la mousse *foam,* or *mousse*
le moustique *mosquito*
la moutarde *mustard*
moyen(ne) *average,* or *medium*
le mur *wall*
mûr(e) *mature,* or *ripe*
le muscle *muscle*
la musculation *gym* (with weights)
le musée *museum*
le/la musicien(ne) *musician*
la musique *music*
musulman(e) *Muslim*
myope *short-sighted*

nager *to swim*
naïf (f: naïve) *naïve*
la naissance *birth;* **la date de naissance** *date of birth*
la nana** *girl*
la natation *swimming*
la nationalité *nationality*
nature *plain*
la nature *nature*
naturel(le) *natural*
navré(e) *terribly sorry,* or *distressed*
naze** *exhausted*
ne ... pas *not* (see also Negatives p. 60)
nécessaire *necessary*
la neige *snow*
neiger *to snow*
le nerf *nerve;* **taper sur les nerfs* (de quelqu'un)** *to get on (someone's) nerves*
le nez *nose*

n'importe *it doesn't matter;*
n'importe quel(le) *any;*
n'importe qui *anyone;*
n'importe quoi *anything,* or (slang) *nonsense*
le niveau *level* or *standard*
Noël *Christmas*
noir(e) *black;* **il fait noir** *it is dark;* **broyer du noir** *to be down in the dumps*
la noisette *hazelnut*
la noix *walnut;* **la noix de cajou** *cashew nut;* **la noix de coco** *coconut;* **la noix du Brésil** *brazil nut*
le nom *name;* **le nom de famille** *last name*
non *no*
le nord *north*
nos *our*
la note *note,* or *mark,* or *bill*
notre *our*
nouer *to knot,* or *to tie*
les nouilles [f] *noodles*
la nourriture *food*
nous *we,* or *us*
nouveau (f: nouvelle) *new;* **de nouveau** *again;* **le nouvel an** *new year;* **la Nouvelle-Zélande** *New Zealand*
nouvel(le) (see 'nouveau')
les nouvelles [f] *news*
novembre *November*
nu(e) *naked*
le nuage *cloud*
la nuit *night*
nul(le) *nil,* or *lousy,* or *naff;* **nulle part** *nowhere;* **le match nul** *draw (equal score)*
le numéro *number*

l'objectif [m] (camera) *lens*
l'objet [m] *object;* **les objets trouvés** *lost-property*
obligatoire *compulsory*
l'occasion [f] *opportunity;* **d'occasion** *second-hand*

occupé(e) *busy,* or (toilet) *engaged*
s'occuper de *to take care of,* or *to take charge of*
octobre *October*
l'odeur [f] *smell*
odieux (f: odieuse) *obnoxious*
l'oeil [m] *eye*
l'oeuf [m] *egg;* **l'oeuf à la coque** *soft-boiled egg;* **l'oeuf au plat** *fried egg;* **les oeufs brouillés** *scrambled eggs;* **l'oeuf dur** *hard-boiled egg;* **l'oeuf poché** *poached egg;* **les oeufs à la neige** *dessert of whipped egg whites in custard*
officiel(le) *official*
offrir *to offer*
l'oignon [m] *onion*
l'oiseau [m] *bird*
l'olive [f] *olive*
l'ombre [f] *shade*
l'omelette [f] *omelette*
on *we,* or *people* e.g. **on dit que ...** *people say that ...*
l'oncle [m] *uncle*
l'opticien(ne) [m/f] *optician*
optimiste *optimistic*
l'orage [m] *thunderstorm*
l'orange [f] *orange*
l'orchestre [m] *orchestra*
ordinaire *ordinary*
l'ordinateur [m] *computer*
l'ordre [m] *order*
les ordures [f] *rubbish*
l'oreille [f] *ear*
l'oreiller [m] *pillow*
organiser *to organize*
l'organisme de charité [m] *charity organization*
original(e) *offbeat,* or *original*
l'os [m] *bone*
oser *to dare*
ou *or*
où *where*

oublier to forget
l'ouest [m] west
oui yes
l'outil [m] tool
ouvert(e) open
l'ouvre-boîte [m] can opener
l'ouvre-bouteille [m] bottle opener
ouvrir to open

la pagaille* mess, or chaos
la page page
le pain bread; **le petit pain** bread roll; **le pain complet** wholemeal bread; **le pain grillé** toast; **le pain au raisin** bun with raisins; **le pain au chocolat** like a croissant but with chocolate filling
la paix peace
le palais palace
la palme (diving) flipper
le/la pamplemousse grapefruit
le panaché shandy
le panier basket
la panique panic
la panne breakdown; **en panne** out of order, or broken down
le panneau sign
le pansement plaster
le pantalon trousers
la papeterie stationer's shop
le papier paper; **le papier hygiénique** toilet paper
les papiers documents
le papillon butterfly
Pâques Easter
par by, or through
le parachute parachute
le parapluie umbrella
le parasol parasol
le paravent windbreak
le parc park; **le parc d'attractions** theme park

parce que because
pardon sorry, or excuse me; **demander pardon** to apologize
pardonner to forgive
le pare-battage (boat) fender
le pare-brise windscreen
les parents [m] parents
le pare-soleil (camera) lens hood
paresseux (f: paresseuse) lazy
parfait(e) perfect
le parfum perfume, or flavour
parier to bet
le parking car park
parler to speak, or to talk
la parole word
partager to share, or to split
le/la partenaire partner
le parti (political) party
participer to take part
particulier (f: particulière) particular, or private
la partie part; **la partie de cartes/tennis** game of cards/tennis
partir to leave, or to go away
partout everywhere
pas not (see Negatives p. 60)
le pas footstep
le passage passage
le passager (f: la passagère) passenger
le passeport passport
passer to pass, or (film) to be on/showing
se passer to happen
la passerelle footbridge or gangway
passionnant(e) exciting, or fascinating
le/la passionné(e) fan, or enthusiast

la pastèque watermelon
le pastis alcoholic drink tasting of aniseed
les pâtes [f] pasta
le patin skate, or skating; **le patin à glace** ice skate/skating
la patinoire ice rink
la pâtisserie cake shop
le/la patron(ne) boss
la paupière eyelid
pauvre poor
la paye wage
payer to pay
le pays country, or nation; **le pays de Galles** Wales
le paysage scenery
PCV (phone) reversed charges
le péage toll
la peau skin
la pêche peach, or fishing; **avoir la pêche*** to be on top form
la pédale pedal; **perdre les pédales**** to get mixed up, or to lose your grip
le peigne comb
peindre to paint
la pellicule film (for camera)
la pelouse lawn; **pelouse interdite** keep off the grass
pendant during, or while
penser to think
la pension small hotel, or guest house; **pension complète** full board; **demi-pension** half board
le pépin pip
perdre to lose
perdu(e) lost
le père father
périmé(e) no longer valid
le périphérique ring road
le permis licence; **le permis de conduire** driving licence
le personnage character (in play/cartoon/novel)

personne *nobody*
la personne *person*
la perte *loss;* **la perte de temps** *waste of time*
perturbé(e) *disturbed*
pessimiste *pessimistic*
la pétanque *game of bowls played mostly in southern France*
petit(e) *small*
les petits pois [m] *peas*
peu *little,* or *not much*
la peur *fear*
peut-être *perhaps*
le phare *headlight,* or *lighthouse*
la pharmacie *chemist's shop* or *pharmacy*
la philosophie or **la philo*** *philosophy*
la phobie *phobia*
la photo *photo*
le/la photographe *photographer*
le piano *piano*
le pichet *jug*
la pièce *coin,* or *play,* or *room;* **la pièce de rechange** *spare part*
le pied *foot;* **pieds nus** *barefoot*
la pierre *stone*
le/la piéton(ne) *pedestrian*
piger** *to catch on,* or *to get* (a joke)
la pile *battery;* **jouer à pile ou face** *to toss a coin*
le pilote *pilot*
la pilule *pill*
la pince à épiler *tweezers*
le pinceau *paintbrush*
le pin's *pin badge*
la pintade *guinea fowl*
le pique-nique *picnic*
piquer *to sting,* or (slang) *to nick* (steal)
le piquet *peg*
la piqûre *injection,* or *sting*

pire *worse*
la piscine *swimming pool*
la pistache *pistacchio*
la piste *track,* or (ski) *run*
le placard *cupboard*
la place *space,* or *seat,* or (town) *square*
la plage *beach*
se plaindre *to complain*
plaire *to please;* **plaire à** *to be fancied/liked by* e.g. **elle plaît à Eric** *Eric fancies her*
plaisanter *to joke*
la plaisanterie *joke*
le plan *plan,* or *map*
la planche *board;* **la planche à voile** *windsurfer* (board); **la planche de surf** *surf board*
le/la planchiste *windsurfer* (person)
la plante *plant*
se planter** *to get it all wrong,* or *to land yourself in it*
plaquer** *to chuck,* or *to dump* (a girl/boyfriend)
le plastique *plastic*
plat(e) *flat,* or (water) *still*
le plat *dish;* **le plat du jour** *dish of the day;* **faire tout un plat**** *to make a fuss*
plein(e) *full,* or (slang) *drunk;* **faire le plein** *to fill up*
pleurer *to cry*
pleut: il pleut *it's raining*
pleuvoir *to rain*
plier *to fold*
le plomb *lead*
la plongée *diving;* **la plongée sous-marine** *scuba diving*
le plongeoir *diving-board*
plonger *to dive*
le plongeur (f: la plongeuse) *diver*
plouc** *derogatory term meaning unsophisticated*
la pluie *rain*

la plupart *the majority*
plus *more*
le pneu *tyre*
la poche *pocket*
la poêle *frying pan*
le poème *poem*
le pognon** *dosh* (money)
le poids *weight*
la poignée *handle*
le poignet *wrist*
le poil *hair* (on body)
le point *point,* or *dot;* **à point** (steak etc.) *medium*
la poire *pear;* **la poire belle Hélène** *pear with vanilla ice cream and chocolate sauce*
le poireau *leek*
le pois *pea*
le poisson *fish*
Poissons (star sign) *Pisces*
la poitrine *chest,* or *breast*
le poivre *pepper*
poli(e) *polite*
la police *police*
la politique *politics*
la pollution *pollution*
la pomme *apple;* **tomber dans les pommes*** *to faint;* **la pomme de terre** *potato;* **pommes de terre en robe des champs** *baked/jacket potatoes;* **pommes vapeur** *steamed potatoes*
la pompe *pump,* or (slang) *shoe*
les pompiers [m] *fire brigade*
le pont *bridge,* or *deck*
populaire *popular*
le porc *pork,* or *pig*
le port *harbour*
la porte *door,* or (airport) *gate*
le portefeuille *wallet*
le porte-monnaie *purse*
porter *to carry,* or *to wear*
positif (f: positive) *positive*
possible *possible*

la poste post office
le pot jar, or pot, or (slang) luck; **prendre un pot*** to go for a drink; **pas de pot*** hard luck; **le pot-au-feu** meat and vegetable hotpot
potable drinkable; **non potable** not drinkable
le potage vegetable soup
la poubelle rubbish bin
la poule chicken, or hen
le poulet chicken
pour for
le pourboire tip
pourquoi why
pourri(e) rotten
pousser to push, or to grow; **pousse-toi!** move over!
pouvoir (see p. 59) to be able to, or can
pratique practical
préféré(e) favourite
premier (f: première) first
prendre to take, or (food, drink) to have
le prénom first name
près de near; **tout près** close by
présenter to present, or to introduce (someone)
le préservatif or **le préso*** condom
presque nearly
pressé(e) in a hurry; **le citron/l'orange pressé(e)** drink of fresh lemon/orange
la pression pressure, or beer on tap
prêt(e) ready
prétentieux (f: prétentieuse) pretentious
prêter to lend
la preuve proof
principal(e) main
le printemps spring
la priorité right-of-way; **priorité à droite** give way to the right

pris(e) taken, or busy
la prise plug
la prison prison
privé(e) private
le prix price, or prize
probable probable, or likely
le problème problem
prochain(e) next
proche close
le professeur or **le/la prof*** teacher
profiter de to make the most of, or to take advantage of
profond(e) deep
le progrès progress
la promenade walk, or outing
se promener to walk about/around, or to go for a walk
la promesse promise
proposer to suggest
propre clean
le/la propriétaire owner
le/la prostitué(e) prostitute
protéger to protect
le provocateur (f: la provocatrice) trouble-maker
provoquer to cause trouble
prudent(e) careful
la prune plum
PTT (or P et T) post office
la pub* advertising, or publicity
le public audience
puer to stink
le pull-over or **le pull** sweater
pur(e) pure
la purée (de pomme de terre) mashed potato

le quai quay, or platform
la qualité quality
quand when
la quantité quantity
le quart quarter; **neuf heures et quart** quarter past nine

le quartier neighbourhood
que than, or that
quel(le) what, or which
quelque some, or any; **quelque chose** something; **quelques-un(e)s** a few
quelquefois sometimes
quelqu'un somebody
la quenelle a sort of light dumpling made of fish or meat
qu'est-ce que ... ? what ... ?; **qu'est ce-que c'est?** what is this/it?
la question question
la queue tail, or stalk, or queue; **faire la queue** to queue/line up
qui who
la quincaillerie hardware shop
quitter to leave; **ne quittez pas** (phone) hold the line
quoi what

le raccourci short cut
raccrocher to hang up
raciste racist
la raclette dish of melted cheese with potatoes
raconter to tell (a story)
le radeau raft
le radiateur radiator
radin(e)* stingy
la radio radio
la radio-cassette radio cassette player
radoter* to waffle, or to babble
le ragoût stew
raide steep, or stiff, or straight
le raisin grapes; **la grappe de raisin** bunch of grapes
la raison reason; **avoir raison** to be right
raisonnable sensible
ralentir to slow down

râler* to moan, or to complain
ramasser to pick up
la rame oar
ramer to row
le rancard** tip (information), or date (meeting)
la randonnée walking, or hiking
ranger to put away
rapide fast, or quick
rappeler to remind, or to phone back
le rapport relationship; **les rapports (sexuels) [m]** sex, or intercourse
la raquette racket
rare unusual, or rare
ras le bol*: en avoir ras le bol* to be really fed up
se raser to shave
rasoir* boring
le rasoir razor
la ratatouille dish of aubergine, tomato and courgette
rater to miss, or (exam) to fail
rayé(e) striped
le rayon (in shop) shelf, or department
la réception reception
la recette recipe
recevoir to receive
réchauffer to warm up
la recherche research
recommandé(e) (post) registered
recommander to recommend
se réconcilier to make up (become friends again)
reconnaissant(e) grateful
reconnaître to recognize
reculer to move backwards
la réduction discount
regarder to look at, or to watch

le régime diet; **être au régime** to be on a diet
la région region, or area
la règle rule, or ruler
les règles [f] period (menstruation)
régulier (f: régulière) regular
le rein (part of body) kidney
les reins [m] small of the back; **avoir mal aux reins** to have backache
la religion religion
le remboursement refund
rembourser to pay back
remercier to thank
remettre to put back, or to postpone
les remparts [m] city walls
remplir to fill
remuer to stir
rencontrer to meet
le rendez-vous meeting, or appointment
rendre to give back; **ça me rend malade/jalous(e)/dingue*** it makes me ill/jealous/crazy
se rendre compte to realize
les rênes [f] (riding) reins
les renseignements [m] information
se renseigner to get information
la rentrée return, or beginning of term
réparer to repair
le repas meal
répéter to repeat, or to rehearse
la répétition rehearsal
le répondeur (automatique) answering machine
répondre to reply, or to answer
la réponse answer
le repos rest

se reposer to rest
la représentation performance
RER under/overground trains in and around Paris
la réservation reservation, or booking
réservé(e) reserved
réserver to reserve, or to book
le réservoir reservoir, or tank
respirer to breathe
ressembler (à) to look like
le restaurant or **le resto*** restaurant
le reste the rest
rester to stay
le résultat result
le retard delay; **en retard** late
le retour return
retourner to go back
le retrait withdrawal
la retraite retirement
retrouver to find, or to meet (up with)
réussir to succeed, or to pass (an exam)
le rêve dream
le réveil alarm clock
se réveiller to wake up
revenir to come back
le revers reverse (side), or (jacket) lapel, or (sleeve) cuff, or (trousers) turn up, or (tennis) backhand
revoir to see again
la revue magazine
le rez-de-chaussée ground floor
le rhume cold; **le rhume des foins** hayfever
riche rich
ridicule ridiculous
rien nothing; **de rien!** you're welcome! **ça ne fait rien!** it doesn't matter!

rigoler* to laugh, or to giggle
rigolo(te) funny
ringard(e)* old-fashioned
rire to laugh; **pour rire** for fun; **le fou rire** the giggles
le risque risk
la rivière river
le riz rice
la robe dress; **la robe de chambre** dressing gown
le robinet tap
la rocade bypass
le rocher boulder, or rock
le rock rock 'n roll
le rognon (food) kidney
les rollers roller skates
le roman novel
romantique romantic
rond(e) round, or plump
le rond-point roundabout
ronfler to snore
le roquefort strong blue cheese made from ewe's milk
rose pink
le rôti roast (meat)
la roue wheel
rouge red; **le rouge à lèvres** lipstick
rougir to blush
rouler to roll, or to go/drive (along)
le/la routard(e) backpacker
la route road
roux (f: rousse) (hair) red, or auburn
la rue street
les ruines [f] ruins
le rythme rhythm, or beat

sa her, or his
le sable sand
le sabot hoof
le sac bag; **le sac à dos** backpack; **le sac de couchage** sleeping bag
sacré(e) sacred, or (slang) really good, or damned

Sagittaire (star sign) Sagittarius
saignant(e) (steak etc.) rare
saigner to bleed
sain(e) healthy
saisir to grasp, or to get (understand)
la salade salad, or lettuce; **la salade composée** mixed salade; **la salade niçoise** olive, tomato and anchovy salad
sale dirty
salé(e) savoury, or salty
la salle room; **la salle à manger** dining room; **la salle d'attente** waiting room; **la salle de bain** bathroom
le salon living room; **le salon de thé** tea room
la salopette dungarees
salut bye, or hi
samedi Saturday
le sandwich sandwich
le sang blood
la sangle (riding) girth, or (climbing) sling
les sanitaires [m] wash rooms
sans without
les sans-abri [m/f] the homeless
la santé health; **en bonne santé** healthy; **santé!** cheers!
le sapin fir tree
sarcastique sarcastic
la sauce sauce
la saucisse sausage
le saucisson salami
sauf except
le saumon salmon
sauter to jump
sauvage wild
sauver to save
savoir to know
le savon soap
le saxophone or **le saxo*** saxophone

le/la saxophoniste saxophonist
scandaleux (f: scandaleuse) outrageous, or shocking
la scène scene, or stage
la science science
le score score
Scorpion (star sign) Scorpio
le scotch© adhesive tape
les SDF* [m/f] (sans domicile fixe) the homeless
la séance session, or showing (of a film/movie)
sec (f: sèche) dry; **à sec*** broke
le sèche-cheveux hair-dryer
le sèche-linge tumble dryer
sécher to dry, or (slang) to bunk off
la seconde second
le secours help, or rescue; **au secours!** help!
les premiers secours [m] first aid; **la roue de secours** spare wheel
le/la secrétaire secretary
la sécurité safety; **la ceinture de sécurité** safety belt; **en sécurité** safe
séduire to seduce
séduisant(e) attractive
le sein breast; **seins nus** topless
le sel salt
le self-service or **le self*** self-service (restaurant)
la selle saddle; **le tapis de selle** saddle cloth
la semaine week
semblant: faire semblant to pretend
sembler to seem
le sens sense; **ça n'a pas de sens** it doesn't make sense; **le bon sens** common sense; **le sens unique** one-way street/system

sensationnel(le) or
sensass* *great,* or *fab*
sensible *sensitive*
le sentier *path*
sentir *to feel,* or *to smell*
séparer *to separate*
septembre *September*
sérieux (f: sérieuse) *serious*
séropositif (f: séropositive)
HIV positive
le serpent *snake*
serrer *to tighten,* or *to hold tightly;* **serrer (quelqu'un) dans ses bras** *to hug (someone);* **serrer la main** *to shake hands*
le serveur *waiter*
la serveuse *waitress*
le service *service*
la serviette *towel,* or *napkin;* **la serviette hygiénique** *sanitary towel*
servir *to serve,* or *to wait on;* **servir à** *to be (used) for*
se servir *to help yourself;*
se servir de *to use*
seul(e) *alone,* or *lonely,* or *only*
seulement *only*
le sexe *sex,* or *genitals*
le shampooing *shampoo*
le short *shorts*
si *if,* or *yes,* or *so,* or *such*
le SIDA *AIDS*
le siècle *century*
le siège *chair,* or *seat*
siffler *to whistle,* or *to boo*
la signature *signature*
le signe *sign*
le silence *silence*
s'il te/vous plaît *please*
simple *simple,* or *(ticket) single*
sincère *sincere,* or *truthful*
sinon *otherwise,* or *if not*
le ski *ski,* or *skiing;* **le ski de fond** *cross-country skiing;*
le ski nautique *water-skiing*

skier *to ski*
le slip *briefs,* or *knickers,* or *underpants*
la SNCF *French railways*
la soeur *sister*
la soif *thirst;* **avoir soif** *to be thirsty*
soigné(e) *neat;* **peu soigné(e)** *scruffy*
soigner *to look after*
le soir *evening;* **ce soir** *tonight;* **hier soir** *last night*
le soldat *soldier*
soldé(e) *reduced*
les soldes [f] *sales*
le soleil *sun*
sombre *dark*
son *his,* or *her*
le son *sound;* **le son et lumière** *sound and light show* (*takes place in historic locations on summer evenings)*
sonner *to ring*
la sortie *exit;* **la sortie de secours** *emergency exit*
sortir *to go out*
le sou *coin;* **la machine à sous** *slot machine*
souffrir *to suffer*
souhaiter *to wish,* or *to hope*
soûl(e) *drunk*
le soulagement *relief*
se soûler *to get drunk*
la soupe *soup*
la source *spring* (source of water)
sourd(e) *deaf*
le sourire *smile*
la souris *mouse*
sous *under;* **sous-marin(e)** *underwater;* **le sous-sol** *basement;* **le sous-titre** *subtitle;* **les sous-vêtements [m]** *underwear*
souterrain(e) *underground*
le soutien-gorge, or
le soutif** *bra*

le souvenir *souvenir*
se souvenir de *to remember*
souvent *often*
la spécialité *speciality*
le spectacle *show;*
le guide des spectacles *entertainment guide*
la spéléologie or
la spéléo* *caving*
le spinnaker or **le spi** *spinnaker*
spontané(e) *spontaneous*
le sport *sport*
sportif (f: sportive) *sporty*
le stade *stadium*
le stage *training course,* or *work experience*
le stand-by *stand-by*
la station (metro) *station;*
la station-service *petrol station;* **la station de ski** *ski resort;* **la station de taxis** *taxi stand*
le stationnement *parking*
la statue *statue*
le steak *steak;* **le steak frites** *steak and chips/French fries;* **le steak haché** *minced beef;* **le steak tartare** *raw minced beef mixed with a raw egg*
le stop* *hitch-hiking;* **faire du stop*** *to hitch-hike*
stupide *stupid*
le stylo *pen*
le succès *success*
sucré(e) *sweet*
le sucre *sugar*
le sud *south*
la sueur *sweat*
suisse *Swiss*
la Suisse *Switzerland*
suivre *to follow*
le sujet *subject*
super* *great,* or *fantastic;*
super-bon*/beau* *really good/good-looking*

le super *four-star petrol*
superbe *superb,* or *beautiful*
superficiel(le) *superficial*
le supermarché *supermarket*
superstitieux (f: superstitieuse) *superstitious*
le supplément *supplement,* or *excess fare*
supplémentaire *extra*
supporter *to support,* or *to put up with,* or *to bear;* **je ne supporte pas ...** *I can't stand ...*
le supporter *(football) fan*
supposer *to suppose*
le suppositoire *suppository* (often prescribed in France)
sur *on*
sûr(e) *sure;* **bien sûr** *of course*
le surf (on water) *surfing,* or (on snow) *snowboarding*
surfer *to surf* (sport/Internet)
le surfeur (f: la surfeuse) *surfer,* or *snowboarder*
le surnaturel *supernatural*
le surnom *nickname*
la surprise *surprise*
le/la surveillant(e) de baignade *lifeguard*
surveiller *to watch,* or *to keep an eye on*
le survêtement or **le survêt*** *track suit*
sympathique or **sympa*** *friendly,* or *nice*
le syndicat d'initiative *tourist office*
le synthétiseur or **le synthé*** *synthesizer*

ta *your*
le tabac *tobacco,* or *shop where you can buy cigarettes, stamps, phonecards, etc.*
la table *table*

le tableau *picture,* or *board;* **le tableau des arrivées/départs** *arrivals/departures board*
la tache *mark,* or *stain*
les tags* [m] *graffiti*
la taille *size,* or *waist*
le tailleur (woman's) *suit*
se taire *to be/keep quiet*
le tampon *tampon*
tant pis! *too bad!*
la tante *aunt*
taquiner *to tease*
tard *late*
taré(e)** *crazy,* or *sick*
le tarif *price,* or *rate;* **le plein tarif** *full fare;* **le tarif réduit** *reduced fare*
la tarte *tart;* **la tarte aux pommes** *apple pie;* **la tarte Tatin** *hot caremelized apple pie*
la tartelette *small tart*
la tartine *piece of bread spread with butter/jam/pâté, etc.*
le tas *heap;* **un/des tas de** *heaps/loads of*
la tasse *cup*
Taureau (star sign) *Taurus*
le taxi *taxi*
tchao* *bye*
la télécabine *cable car*
la télécommande *remote control*
le téléphone *phone;* **le téléphone à carte** *card phone;* **le téléphone à pièces** *coin phone*
téléphoner *to phone*
le télésiège *chair lift*
le téléski *drag lift,* or *poma© lift*
la télévision or **la télé*** *television*
tellement *such,* or *so*
la température *temperature*

la tempête *storm*
temporaire *temporary*
le temps *weather,* or *time;* **quel temps fait-il?** *what's the weather like?* **avoir le temps** *to have time;* **la mi-temps** *half-time;* **le temps libre** *spare time*
les tenailles [f] *pliers*
tendu(e) *tense,* or *up-tight*
tenir *to hold*
le tennis *tennis;* **le tennis de table** *table tennis*
les tennis [f] *tennis shoes,* or *trainers*
la tension *blood pressure*
tentant(e) *tempting*
la tente *tent*
le terrain *plot of land,* or *site,* or *(sport) pitch,* or *field*
la terrasse *terrace*
la terre *ground,* or *earth,* or *land;* **par terre** *on the ground*
terrible *terrible,* or *(slang) out-of-this-world*
la tête *head;* **avoir la tête qui tourne** *to feel dizzy;* **ça va pas la tête?**** *are you crazy?*
têtu(e) *stubborn*
le TGV (train à grande vitesse) *very fast train*
le thé *tea*
le théâtre *theatre*
le thermomètre *thermometer*
le/la thermos© *Thermos© flask*
le thon *tuna*
le/la tien(ne) *yours;* **à la tienne!** *cheers!*
les tifs* [m] *hair*
timbré(e)* *mad* or *crazy*
le timbre *stamp*
timide *shy*
le tire-au-flanc* *skiver*
le tire-bouchon *corkscrew*
le tire-fesses* *drag lift*

tirer to pull, or to shoot;
tire-toi de là!** get lost!
la tisane herb tea
le tissu fabric
le titre title, or headline
toi you; **à toi** your turn
les toilettes [f] toilet
le toit roof
la tomate tomato
tomber to fall; **tomber
amoureux (f: amoureuse) de**
to fall in love with; **tomber
en panne** to break down;
tomber sur to bump into (by
chance)
ton your
la tonalité dialling tone
le tonnerre thunder
le top* the best, or the
in-thing; **le top 50** charts
(top 50 hit songs)
le torchon cloth, or tea
towel
le tort wrong; **avoir tort**
to be wrong
tôt early
la touche key, or button;
avoir/faire une touche* to
make/be a hit (with someone)
toucher to touch
toujours still, or always
la tour tower
le tour turn, or magic trick;
faire un tour to go for a ride
le tourisme tourism, or
sightseeing; **l'office du
tourisme [m]** tourist office
le/la touriste tourist
touristique touristy
le tournedos type of steak
la tournée round of drinks,
or (music/concert) tour
tourner to turn
le tournevis screwdriver;
le tournevis cruciforme
Phillips© screwdriver
la tourte pie (meat or fish)
tousser to cough

tout(e) all, or everything;
tout à coup suddenly; **tout à
fait** exactly; **tout de suite**
immediately; **tout le monde**
everybody; **tout le reste**
everything else; **tout près**
close by; **tout(e) seul(e)** by
my/your/him/herself; **tous les
autres** everybody else;
tous/toutes les deux both
(of them); **tous les jours**
every day
toxique poisonous
le trac: avoir le trac* to
have butterflies
traditionnel(le) traditional
la traduction translation
traduire to translate
la tragédie tragedy
le train train
traîner to drag, or to hang
around/out
le traitement de texte
word processing
le traiteur delicatessen
selling ready-made dishes
la tranche slice
tranquille peaceful, or quiet
le transat deck chair
transpirer to sweat
le travail work, or job
travailler to work
travaux (on sign) roadworks
le traveller's chèque
traveller's cheque
à travers through
la traversée crossing
traverser to cross, or to go
through
très very
la trêve truce
tricher to cheat
le tricot knitting or knitted
fabric
le trimestre term
les tripes [f] tripe
triste sad
le trognon (apple) core

le trombone trombone, or
paper clip
se tromper to make a
mistake
la trompette trumpet
trop too, or too much;
en trop spare
le trottoir pavement
le trou hole
la trouille**: avoir la
trouille**** to be/feel scared
la trousse kit, or case;
la trousse à pharmacie first
aid kit
trouver to find
le truc* thing, or tip, or hint
tu you (see also p. 58)
le tuba snorkel
le tube* hit song
tuer to kill
les tunes** [f]** money, or
dosh
la Tunisie Tunisia
le tunnel tunnel
tuyauter* to give a useful
tip
la TVA VAT (value added tax)
le type* bloke, or guy
typique typical

un(e) a, an, or one
unique unique, or the only
one; **la fille/le fils unique**
only daughter/son
l'université [f] university
l'urgence [f] emergency
urgent(e) urgent
user to wear out
l'usine [f] factory
utile useful

les vacances [f] holiday
les grandes vacances
summer holidays/vacation
la vaccination vaccination
vache** mean, or bitchy;
c'est vache** it's tough/
rotten

la vache cow; **la vache!**** wow!

vachement** very, or really

la vague wave

la vaisselle washing-up

valable valid

la valeur value; **les objets de valeur [m]** valuables

la valise suitcase; **faire les valises** to pack

la vallée valley

la vanille vanilla

se vanter to boast

la varappe rock-climbing

varié(e) varied

le veau veal

la vedette (film/movie) star

végétarien(ne) vegetarian

la veille the day before

le vélo bike; **le vélo de course** racing bike

les vendanges [f] grape harvest

le vendeur (f: la vendeuse) shop assistant

vendre to sell; **à vendre** for sale

vendredi Friday

se venger to get your revenge

venir to come; **venir de (faire quelque chose)** to have just (done something)

le vent wind; **il fait du vent** it's windy

le ventilateur fan

le ventre tummy

le verglas black ice

vérifier to make sure

la vérité truth

le verre glass

vers towards

Verseau (star sign) Aquarius

le versement deposit, or payment

vert(e) green

la veste jacket; **la veste d'équitation** riding jacket

le vestiaire changing-room, or cloakroom

les vêtements [m] clothes

vexé(e) offended

la viande meat

vide empty

la vidéo video

la vie life; **mener la grande vie** to live it up

vieille (see 'vieux')

Vierge (star sign) Virgo

vieux (f: vieille) old

vif (f: vive) bright, or lively

la vigne vine

le vignoble vineyard

le village village

la ville town, or city

le vin wine

le vinaigre vinegar

la vinaigrette salad dressing made from oil and vinegar

le viol rape

le violon violin

le violoncelle cello

le virage bend

virer to turn, or (slang) to fire, or to throw out

la vis screw

le visage face

la visière visor

la visite visit; **rendre visite à** to visit (a person)

visiter to visit (a place)

vite quickly

la vitesse speed, or gear; **à toute vitesse** at full speed

la vitrine (shop) window

vivre to live

VO* (version originale) original version (of film/movie)

le voeu wish

voici here is/are

la voie (railway) track

voilà there is/are

la voile sail, or sailing; **la grand-voile** main sail

le voilier sailing boat

voir to see

le/la voisin(e) neighbour

la voiture car

la voix voice

le vol flight, or theft

la volaille poultry

le volant steering wheel

voler to fly, or to steal

le volet shutter

le voleur (f: la voleuse) thief

le volley(-ball) volleyball

vomir to be sick (vomit)

le vote vote

votre your

le/la vôtre yours; **à la vôtre!** cheers!

vouloir (see p. 59) to want; **vouloir dire** to mean

vous you (see also p. 58)

le voyage journey, or trip; **le voyage organisé** package tour; **bon voyage!** have a good trip!

voyager to travel

le voyageur (f: la voyageuse) traveller

le voyou thug

vrai(e) true

vraiment really

le VTT (vélo tout terrain) mountain bike

la vue view, or sight

le wagon wagon, or (train) carriage; **le wagon restaurant** restaurant car; **le wagon-lit** sleeping car

les WC [m] loo, or toilet

le week-end weekend

le yaourt yogurt

les yeux [m] eyes

zéro zero

le zoo zoo

le zoom zoom lens

zut* damn